I'll never feel like this again, Brody thought

He buried his head in Amanda's hair and took in a deep, cleansing breath. God help him, for just a moment he latched on to the fantasy that she was his girlfriend. Not this summer or next winter or whenever it was they were finished with their goals, but here and now. He imagined he could take her out in public, today, and have people respect them as a couple.

None of these setups of her with other people.

Nobody assuming he was dogging her because that's what skiers did.

It felt good being with Amanda Jensen.

He could get used to this feeling.

Dear Reader,

I confess, I love heroes. I also love stories where the emotion between the hero and heroine takes center stage.

The idea for this story—my first published book— came in the months before the Winter Olympics. The elite athletes who train their whole lives for the love of their sport intrigue me. What if guilt over a past mistake drives a retired champion back to his sport for a shot at redemption?

Brody Jones is an alpine skier with something to prove. He and reporter Amanda Jensen share similar values of family, integrity and work that fulfills them.

But Brody has a career-ending secret he needs to keep hidden, and Amanda needs to uncover Brody's secret in order to excel at her job. It's an emotional dilemma that isn't easily solved. As they're drawn together during a week on the ski tour at close quarters, they're tested to the utmost. But like all my favorite stories, the power of love shines through and heals all.

Thanks for picking up my first Harlequin Superromance. I hope you enjoy the romantic Italian Alps setting and the company of elite competitors. Drop me a line at www.CathrynParry.com and let me know what you think.

Best wishes,

Cathryn Parry

Something to Prove
Cathryn Parry

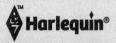

TORONTO NEW YORK LONDON
AMSTERDAM PARIS SYDNEY HAMBURG
STOCKHOLM ATHENS TOKYO MILAN MADRID
PRAGUE WARSAW BUDAPEST AUCKLAND

Recycling programs
for this product may
not exist in your area.

ISBN-13: 978-0-373-71756-9

SOMETHING TO PROVE

www.Harlequin.com

Printed in U.S.A.

ABOUT THE AUTHOR

Cathryn Parry lives in New England where she loves to dote on her husband, Lou, and her neighbor's cat, Otis (in that order). She enjoys traveling, sports of all kinds (but especially winter sports) and genealogy. After writing stories for nearly her whole life, she is thrilled to publish her debut novel with Harlequin Books.

For Lou, first and always. You've supported me as I reach for my dreams, and your faith in me always lifts me up.

Acknowledgments

A debut novel takes many fairy godmothers to bring to fruition. Most important was my editor, Megan Long, who saw the spark of promise in the manuscript and worked patiently with me to bring it to form. I can never thank you enough!

Also, thanks to Laurie Schnebly Campbell, writing teacher extraordinaire, whose classes helped me develop the characters, and to Brenda Chin, who, through one of her famous workshop contests, gave me my first shot at submitting my manuscript to Harlequin. I appreciate you both so much!

Much gratitude goes to my nephew Charles, who, as a ski racer on an alpine team, inspired me to write about a downhill racer.

Where would I be without my writing friends? Thanks to Karen Foley, Denise Eagan, Barbara Wallace, Nina Singh, Michelle Drosos and Dani Collins. Thanks as well to my blogging partners at www.MoodyMuses.com: Barbara, Katy Cooper and Becca Wilder; and to the members of the New England Chapter RWA, for your encouragement and support.

CHAPTER ONE

THEY HAD TRACKED HER DOWN, even at her sister's Italian wedding hideaway.

Amanda Jensen disconnected the call from her boss and jammed her phone inside the pocket of her spa robe. Wouldn't she love to shut off the thing completely? But since the magazine she worked for was going through layoffs and she was the last person hired, she couldn't take chances.

"Sorry, but I have to go." She wiggled her foot, hoping to gain the attention of the impossibly beautiful European woman with the glossy bun, wearing a white lab coat, who knelt over Amanda's toes, meticulously applying a thin layer of French nail polish.

"But, madam, I have finished only one foot."

She had, and it looked silly. Amanda stifled a laugh. "It's okay, I'll come back tonight to get the rest of the pedicure."

"But, madam, our resort spa is full with the wedding guests."

True. Jeannie's wedding weekend had created a logjam of skiers, coaches, friends and ski fans, all clamoring to be made beautiful for the event of the season. Amanda's stomach dropped. She was reminded of the subject of her interview assignment, and she felt queasy.

"Madam?"

"What? Oh, never mind my foot. It's winter—I'm wearing closed-toe shoes."

The European woman turned her doe eyes up at Amanda, insinuating what only doe eyes could insinuate.

Amanda shook her head. "No one's going to be sucking on my toes anytime soon."

Which was depressing now that she thought about it, but what could she do?

"It is winter in the Italian Alps, madam. Anything can happen."

"Yes. Yes, it can." That was how it had happened for her sister, and in this very resort.

Smiling, Amanda glanced through the plate-glass window at the glistening white slope dotted with pine trees, and for a moment she felt that old familiar tug in her heart. Mountains had been her home from her earliest memories. Now she lived in a concrete city, bustling, alive and powerful. And the demands of New York followed her, even to this snowcapped paradise.

Shaking off her wistful mood, she took one last inhalation of the siren's call of cedar-and-rosemary-scented massage oil. She felt bad enough as it was, cutting out on her pampering afternoon with Jeannie, but work gave her no choice. She hoped Jeannie would understand.

Amanda pushed off the lounge chair in search of her younger sister, trying not to dwell on what she was missing. She and Jeannie had so little time together as it was. For months Jeannie had been recuperating in a hospital in Milan, healing from a horrific ski-racing crash. Amanda had been in the States, shuttling between her magazine job in Manhattan and their mother's hospice in New Hampshire.

Home, she thought. Or what used to be home. Now her home was the place that employed her.

Jeannie's home was Massimo Coletti.

"Ciao, bella." Massimo ducked his head inside the herb-laced, steamy room, and immediately sent the temperature rocketing upward another few degrees. Her sister's Italian skier fiancé was a knockout. Chiseled cheekbones, sleek shiny hair, glowing green eyes, dimples and a hard body that didn't quit. But his sexiest trait, in Amanda's eyes, anyway, was the way his gaze softened when he looked at her sister.

"Have you seen my Jeannie?" Massimo asked.

My Jeannie. Amanda sighed. Here was the man who made all the difference in healing her sister's difficult past. "She's in the massage room. I was just going to look for her."

But Massimo beat her to it. He swooped in as the masseuse was leaving and gave Jeannie's massage-radiant skin a hug. Then he leaned closer and kissed her on both cheeks. Amanda's heart both gladdened and pounded. Jeannie giggled and threw her arms around Massimo's neck, not shy about the towel that dropped to her waist.

It was the scar that undid Amanda. A long, jagged cut from a surgeon's scalpel, winding its way down her sister's left leg.

The old fury came back. This was her father's fault. And Amanda hated skiing, she truly did. Hated it with a passion.

"Amanda, are you almost ready for the rehearsal luncheon?" Jeannie asked, gently touching her on the arm. "Because there's this great guy I want to introduce you to. His name is Marco and he's a friend of Massimo's."

"Marco is a writer like you," Massimo explained, his arms around his beloved wife-to-be.

"He won the Milan Prize for literature. He's very accomplished." Jeannie squeezed Massimo's hand and then looked at Amanda hopefully.

They wanted her to be happy. They truly did.

"You guys are sweet, but I'm an investigative reporter." Okay, a fledgling investigative reporter. "There's a world of difference in the kind of writing your friend does and what I do."

Massimo's brow scrunched. To a guy who sped down icy mountainsides at eighty-five miles per hour, one keyboard jockey was pretty much the same as the next.

"Just tell him I'm on deadline," Amanda said. "If he's a writer, he'll understand."

"Deadline?" Her future brother-in-law was so smooth that sometimes she forgot English was his second language.

"That means she can't make it," Jeannie said. "Why, Mandy? What happened?"

Amanda looked at her beautiful sister's disappointed face. "*Paradigm* gave me an interview assignment here in the hotel. I'll come back as soon as I'm finished, Jeannie, I promise."

"I know you will." The look of faith never left her eyes. Sometimes Amanda didn't deserve her sister. "And this will give you incentive to come back." Jeannie leaned over and rustled inside her purse, as if her upcoming rehearsal luncheon wasn't reason enough for Amanda to hurry.

She felt guilty and sick. Why did her father have to be a famous ski coach, and why did she let it slip to her boss, who took advantage of it to make her interview a skier, of all people?

And not a sweet, hunky Italian skier, but an arrogant, aloof American skier who, her boss informed her, had once skied under her father's tutelage.

Strike one, strike two. Could anything be worse about this assignment?

But her anger was erased by the photo Jeannie held up of one Marco D'Angeli. Marco of the Angels. Jeannie's setup for her looked like an angel, with a cherubic face, the same glossy hair as Massimo, and the same soulful brown eyes. Unlike her sister's fiancé though, Marco was thin and serious and...writerly. He posed with a pen in hand and not a stitch of clothing on his slight, studious frame.

Oh, my. "Is this one of those naked charity calendars?"

"His writers' club is raising money for diabetes research."

"Okay," she joked, "sign me up for two copies. One for home and one for work."

"Are you sure you can't postpone the interview until tonight? Because then you could meet Marco in person."

Amanda glanced at her younger sister's pleading eyes. The younger sister who only wanted her to share some of the happiness and peace she'd finally found. Then she glanced at the hunky photo of the cute, non-threatening Italian.

"I'm sorry, but I can't right now. Chelsea made an appointment with the agent. I have twenty minutes for the interview, then I'll need an hour or two to write up something quick. It won't take me long, I swear."

Jeannie's head tilted. She would never understand

Amanda's drive—not completely. But how could she be expected to understand when she hadn't been home when Mom was in hospice? When she hadn't been there when Amanda couldn't get their father to cover one godforsaken doctor's bill?

Because in his world, their mother was a nobody. Just like Amanda was a nobody. Jeannie would never know that feeling, because Jeannie was a *somebody*.

"I need to secure my job, Jeannie." Being an investigative reporter at *Paradigm* magazine was power. It was status. It was the ultimate trump card against people like her father. "Marco is a big shot like you and Massimo. I'm still on my way up in the world."

"Amanda," Jeannie said softly. "The right man will love you for who you are inside."

Easy for her to say. "Sure he will," Amanda said cheerfully. "Right after I nail this five-hundred-word profile. Now, will you help me prepare my interview questions? Because I have no clue who this guy is."

"I'll bet I know," Jeannie said, the smile in her eyes again. "If they want to profile a skier in a glossy American magazine, there's only one person."

Massimo nodded. "Brody Jones. There is no other American skier."

Amanda had never heard of Brody Jones before today. But that wasn't saying much. When skiing came on television or showed up in the newspaper, then Amanda Jensen, daughter of the famous alpine ski coach, MacArthur Jensen, tuned out and turned the page.

Jeannie studied her nails. "Brody won't be happy when you tell him who your father is."

"No problems there," Amanda said dryly. "Because I'm telling Brody Jones nothing."

"And I wouldn't expect him to give you any quotes."

Amanda just stared. Her sister knew as much about being a reporter as Amanda knew about ski racing. "That's what interviews are for, giving quotes. I scratch your back, you scratch mine. I give you print space to please your sponsors and attract fans, and in return, your exposure gives me readers and advertising. It's an age-old deal."

"She really doesn't know Brody," Jeannie murmured to Massimo.

"Doesn't matter," Amanda said. "He signed up for this interview, so he should know he's expected to give quotes in return."

Massimo laughed. Rather loudly, Amanda thought. Which was strange, considering she could see Massimo encouraging any media attention sent his way. As all the top-ranked skiers she'd known from childhood would have done.

Massimo turned to Jeannie and smiled gently. "Do you want to tell your sister about the American skier, or should I?"

BRODY PAUSED AFTER HIS THIRD set of single-leg squats and poured the last of the water in his bottle down his throat. The tiny resort gym was like a sauna inside.

"Um, are you Brody Jones?"

He glanced down to see a gangly American teen, his ski-team vest too big for his frame, standing beside the bench gawking at him as though he was his everlasting hero.

Brody shriveled inside. He wasn't anybody's hero. But he smiled at the kid anyway. Why disillusion youth? They grow up soon enough. "Yeah, I'm Brody. What's your name, kid?"

"Aiden." The teen shifted. "I, uh, want to be a great ski racer too."

"Do you like to work hard?" At the kid's awkward nod, Brody figured he'd spare him the lecture and just sign the autograph pad the kid was shoving in his face. Brody made a scrawl approximating his signature. Depending on his next race, the thing might end up on eBay.

Or not. Depending on his next race.

He smiled at the kid and handed it back. He really didn't care where the autograph ended up. That was the beauty of it.

"You gonna win next week, Brody?" the kid asked.

"Of course. Are you gonna win your next race, Aiden?"

Aiden blinked at him. "Yes?"

"Say it proud, brother."

"Yes!"

Brody high-fived him and the kid laughed, which made him laugh too. The world thought Brody was washed up, but he wasn't. He had just one more race he needed to compete in, but that was nobody else's business but his own.

"Can I take a photo of you, Brody?" The kid held up his phone.

"Sure." He looked like crap, but he obliged Aiden with the photo op. Even smiled for the camera.

A throat cleared behind him. "We need to talk strategy."

Brody turned from the kid to his longtime agent, Harrison Rice, hopping from one foot to the other, looking as if he was being raked over the coals, which he usually was.

"Yeah?" Brody picked up his dumbbells and decided

to let Harrison say whatever he needed to say. Brody didn't need to talk anything with him. He had his own strategy. Always had had.

He lifted the weights and blew out the tension. One more set. He knew the routine cold, and nothing and no one could snap him out of it.

Harrison sat on the bench beside him and wiped his brow with his handkerchief. It was hot in here, but Harrison was the only guy Brody knew who actually carried a handkerchief in his pocket.

"Here's the deal, Brody—you can't say anything this afternoon. If the reporter starts digging too much about your last season with MacArthur, or about your injury, then we're screwed."

Brody paused in his reps. "Exactly why did you agree to this interview, Harrison?"

"Because the Xerxes people wanted it."

Right. Brody rolled his eyes. "You don't see the irony of my sponsoring an energy drink?"

"It's an excellent deal they're offering." Harrison spread his hands. "What am I supposed to do? If you want a comeback, you need training money. If you need training money, you need sponsors."

True. Though Brody didn't want a comeback, not a full-fledged one, anyway. Harrison knew that. Of everyone on his business team, Harrison was the one guy who'd been with him since the beginning when Brody had been a pimply rebel teen fleeing a lousy home life to the ski slopes of a New England prep school.

He lifted the weights again. There weren't too many people he trusted and he surrounded himself with the few he did as coaches and equipment specialists. And Harrison, who was both agent and business manager. "Do we have any other options?"

"No. And I would tell you if we did."

Brody breathed out and set down his weights. "Who's the reporter?" he asked quietly.

"A woman from *Paradigm* magazine."

"*Paradigm*? The monthly New York glossy?"

"They have reporters who cover sports stars," Harrison said defensively.

"Great." He felt like spitting. "A celebrity reporter. Even worse."

"It's what Xerxes wants, and it's a puff piece. It's tailor-made for our purposes." Harrison shifted. "I've been thinking about it, Brody, and here's how we'll handle it. I'll write up some quotes and put them on index cards for you. When the reporter turns on her tape recorder, you read from the cards. Better yet, memorize them. That'll satisfy her, and get us what we want."

Brody just stared at his agent. If Harrison wasn't such a miracle worker with the sponsors—which unfortunately he really couldn't afford to give up—then he would've told him to forget it. The same way he'd cut himself loose from his former coaches, trainers and the whole national ski-team organization in favor of forming his own team.

"So, are we on board?" Harrison adjusted his cuff links, and Brody couldn't help smiling. Yes, his agent was a slick suit inside a sweaty gym. But he'd never turned his back on Brody after the accident, unlike almost everybody else in his life.

He curled a clean towel around his neck and headed over for his cool-down stretch. As a young hotshot, he hadn't believed in stretching. But at thirty-two, with two debilitating crashes and rehabs behind him, he'd learned that wisdom was better than bravado.

Not always, but usually.

"Brody? Are you even listening to me?"

He gave Harrison a look. "Freaking journalists." They mangled quotes. They chopped up quotes. They quoted out of context. They took old quotes and applied them to new situations. "Why don't we just tell her to write what she wants, because that's what those guys do anyway."

"Yeah, I know. Everybody's a lying jerk." Harrison sighed.

But Brody grinned at him. "Everybody except you, Harrison. You're the real deal."

"That's why you love me, Brody."

"Don't make light of it, or I'll drop you, too," he joked.

"Whatever." Harrison wasn't in a joking mood. "You just make sure the reporter doesn't find out what we have to hide, not unless you want your reputation to go down in flames. Because sometimes I wonder."

Brody's knuckles went white as he gripped the water bottle. He suddenly couldn't breathe.

"Yeah, something you care about," Harrison said. "That's good. You remember that, Brody."

And then Harrison was gone. But his threat hung in the air—poisoning the rest of Brody's cool-down.

AMANDA STOOD AT THE SINK in her hotel bathroom and sucked in deep, cleansing breaths. It wasn't like her to be nervous. Then again, maybe it was finally sinking in that she could be facing her career Waterloo, and before her career had ever gotten off the ground. Because, knowingly or not, Chelsea had given her the one assignment that hit too close to home.

He's a skier, she thought. *And he's just like Dad.*

Therein lay her problem.

According to Jeannie, Brody Jones had a reputation for walking out on reporters without saying a word. He was aloof and disrespectful of anyone with a pen and microphone.

From long experience, Amanda knew what a losing proposition it was to deal with arrogant competitors like that. Her father—case in point. The last time she'd met with him, in his office in Colorado Springs near the Olympic training center, had been a disaster. She'd completely failed. She'd received nothing she'd needed from him, and their mom had been the one to suffer for it.

Grabbing Jeannie's hairbrush from their mixed jumble of toiletries on the countertop, Amanda vigorously brushed her hair until it crackled with static electricity.

Slow down. Breathe.

I've learned since then.

She held on to the edges of the countertop and stared at herself in the mirror, struggling to find calm. This would be different. She'd done her homework and had thought through all the angles for her interview approach. She'd even dressed in full body armor for the event. Today she wore one of Jeannie's feminine silk-and-Spandex shells over her thinnest lace bra. That was a new tool in her repertoire and one that wasn't entirely comfortable, but she'd seen how the celebrity reporters in her office dressed, and she would do what she must.

By rote, she ticked through her habitual, pre-interview routine. She dabbed on her lip balm. Pulled her hair back from her face. Tested the batteries in her never-fail, top-of-the-line digital voice recorder.

The tiny gadget was inconspicuous and quiet; she

would place it on the table beside her oversize purse and hope that Brody Jones would forget it was there and would open his mouth, just once. One good quote, that was all she needed from him, and then she could return to her sister and the safe, non-skiing man her sister had lined up for her to meet.

She glanced at her phone. Three more minutes. And she'd better set it to silent mode, because the fewer distractions to spook Brody, the better. That was why she'd memorized what she needed to ask him, because she'd figured it was best not to face him with a notepad. Or a pencil. Or anything that screamed Interview with a capital I.

No, with any luck, Brody would forget she was a reporter and would instead consider the twenty minutes as coffee with a friendly person he could chat with.

Taking a short, careful swig from her ever-present water bottle, she considered the major flaw in her plan. Her father, per usual. Under no circumstances could she let Brody discover she was MacArthur Jensen's daughter. Jeannie had implied that would send Brody fleeing faster than the roadrunner on skis. Amanda had no problem with that aspect of his personality. Anyone who distrusted her father was wise in her book.

She shook off the last of her nerves and strode down the corridor, the air cool against her bare legs because she was wearing one of Jeannie's pre-injury outfits— a short, trendy skirt and a pair of her formerly favorite heels. Despite Jeannie's admonition "to be herself," whatever that was, Amanda was a celebrity profiler today, so she'd better act like one. Which gave her two choices for an approach strategy, as far as she could see.

Plan A was to keep the celebrity-reporter persona she'd prepared for. Disarm the recalcitrant skier with a nonthreatening approach. Plan B was her regular, hard-hitting interviewing style. Grill 'em and stick 'em and then serve up the painful truths.

Depending on how Brody reacted, she would adopt one tactic or the other. There was more than one way to open up a closemouthed celebrity.

Please, just give me one decent quote...

She stood outside the conference room and wished there was a window she could see through, but since there wasn't, she pasted what she hoped was a vacant smile on her face and swung open the door like someone who meant business. Plan A and plan B, in combination. Once she met Brody, she would choose her final course.

Immediately, she needed to shield her eyes from the blinding afternoon sun slanting through the window. For a moment, she couldn't see.

"Um, are you Amanda? From *Paradigm* magazine?"

She blinked to see a short man in a rumpled suit standing behind a conference table, his hand extended. He must be Harrison Rice, the agent. And next to him...

Amanda swallowed. Like a warrior prepared for battle, she thought.

Jeannie had showed her a photo of Brody Jones, downloaded from her phone's internet connection. In it, he was dressed in a black helmet and tight racer's uniform, his body bent so he was impossibly close to the slope, his powerful thighs straining while his biceps bulged, gripping a ski pole as he surged past a giant slalom gate.

Amanda hadn't been able to see his face, but she'd seen his power and his sex appeal. She'd understood his charisma.

And now here he was in the flesh. Six feet one, two hundred pounds—she could recite his stats in her head. He was built. Hard. Powerful. And recklessly daring.

But he wasn't behaving recklessly now. Like her, he wore body armor—in his case, a hat with a brim so low she couldn't see his eyes clearly. Several days of stubble obscured his facial expression. He wore a tight black T-shirt that showed off his powerful neck, and over that, a team sweat jacket that read *Italia*—great. Did he know about her connection with her sister?

Stop that. You're psyching yourself out before you've even started.

She gripped the agent's fleshy paw, giving him both a friendly wink and a hardnosed MacArthur Jensen squeeze. "Hello there, I'm Amanda Jensen. I'm pleased to meet you, Harrison."

She still hadn't decided yet which plan to choose, A or B, and so was fluctuating wildly between them. While Harrison winced, clutching his hand, she switched her gaze to Brody. What should she say to him? How would he react?

Before she could decide, his chair slid leisurely back. As he moved, preparing to rise, his head slowly came up. The visor of the sponsor's ball cap came off. And the most amazing pair of baby-blue eyes stared at her, sizing her up.

Amanda felt the shock zing up and down her anatomy. This guy had *It.* The physical key to setting her hormones on fire.

Because, oh, God, there was something about his eyes. They were probing eyes. Intelligent eyes.

Eyes that sucked her in.

He braced his hands on the table and fixed that quiet stare on her. He didn't feel like a skier to her, not like any skier she'd ever known, anyway. Nothing Jeannie had told her could have prepared her for this. Without a trace of a smile on lips that were tense, yet still so full she could easily picture herself leaning over the table and kissing him, he said to her, "Amanda Jensen. Are you related to MacArthur Jensen?"

Oh, she was definitely going for plan A. *Hard* wouldn't work with him. Best to play soft and dumb with this powerful, guarded man.

"Who's MacArthur Jensen?" she asked.

SHE WAS LYING. BRODY KNEW IT, but what he really wanted to know was why she was bothering.

He shifted in his seat, purposely tuning out the words she was saying and concentrating on her actions. Her essence.

She smelled amazing, like pine trees and winter. And…cooking? Rosemary, yeah, that was the herb he was catching. But that couldn't be right. Her presence brought to mind good food and companionship. A hearty meal in the company of true friends. Wine and humor.

He glanced at her mouth and watched her lips move as she spoke. He could easily kiss that mouth. She had the clearest porcelain skin he'd ever seen, and long, dark hair like Snow White. He imagined running his hands through it, feeling it drag across his chest. Every cell, every nerve in his body was straining toward her, and that wasn't good.

He pushed back his chair and jammed on his ball cap again. Pulled the visor down low. Crossed his arms against her.

That was better. She stiffened, the Miss Airhead persona falling away. For a split second her gaze narrowed. She was a helluva lot sharper than she wanted him to see.

"Brody, what do you think about Amanda's question?" Harrison grinned madly and dug him in the arm. What do you know, he was completely snowed by Amanda's phony routine.

"What do I think about what?" Brody said.

"Amanda has been asking about your record. Remember what we talked about?" Harrison coughed into his hand. *Pull out the cards with the phony quotes,* he was hinting. But Brody shook his head because he had already tossed the cards out.

Instead he pinned his gaze on the reporter, which was a bad idea because his heart had already softened toward her. *Trust her,* his intuition said.

His intuition had failed him before.

"You said you're no relation to MacArthur Jensen?" he asked.

On the table, the voice recorder flashed its red light. She followed his glance and then looked back at him.

"Yes," she said calmly, "I have no relationship with that Jensen."

"What about Jeannie Jensen? Aren't you here for the wedding?"

"The wedding…" Amanda licked her lips. Beside him, Harrison inhaled sharply. Brody could relate. She was stunning. So stunning, he literally ached.

She gave a small smile and stared full at him. Her eyes were the most amazing hazel-green. Playful, and yet as somber as he'd seen.

She smiled again, sadly this time. "I have to admit, Jeannie and I go way back. We went to boarding school together. We were assigned to the same dorm room, probably because of our last names. We had a hard…"

She faltered, and there it was, that accent. Her *A*s were distinctive, from the north country. It came out when she was caught off guard, when she wasn't concentrating on fooling him.

"You're from northern New England, aren't you?" he asked.

She looked up, genuine pleasure in her eyes for the first time. "You're talking to me, I like that."

"Where did you grow up?"

Her gaze never left his. "New Hampshire."

His pulse picked up. Few people knew it, but he'd lived there as a kid for a while. It was where he'd first tried skiing, where he'd first found his escape. "Where in New Hampshire?"

She nibbled the inside of her lip, as if debating whether to tell him. "Deanfield," she finally said. "It's a really beautiful place in the mountains."

He stared at her. She'd grown up right down the road from him. What had she looked like as a child?

Haunting. With inquisitive eyes that saw through a person, and luminous skin. The two of them created some kind of magnetic vacuum that sucked all the air from the room. Under the table, her bare legs crossed and uncrossed. He could practically feel her heat.

In the old days, if Harrison hadn't been present, Brody knew exactly what he'd have done next. He would have already been across the table, settling her into his lap, kissing her...

He shook off the vision. This wasn't what he needed in his life anymore. He'd been through hell these past few years, and as a result, he'd changed every concept of what was meaningful and real to him. Meeting a woman and hooking up with her before he knew anything about her was the last thing he could afford to do.

But, he noticed, despite her former reticence toward him, she was leaning forward, not fighting the connection. Obviously she felt the pull, too.

He doubted she was lying to him, at least not about that. No, she seemed to have dropped her mask altogether and was being herself.

The way she really was.

The way he was glad she was.

CHAPTER TWO

AMANDA FELT A HUMMING INSIDE her and willed herself to stop looking at Brody's mouth.

Instead, she gazed out the window at the mountainside punctuated with tall pines. And skiers. But none of them were solid and haunting, with lips that were flat on the bottom and bow-shaped on top. The kind she could feel herself kissing...

What was she doing? Fantasizing about an interview subject was wrong, and completely unlike her. She needed to get a grip.

"So..." Shifting in her seat, she aimed the voice recorder at him. Time to get to work. "I understand you have an amazing record, Brody, ten years and fifty World Cup podiums. You're the most accomplished skier from North America in quite a while. You've won everything there is to win. Nobody is even close to your record. I'd like to know why you've come back after being gone from the circuit for two years, and what you hope to accomplish this season."

He eyed her. He eyed the recorder.

Please, Brody. Talk to me.

"I'm here to win my next race," he said.

Good, that was good. She nodded. *Please keep talking.*

"I'm here to win it my way."

"What does that mean?" she asked softly. "I really would like to know."

His agent grew nervous, fidgeting with his pockets. "Brody means he feels privileged to be back, and he's looking forward to having a great season."

Brody met her gaze and held it. Her insides heated. She felt that invisible line again, tugging her to him.

No. She couldn't give in. Obviously, something was going on, something he and his agent were hiding. She wasn't an investigative reporter for nothing. She had intuition. Gold-plated hunches, the editors called them in the newsroom of her first reporting job, back when she'd been still in high school.

She leaned forward on her elbows. "Brody," she said, purposely ignoring the agent's coughing fit on the other side of the table, "what makes you different from the other competitors in the circuit? In the way you ski, I mean? What makes caravans of people follow you from race to race just to catch a glimpse of you in action?"

As if you don't get it, Amanda. It's called world-class sex appeal, and you can't buy that in Walmart.

"Have you ever been on skis?" he asked intently, his smile slowly forming again, his hands inches from hers.

She held her breath, not wanting to go there. But his eyes were insistent. And if she wanted to get her story, she needed to keep him talking. "Yes," she admitted, "but not since I was little."

"Do you remember how it felt?" His voice was low. "To go fast? To feel the wind in your hair? To feel like nothing could stop you and you were part of heaven and earth?"

Her gaze felt tied to his. She couldn't help swallowing, because those visual cues—the intensity of his facial expression, his strong athlete's neck, the proud affiliation of his ski-team jacket—brought back the *bad* parts of skiing, the things she'd always hated and felt terrorized by, growing up. For too long, skiing had been about failure, humiliation and shame. And now, her sister's broken, ruined body.

She swallowed again, but she could never get rid of the bad taste in her mouth; it always came back to haunt her. There was no solution, even though Brody Jones seemed to sense her discomfort.

"What's wrong?" he asked.

"Nothing." But tears were threatening, so she blinked fast. She had one strong point in her life to fall back on—her job—and here, with this skier, she couldn't even do that properly.

Exhaling, she lifted her chin. She needed to hold on to whatever shred of an interview she had left. "We all grow up, Brody. Life changes. Nobody can help that."

"True." His brow creased as he looked not at the voice recorder, but directly into her eyes. "But we can remember when life was simpler. At heart, I think people want to recapture that. Maybe that's why they go to mountain races—to breathe in the air and soak up the sun and ring cowbells like they're kids again. You could, too, if you wanted."

She dropped back in her seat and stared at him.

He smiled, embarrassed this time. "Or not. It's a theory, but you asked."

He's giving me amazing quotes, the reporter part of her brain said. Brody hadn't said anything like this, not that she'd read, to any other reporter.

"You...stayed away from the circuit for two years," she pressed on. "Even after you were healthy. You said you were finished, that you'd accomplished all you wanted to accomplish. What made you come back to the tour?"

"Time is up." The agent stood. "Miss Jensen, it's been a pleasure to meet you."

But Amanda looked to Brody. Her hunch was right. His mask was back in place, as if he regretted opening up to her. Something was wrong, and he was hiding whatever it was.

"I'm not going to screw you over, Brody," she murmured. How could she, after the kindness that he'd shown her?

He reached over and turned off her digital recorder. "You're a journalist," he said with an edge to his voice. "It's what journalists do."

"Some journalists maybe, but not me." She pointed at him. "Let's get something straight. You talk about the joy of youth. Well, I've known since I was a kid that I was a born writer, and that I loved doing it. I caught the enthusiasm for reporting early, and I never lost it. Believe me, I don't compromise my journalistic integrity for anyone, including my employer."

He smiled widely at her. "Then you're the first of the breed I've met."

"You don't believe me?"

"We'll see, won't we? I gave you quotes. Let's see what you do with them."

"Cynical, aren't you?"

He shrugged. "I've had my words twisted by all the so-called nicest journalists. They write what they want to write, for whatever agenda they have. I've learned better than to try to control it."

"Refusing to speak—is that the way to control it?"

He shook his head. "Even that doesn't work. Stuff still gets made up."

"Believe it or not, Brody, I take my job seriously. I might go undercover now and then, I might bust a person's chops, but I never, ever mess around with quotes. Are you kidding me? That's for hacks, and I don't care how many awards they might have won, it's still hack reporting. That's like, like…" She was so mad she was stuttering.

"Cheating?" Brody asked.

That was it. Cheating. She nodded in excitement. "Exactly. You understand."

"Yeah." He smiled sadly. "Yeah, I understand."

"Well, that's good." Harrison clapped from where he stood. "Time is definitely up."

"Amanda Jensen." Brody stood and moved around the table, then held the door for her. Her knees were suddenly weak and she wobbled on her too-high shoes. "It was a pleasure to meet you."

And then he leaned close and kissed her first on one cheek, and then the other. She felt the electricity from his kiss ricochet all over her body. By reflex, she reached up and touched his arm. It felt rock-solid.

He grinned at her sheepishly. "Sorry. When in Italy…"

Her cheeks flamed.

"Yes," she breathed.

And then he reached up and tipped the brim of his hat to her.

Like a wayward cowboy, he was out of there. Taking all the air in the room with him.

BRODY SPLASHED COLD WATER on his face, the back of his neck, his forearms. He leaned over the sink, feeling wired, as if he'd just finished a challenging run and wanted to go back up the mountain and do it again.

Because he did want to do it again. He wanted to see more of Amanda Jensen, and outside the interview room.

He reached for the paper towels. Unfortunately that was off the table. Maybe someday they could get together, after he'd finished what he'd come to accomplish, but not now. He had so little free time as it was. Harrison was a pain about scheduling him.

"You have got to be kidding me," Harrison muttered, his voice echoing off the tile in the empty men's room. He'd already attempted to chew Brody out for being needlessly open with a reporter, but Brody had shut him down, reminding him there were times when going off-script was the best strategy. When he followed his intuition on the race course, good things happened. It was the reason for his wins, and nobody could deny that, especially his agent.

"Don't worry about her. She isn't going to screw us," Brody said, but Harrison just grunted. Brody wadded the wet paper towels and turned, realizing that Harrison was preoccupied with reading text messages on his phone. He mopped perspiration from his forehead and cursed under his breath.

"What's the matter?" Brody asked. "Xerxes yanking your chain?"

"No. Give me a minute," Harrison said, furiously typing a text message.

"Not a problem." He thought of Amanda again. Something about her niggled at him. What had upset her and tripped her up, enough to almost throw that one part of the interview?

"Why haven't I heard of her before?" he muttered, though it was likely Harrison wasn't listening. "News of a reporter like her would have gotten around on the circuit."

"We could be in deep trouble here, in case you haven't noticed." Harrison snapped his phone shut and scowled at him.

His agent was always the jumpy type, but today he was excessively nervous. He'd been sticking to Brody in full-on babysitter mode, and Brody had taken enough. "Cut her some slack," he said, more sharply than he'd intended.

"It isn't her I'm worried about." Harrison stalked to the far sink and soaped up his hands. "It's you," he said over the spray of water. "You don't seem to grasp what's at stake."

"Are you talking about the note cards?"

"I'm saying I'm not sure we can pull this off anymore."

Brody stilled. Everything in his life depended on them making this race a go. "What is it?" he asked in a low voice.

"You know you're the center of my business, Brody. You always have been."

He waited, his heartbeat slowing until it was a dull thudding in his chest.

"I met you when you were what…eighteen?" Harrison continued. "A local kid at a local race."

Those days were a distant memory. Brody couldn't go back there if he wanted to. He didn't want to, but that was beside the point.

"You had it even then, raw talent compounded with charisma. Only a handful of athletes in any sport have those. But because you skied, the big boys were blind to it, agents bigger than me."

"Why the trip down memory lane?" Brody asked sarcastically.

Harrison wasn't laughing. "People mocked me when I signed you, did you know that? I was a small-time agent at a big agency, scrounging for crumbs. And you delivered, more than any American skier ever had. The sponsor deals rolled in. Companies signed you who hadn't known what skiing was until you lit up their TV screens."

"So what's the problem?" Brody said, his voice hard. "Just spit it out and tell me."

Harrison shook his head. "No, because I don't think you get it. And I want to make sure you hear this from me—*You* crashed and burned, Brody. *You*. Everything ended because people don't like losers or also-rans. They want to see successes."

Brody felt the ice in his veins. He didn't care about the successes. Not really. He didn't even care about losing. That's not what this comeback was about for him. And he couldn't acknowledge the anger that Harrison so obviously wanted him to feel.

"You think I don't know I allowed myself to be manipulated? You think I'm not serious about fixing what happened?" His voice shook. "Everything has changed about me. I'm not that guy anymore, Harrison."

"You were talking about being a *kid* today."

"That's not what I meant and you know it."

"I have as much to lose as you do, which is everything. Not just every deal we've made together, but your entire legacy, demolished."

Brody felt a shudder go through him as if Harrison had sucker-punched him. His name and his integrity were the only reasons he'd come back. To fix the mistakes that he'd made. To make it right this time, in a way he could be proud of.

He walked to the paper towel dispenser, avoiding looking at his reflection in the mirror as he did. To change that feeling—wasn't that the whole point of this exercise?

"Are you chewing me out because I talked with a reporter?" Brody stared at the wall in front of him, doing his best to hold on to the good he felt about Amanda, the good that Harrison was doing his best to stomp flat. "Are you complaining because I dared to trust somebody, just a little?"

"I'm saying you should trust me. *Me,* Brody."

Yeah, he'd ignored Harrison during the interview and maybe that had been out of line. "Okay. I'm sorry about the index cards. I should have told you before I went in that I wouldn't use them. The last thing I'm going to do this time around is be someone I'm not."

Harrison took a long breath. "Understood. And I accept your apology, by the way."

"Good. So tell me what your text message says before I rip that phone out of your pocket and read it for myself."

Harrison took a step back. *Yeah, you should be worried,* Brody thought.

"We need to get you out of this hotel, now," Harrison said.

"Why?"

"Because Jean-Claude texted me that MacArthur Jensen is on his way over."

"What?" Brody felt his anger flare. "That's not funny."

"I'm not joking. There's a cocktail party scheduled in honor of his daughter's wedding tomorrow. He's got one damn daughter, and she has to get married here, of all places. Jean-Claude is following him in the rental car as we speak."

"You have my equipment manager tracking Mac-Arthur Jensen?" Brody shook his head. "Never mind, don't tell me." He paced to the wall and back. It had obviously been a mistake to believe the rumors that his former coach didn't plan to attend his only daughter's wedding.

MacArthur Jensen was their wild card. Neither Brody nor Harrison had any idea what he would do when they bumped into one another for the first time in two years. Every nightmare Brody had was related to the knowledge that his former coach could destroy him whenever he wanted.

The goal had been to have the race long over before they crossed paths again.

"Brody, you know I'll do everything I can to buffer you from the outside pressure." Harrison touched Brody's arm, but Brody backed away. Harrison shook his head. "See, you need to trust me when I give you advice. If you don't trust me, this isn't going to work."

"Then what do you suggest I do?"

CHAPTER THREE

AMANDA FINISHED THE EMAIL to her editor, attached the document containing Brody's five-hundred-word profile, and then pressed Send. The internet connection was slow, so it took a few moments for her email to go through.

Message sent, her laptop screen finally displayed.

She let out a breath and slumped across her keyboard, head in hands. She'd written and edited the piece as if she were in a fever. With every sentence she typed, it became clearer Brody was under her skin, which was confusing. She'd never behaved this way over any interview subject. She felt like a crush-ridden schoolgirl.

She pushed away from the desk and immediately saw Jeannie's wedding dress hanging on the closet door. Her sister's wedding tomorrow had to be playing its part in wreaking havoc with her good sense. Just the idea of couples being paired up for tonight's party had surely put Brody on her mind where he shouldn't be. The fact that he was a skier—and one of her father's former skiers at that—should have been dampening her obviously confused libido.

She stood and walked over to lean her hot forehead against the cool glass of the hotel window. Three stories below, a small group of Jeannie's and Massimo's friends from the ski tour trickled in and out of the courtyard lounge with drinks in hand. The rehearsal luncheon was finished, and now they looked to be gathering for the evening cocktail reception. Couples would be buzzed, chatty and amorous. Did she really want to meet Massimo's and Jeannie's fix-up for her in the state she was in?

I'd rather meet Brody, a rogue voice in her head said.

Stupid voice. Brody was the subject of her *work*. Her future. That was something she could never risk.

She rose and circled the room, glancing at Jeannie's clothes spread over one bed and her own papers, briefcase and notes across the other. Practical, the way she needed to be. If she thought rationally, she knew this pull toward Brody wasn't an attraction of the heart, on either of their parts. Her reaction to him was one-hundred-percent physical, and that was all. She would never invest time in a relationship with him, or he with her, especially once he found out who her father was.

And he *would* find out. Her background, including her father's connection to the American ski racers, would be detailed in a boxed blurb below her byline. When Brody saw it, he would never want to see her again.

Her cell phone rang. *Brody,* was her first thought. Which was crazy. He was leaving in the morning, why would he want to see her again?

Besides, he didn't have her phone number. His agent was the one she'd confirmed the appointment with, after her editor had set up their meeting.

No, the call was more likely from Jeannie. Amanda leaned over and picked up the phone, checking the caller ID as she did so.

Yes, it was Jeannie, calling on Massimo's phone.

"I'll be right down," she said into the receiver, her

heart dropping despite her best intentions to the contrary. "I just sent the profile to Chelsea, so all that's left is to change my clothes, okay, sweetie?"

"Hi, Amanda!" Jeannie's voice was tipsy, as if she'd drunk a glass or two of wine at her luncheon party. Loud, happy laughter sounded in the background, intermingled with festive piano music. "How did it go with the interview? I've been dying to hear."

"It went...well." She settled onto Jeannie's bed, kicking off the heels and drawing her knees to her chin. To keep her hands busy, she picked up one of Jeannie's old sweaters and brought it to her nose. It smelled like her baby sister. "Really well."

"He talked to you?" Jeannie sounded breathless.

"Even more than I'd hoped for. He opened up to me, Jeannie."

"Oh, my God, you *like* him, don't you?"

Like in Jeannie's vocabulary meant *want to hook up with*. Which was the last impression Amanda wanted to give her matchmaker sister. "Don't even say that," she chided. "We have a professional relationship. Are you trying to get me in trouble?"

"Hold on a sec, Massimo wants to listen in. I need to move someplace quiet so we can both hear you, okay?"

Amanda found herself smiling even as she shook her head. Jeannie and Massimo were so sweet together. She'd landed in Italy a week ago feeling exhausted and weepy, still so frustrated over fighting her mom's illness and furious over her father's lack of caring. But Jeannie and Massimo had made her smile again. Amanda had never blamed her little sister for being unable to visit Mom when she'd been sick—those days, Jeannie had been too often hospitalized herself. They'd talked by computer video connection almost every day, though, and Amanda had frequently thanked God for Massimo. This week, especially, he'd brought them around to his big, extended family, fed them pumpkin-filled pasta and goblets of Prosecco, shown her his and Jeannie's new village apartment, and talked incessantly about their future together.

"You should call him, Amanda." The line was calmer now, just Jeannie's voice with no background cocktail chatter. "Since your work is finished, bring Brody down to the party. Everybody else is here, it's only polite."

It would be disastrous, only partly because Amanda hadn't told Brody who she really was. But her sister just wanted to help her.

"And to think, a few hours ago you were setting me up with Massimo's friend," she teased.

"Marco? How can I fix you up with Marco when you're interested in Brody?"

Massimo's assenting murmur came through in the background.

Amanda poked at her one pedicured foot. The truly ridiculous part was, Jeannie and Massimo had bugged out of their own party to huddle over a mobile phone, plotting Amanda's potential hook-up. "Have you two thought of starting a dating service? Because you'd be really good at it."

"You have his number, right? Or do you need me to get it from Massimo? He has it right here." Another murmur of agreement.

Amanda crushed Jeannie's sweater closer. It was apparent Jeannie and Massimo weren't going to let this one go. "Actually, Jeannie," she admitted, "there is a small problem. Brody doesn't know who my father is."

"You didn't tell him?" Jeannie fell silent. Because,

as a consequence, Amanda had also hidden the fact that Jeannie was her sister.

Jeannie's hurt radiated across the phone line, even without speaking.

"You need to talk to Brody and tell him who you are," Jeannie said quietly, "because Dad just called me, and he's on his way over."

Amanda's palm slipped on the silicone sleeve of her phone, nearly dropping it. Dad was coming *here?*

"Amanda? What's going on?"

Cold beads of panic broke across her forehead. *I don't want to see him just yet. I* can't *see him just yet.*

She wasn't prepared. Hadn't thought this far ahead, because she hadn't *wanted* to think this far ahead.

Amanda stood and paced the carpet. How could she explain the situation to her sister? It wasn't fair to drag Jeannie into her problems. Above all, this was Jeannie's big day, and it wasn't Amanda's place to ruin it. If anything, the bastard owed Jeannie an appearance on the night before her wedding, especially after causing her accident.

"I'm…sorry I couldn't tell Brody who you are to me," Amanda said. "He…quizzed me about my last name. Dad must have left a horrible taste in his mouth, because I could tell that if he knew who I was, he was going to shut down. And I couldn't have that, Jeannie. Above all, I couldn't have that."

Her voice sounded pleading, and she felt ashamed of herself. If Jeannie hung up on her, she wouldn't blame her.

"I understand," Jeannie said firmly. "What you need to do is call Brody. Meet with him, tell him the truth, and then give him a chance to react. Afterward, you and I will get together and talk."

No, they wouldn't. This whole situation was too embarrassing to discuss with anyone.

Still, Jeannie was giving her a perfect excuse to skip the close encounter with their father.

"Are you sure you won't mind if I miss your party?" Amanda asked. "How's the dessert bar? Do they have the lemon cake and biscotti you wanted?"

"They do. Massimo's mother smoothed the way between the pastry chef and the restaurant manager. It worked out perfectly."

"I should have been there. I'm a horrible sister."

"You're the best sister ever. You deserve all good things. And right now, you deserve time on your own, without us. You've been smothered by me and the Coletti clan all week, now that I think of it."

"I haven't. They're so adorable, they make me want to cry."

"I'll see you when I get back to the room tonight, okay? Call him, Mandy. Please."

She murmured her assent, knowing full well she wouldn't follow through. Jeannie disconnected the call.

Lovely. Now, in addition to skipping out on her sister, she was also lying to her. Because no matter what Jeannie said, or what Amanda had agreed to, there was no way she could call Brody. Her job was simply too important to risk.

On the other hand, there was no way she could face Dad tonight either, and of all the minefields she needed to avoid this evening, that one was the most important.

Her phone beeped, letting her know she had a text. It was from Chelsea, her traditionally terse, "Got it." Not a phone call, not a make-these-changes-now directive.

From experience, Amanda knew that meant she approved of the profile. As of this moment, her assignment was officially over.

Amanda flopped back on Jeannie's bed and let out her breath with a whoosh. At last, some good news. After all the hassles of the day, all the worry about the layoffs at work and coming face to face with her father, now she had one less thing to stress about. Maybe she should call room service and order champagne so she could celebrate her one small victory in private.

Closing her eyes, she dared to let herself remember the low, sexy timbre of Brody's voice, his interview responses that she'd played over and over as she'd drafted her article. When she thought of him, she felt as warm and comfortable as when she'd held Jeannie's familiar sweater.

She was on vacation now. No one from her office was present. Who would ever know or care if she did call Brody Jones?

Forget the champagne—what if she arranged a short drink with him in the hotel lounge, at the other end of the resort from her sister's pre-wedding party, just to get her through the night and away from her father?

Rolling onto her side, she scrolled through her contact list before she could talk herself out of it. *H* for Harrison, his agent's name…

The house phone rang insistently beside her, that jolting, Italian ring tone she still wasn't used to.

The front-desk clerks were the only people who'd ever called them on this phone. She tucked the receiver between her ear and her shoulder. "Hi," she said to the staff member before he could launch into his business, "are you serving drinks at the lounge yet, or do I have to go to the restaurant to get served?"

A familiar laugh sounded, deep and rich. "I take it

you're finished with work," Brody said. "Good, I was hoping that was out of the way."

"Brody...I...hi..." A speechless reporter, wasn't that nice?

"Amanda." The quiet way he said her name calmed her pulse. Oh, yes, she definitely wanted to see him again. "Are you busy with the wedding, or do you have time to meet?" he asked.

She wrapped the phone cord around her finger. Obviously, they were on the same wavelength. This had to be a sign, didn't it? "I just turned my profile in to the magazine, so, yeah, I'm free. And no, I don't have any wedding things planned either." She licked her dry lips. "Um, why? What did you have in mind?"

"I want to go skiing with you."

Skiing? The word hit her like a knock to the gut. "What?"

"I, ah, need to get away for a while and just...forget about things." His voice was low, as though he wanted to keep the conversation quiet. "I was hoping you'd join me."

"On the mountain? In the snow?"

"Yeah. Do you have skis with you?"

She blinked, her fingers clutching the telephone receiver, pressing the cold plastic to her ear. "No, Brody," she managed to say, "I did not fly ski equipment with me to Italy to be a bridesmaid in my best friend's wedding."

"Okay, then I'll rent you a pair."

Over her dead body. "You are out of your mind, do you know that?"

"You've been talking to my agent, I see."

He thought this was funny? "Brody, you don't understand," she said, her voice shaking. "I can't ski. I'm a lousy skier, in fact. And you professionals aren't known for your patience, or your restraint."

"Are you afraid of me, Amanda?" His voice was shocked.

"No, I'm not afraid of *you,* I'm just not cut out for your sport, is all. Trust me on this."

"If it helps, the slope I'm thinking about has an old-fashioned chairlift like they used to have in Deanfield. We'd be up there for the last hour before they close, so I doubt there'll be many people around." He paused. "I promise to take it easy on you. I won't let you fall."

He didn't get it. And her voice wouldn't work to tell him so. Her *brain* wouldn't work to tell him so. "Why can't we stay at the hotel and have a drink together like normal people?"

"You think I'm normal?" He laughed. "Thanks, I'll remember that. Look, there's something on the mountain I'd really like you to see. I'll carry you up there if you'd rather avoid the skiing part."

Despite herself, she smiled. Carry her up there, huh? Yeah, she was a sucker for guys with warped senses of humor. Though he'd never get her anywhere near a ski-rental shop.

"So what do you say, Manda? Will you come and be a kid again with me for a couple of hours before we both have to leave?"

BRODY LEANED AGAINST THE Italianate marble fountain that stood in the rear of the main lobby. The crashing water did a world of good in helping him regain his center. His conversation with Amanda hadn't gone the way he'd expected, or was used to. He figured it was fifty-fifty whether she'd show up at all.

He stared at the copper-colored coins tossed in the

bottom of the fountain. Truthfully, this woman had knocked him for a loop. She showed real fear about the fact he was a skier. Since he'd turned pro, how many women had had that reaction?

None. He shoved his hands in his jeans pocket. Then again, in ten years he'd never pursued a woman during ski season. In his world, he'd learned there were too many temptations that could trip him up. People whose motives he couldn't trust.

Not that their meeting today was a big deal. It was just a…two-hour date. Above all, he didn't want to rush anything with Amanda. Since he'd been off the tour, he'd turned over a new leaf in his life: no more empty one-night stands. That went along with his skiing comeback. He was here to redo the things he hadn't liked about himself and to make his life the way he wanted it to be. That included avoiding groupies. They were there for the picking, always around. What he wanted was something more substantial.

The elevator door dinged and then opened, causing him to stiffen with anticipation, but the car was empty. It looked as if she wasn't coming after all. When he'd called her, he'd been hoping that if he got her outside, onto the mountain, maybe he could make that light come on in her eyes, the way it did when she talked about her job. Yeah, she was a girl from the north country, but by her own admission she had traveled a long way since those days. He'd needed to know if she could get past her aversion to skiing. For some reason, it was important to him to find out. Judging from their phone conversation, the answer was a resounding no.

Maybe it was better she hadn't shown up.

He turned to leave as the elevator dinged again. This

time, Amanda walked out. He stared at her, his fingers curling into his palms.

Her hair was loose and she wore tight jeans and a sexy red top that perfectly hugged her curves. Those weren't ski clothes by any stretch of the imagination, but she looked amazing enough that it didn't matter.

Then she saw him, and her smile lit up the entire lobby. All the tightness in his chest disappeared and he felt lifted and buoyed.

She marched right up to him. "*Ciao,* Brody." Her smile was slightly higher on one side, devilishly crooked. She rose on her toes, then she was in his space and all he could smell was her amazing spa-forest scent that she carried with her wherever she went. She arrowed her gorgeous lips to his.

"*Ciao,* Amanda." He bent his head. He was six feet one to her—maybe—mid five feet. *She's gonna tease me with one of those European double-kisses,* he figured. But, nope, she shocked him and pressed her lips to his, kissing him firmly on the mouth. A hot, honest North American kiss.

Damn. His soul seemed to corkscrew, and he lost his equilibrium. Which for a skier was unheard of.

She stared up at him, her eyes wide, her lips parted. This was where, two years ago, he would have led her out to his motor home. Maybe she would have stayed for an hour or two, but then he would have helped her dress and leave, never to see her again.

He didn't want that from her. This time, everything felt different.

Leaning his hands against the fountain, he steadied himself. "I, ah, wasn't expecting that."

"I know." Her eyes sparkled. "Now what's this about something on the mountain you want me to see?"

"It's a surprise. You don't want me to ruin a surprise, do you?"

She crossed her arms. "Did Jeannie put you up to this?"

"Jean—?" He shook his head. No, it was better to be honest with her. He wasn't setting himself up for anything that could come back to haunt him.

"Truthfully, I'm, ah, under orders to get away and go free skiing." He saw the confusion on her face. "That means to relax and enjoy myself. Naturally, you were the first person I thought to call."

She tapped her foot as if skeptical, but he could tell she was pleased with his answer. "You couldn't go skiing alone and then give me a call afterward?"

"Nope. Too dangerous to ski alone."

"And everybody else is busy?"

He hoped so. By reflex, he gave a furtive glance around the lobby, but the floors echoed with the footsteps of a lone guy headed in the direction of the cocktail party. The guy waved at Brody. "Welcome back," he called with a German accent.

Brody nodded to the skier. He wasn't sure who he was, someone new on the circuit probably, but they'd catch up next week.

He turned to Amanda and gave her a wide smile. "Looks like it's just us. Will you trust me to get you down the slope safely, or are you going to give up and go back to your room without even trying?"

A crease appeared across her brow. His hunch was right; she was too competitive to let him get the best of her, even if it meant facing her fears on the slope. Good—she had guts.

She smiled back at him. "Actually, that depends on you, Brody. Do you think your manhood can handle your fans seeing you taking the baby bunny trail down the mountain?"

"The baby…" Did she mean the easy slope? "Of course, Amanda, I will absolutely follow your wishes."

"No matter how bad it makes you look to your friends?"

"Standing next to you, it's impossible to look bad."

She laughed and made a show of rolling her eyes, but beneath her joking exterior he did sense real vulnerability. "Sure, Brody, that's what you say now. Just wait until you get to know me better."

He was hoping he got to know her a lot better; that was the whole point.

But right now, he had a feeling she was far more fragile inside than she wanted to admit. So he led the way to the rental shop, taking it slow.

CHAPTER FOUR

TWENTY MINUTES LATER, Amanda stood outside the rental shop by the ski lift to the bunny slope. Was she nuts? When she'd come down to the lobby to meet Brody she'd been fully determined to talk him out of his crazy plan. Never in a million years had she intended to actually go through with it.

And now look at her. Her feet were encased in boots as heavy as Frankenstein's clunkers, and the skis made a hollow pinging sound when she stomped on them.

At least Brody had promised they wouldn't tackle the difficult black diamond slopes. Her knees were shaking. Her hands were sweating inside her gloves, and she'd already dropped her ski poles twice. She was reminded why her ski-coach father had disgustedly given up on her years ago.

But Brody leaned over, patiently buckling her feet into the bindings on her skis. The one sweet spot in the last twenty minutes was in watching this new side to him. As he leaned over, the muscular curve of his back was visible even beneath his black parka. He glanced up at her, his skin flushed from the cold air, his baby blues on fire, and a longing for something she couldn't define washed over her.

"How does that feel, Manda? Are you comfortable?"

"If you call being strapped into a death contraption comfortable," she joked.

His brow crinkled. "What happened to the New Hampshire girl who used to ski as a kid?"

"She moved to New York and discovered the subway and all-night taxi service."

He laughed and straightened, settling his dark, bad-ass sunglasses over his eyes. "Do you ever miss the fresh air? Or does concrete and smog make you happy?"

"I wouldn't be here if I couldn't handle it."

He smiled and guided her up the gentle slope toward the chairlift, his hand on her elbow. His touch, even through layers of clothing, sent heat flooding through her.

She had officially lost her mind. "Uh, Brody, I wasn't lying when I told you I don't know how to ski anymore. Sorry."

He gave her a look that said he didn't believe her. "You skied before. Once you learn, it never leaves your muscle memory."

"Then I must be the exception to the rule." She hastened to keep up beside him. "Because the only memories I carry in my muscles are typing and the occasional yoga class."

"You take yoga?" He gazed at her with interest.

"Yep." She nodded proudly. "Downward dog and the warrior pose. That I can do."

His mouth quirked. "I'd like to see that."

"Great. Then let's go back to the hotel and forget this skiing stuff."

He shook his head slowly but his smile was wide. "Because you think you can't do it anymore?"

"I *know* I can't. I'm no Jeannie Jensen, you know."

He stopped and pointed behind them. "If you can't ski, Amanda, then what do you call that?"

She blinked behind them at the dual trail of ski tracks in their wake. They'd covered about forty yards together across the snow. She hadn't even realized.

"You grew up in the mountains," he said. "You don't lose what was part of you, deep down." He stamped his skis on the hard-packed snow. "And you can trust my professional opinion, because I've taught clinics with newbies in the sport. Some of them can't go five yards without falling on their duffs. Obviously, you don't have that problem."

She looked behind her again. The skis had shushed beneath her seemingly of their own accord. It had felt... natural. Beside him she'd flowed, without struggling and fighting the way she usually did.

Could it really be an instinct from a long time ago that had lingered inside her without her even knowing it?

She fell into silence as Brody helped her along the last few yards, easing her between the ropes of the corral line and distracting her with his dimples.

She hated to admit that maybe he'd been right.

But then the heavy clanking of the chairlift machinery drilled into her subconscious, and ever fiber in her body seized up and resisted.

"Um, no. Just no, Brody."

"They have chairlifts in Deanfield, Amanda. I rode them often."

"I can't remember the last time I went up in one of those things. Honestly." She shook her head. "They've been erased from all my memories, muscle and brain."

"Then I'll help you remember." He guided her to the spot where skiers were supposed to stand, waiting for the chair that would bump beneath their backsides, scooping them onto their seats for the long, cold ride up the mountain.

"I don't think so, Brody." It had been so long since her body knew what to do here. And she was going up the lift with the master of his sport.

"You're doing great." Just as the automated chair brushed against the backs of her thighs, he lifted her effortlessly onto the bench seat. She hadn't realized she was frozen, stammering, her mouth gaping open.

He murmured into her ear. "The pain will be worth it, Manda. You'll see."

His warm, sexy breath sent shivers up her spine. Why did he have to have this sweet side to him, too?

And why did she have to want to be with him so much? She'd talked herself into trying on the rental skis in the first place by convincing herself that it might prove useful with some mythical future article. After all, few people could say they'd skied with the great Brody Jones.

But she was fooling herself if she thought that was really why she'd followed him out here.

She blew out her breath as he settled the chairlift bar around them. Reaching across her waist, he gathered her poles, clasping them together with his. "Hang on," he said. "It's an old-style lift and it's going to swing in the wind a bit."

She nodded, her teeth chattering, and he tucked his free arm around her, holding her securely. Despite the danger, she felt protected, even as their chair swung and dipped in the air, as though they were riding a roller coaster.

To her surprise, sensations came flooding back to her from years past, bittersweet in their memories. Feelings and images she must have hidden deep.

Riding a lift like this one with her mom and sister as a child, Jeannie in the middle seat.

"I forgot how much I liked this part," she blurted out. "Starting at the bottom of the hill with the whole journey ahead of us."

"Yeah, it's the anticipation of things to come," he agreed.

Amanda drank in the view of the valley and the church-like quiet as they rose higher, their skis skimming along above the treetops. As far as she could see, the mountain and its snowy outcroppings never ended. The line ahead was long, with dozens of empty chairs in front of them and empty chairs behind. She heard Brody's contented sigh, his deep intake of the clean, cold air that smelled of freshly fallen snow.

She'd missed afternoons like these. Buried beneath all the memories of the fights and humiliations with MacArthur, there had been earlier days when she'd felt happy on the slopes. A flash of her mom's face shone clearly in her mind. She had worried she would forget what her mom looked like, but sitting on this old-style chairlift, in this old-style resort, how could she? Not while she was in the winter and the snow and the mountains, Mom's favorite place.

Leaning into the warmth of Brody's body, she gazed up at him. Without him, she never would have realized these things. He smiled down at her, too, with eyes as blue as the sky. There was no doubt in her mind that Mom would have liked him. Above all, he was kind.

"Thank you," she said quietly.

He exhaled and his head lowered. It was the most natural thing in the world to meet him halfway.

His lips brushed hers, a light touch considering all his coiled power. Everything physical about him—his arm around her shoulders, his chest close to her chest, his muscular thigh nestled against hers on the bench— bled into her consciousness. Sighing, she parted her lips.

And that was it, the warmth burst into sparks. Brody gave a low groan. She opened her mouth and he kissed her deeply, his lips catching her upper lip while she gently sucked and drew him in. It felt so erotic and sensual kissing him that her head swam. All she could do was gasp. Her sexual feelings, so long stifled, were swamping her.

For months and months she'd been deliberately clos-ing herself off, listening to Jeannie tell her how great it was with Massimo. For months and months she'd been fighting to establish herself in her chosen career by weekday, and advocating for her mother's care by weekend.

Now it was her turn to enjoy some romance. She sighed and held Brody tighter, kissing him as if he was hers. And groaning, he kissed her back. Under the heavy parka, sweater, turtleneck and bra, her nipples came awake and peaked. Wriggling on the bench, she pulled off her glove to unzip her jacket, to settle herself closer to him.

"Manda—"

"Hmm?" Just as a wave was beginning to hit her, he broke away and raised the chairlift bar, then lifted her by the waist and glided with her down the short exit slope.

She felt breathless and dizzy, trying to orient herself, clinging to Brody. At the end of the path, he set her on solid ground.

Except it wasn't solid ground. It was slippery, frozen snow. With her weak knees, her skis went out from under her. What a metaphor, she thought, but then Brody caught her and smoothly held her upright.

She inhaled a breath of cold mountain air and gazed up at him. His face was flushed.

"You kiss really, really well," she said.

Humor was always good. Worked in every situation.

"I'm, ah, sorry about that." He wiped his mouth. "I didn't mean for that to happen."

"Don't ruin it. I've never been kissed so well."

BRODY SHOOK HIS HEAD. Was he out of his mind? He hadn't intended anything physical with Amanda, not at all. Maybe that was why his pulse raced as if he'd just finished a slalom run. And stupidly, all his body could think of was going back and doing it again.

Forget it. He swiveled and looked for the marker pointing to the Leopardo trail. Four trails originated at this lift, but he'd made a lousy decision because not only were the snow conditions icy and hard, but the Leopardo trail was too steep for a novice. He really would have to carry her to the ledge he'd wanted her to see, a loaded proposition given the way he'd already kissed her, but what choice did he have?

"Ah, Amanda, sometimes I ski with blind kids. I have them ski in front of me, and I hold their waists and guide them down the slope. Are you game to try that?"

"You do charity work?" she asked, that inquisitive reporter's look wrinkling her nose.

"Don't even go there," he warned.

"Why? I'm interested in what you do."

He glanced away so as not to get trapped by those probing hazel-green eyes of hers. "I have a foundation that works with kids—not just blind kids—but I don't want to talk about it with a journalist."

"Is that how you think of me?" She crossed her arms and frowned at him. "We just kissed, Brody."

Yeah, no kidding. His body was screaming at him to take that one last step toward her and kiss her again, here in the snow at the top of the cold, darkening peak. Because he was burning so hot, he needed to cool down.

Two skiers came off the chairlift and turned toward them. "Hey, Brody," one of them called. "Get a room!"

He muttered a curse. Which was a mistake. Because at the word, Amanda sucked in her breath and pointed her skis down the Leopardo trail. Planting her poles, she pushed off with a cry, tucking her body in a fair approximation of an alpine ski racer.

And damned if something about her form didn't remind him of Jeannie Jensen. He'd seen the video—like thousands of people he'd watched the internet clip of Jeannie's horrific, head-over-heels crash run last winter.

That's why Amanda is afraid of skiing. Kicking himself, he followed her down the slope. He caught up to her within seconds, and the sight of her cute bottom in the tight black pants, wiggling from side to side, made his mouth drop open.

Yeah, she was hot, but it was her technique that shocked him. Somebody who knew their stuff had taught her to ski, whether she wanted to admit it or not. Maybe she wasn't fast or aggressive—certainly not reckless like him—but she knew how to turn cleanly and plant her poles.

He was about to pass her so he could motion her to stop at the outcropping at the base of the hill, but when she saw what he'd brought her up here to see, she abruptly halted.

A MAGNIFICENT WINTER SUNSET spread orange and gold rays across the valleys of the Alps. Amanda stood on the ledge, her breath puffing in front of her, and thought she'd never seen anything so beautiful.

The scrape of skis against snow sounded behind her, and she knew without turning that it was Brody. She heard the clank of metal against plastic as he released his feet from his ski bindings, then the crunch of hard-packed snow as he stabbed the ends of the skis into the mountainside.

He stalked toward her and stepped between the backs of her skis. "What was that all about?" His voice was rough against her ear.

With a sigh she leaned back into his chest. "This is a beautiful sunset."

"Someone taught you," he insisted. "You have text-book technique."

She nearly laughed. "You don't know how ironic it is to hear you say that."

And then, because she owed him an explanation, she did the difficult thing and told him the truth. "Okay, I'm just...upset because my mom would have loved it up here. That's all."

Brody's cheek pressed against the side of her cap and his hands went to her waist. "Is she the one who taught you to ski?"

Her heart was going to break wide open if she wasn't careful.

"Y-yes." She bit the inside of her cheek and turned to him. "I told you, I'm a girl from the north country, and so was my...mom. Like you said, we all grow up learning to ski." She faked a shrug.

"How long ago did you lose her?" he asked quietly.

She thought about deflecting him, but couldn't. "Sh-she died two months ago."

He pulled her close and kissed her on the cheek. "Manda, I'm sorry."

"Why? It's not your fault. I've been putting it out of my mind, but being in the mountains, it was bound to come back." She blinked quickly, forcing herself past the rawness of her grief. "What about you?" she said with a phony smile. "Do you often come up here just to visit the sunset?" She kept it as light and teasing as she could, because she didn't want him to know how badly losing her mom had hurt. The wound was still too fresh, too raw, so she simply did her best to pretend it didn't exist.

She laughed and rolled her eyes at him. "I'll bet you bring a different woman with you up here every time you ski this resort, don't you, Brody?"

But he just looked at her as if he understood the emotion she'd been fighting and didn't judge her for it. "I've been training on this mountain for over ten years, Manda, and this is the first time I've brought anyone here."

She might not have believed him if she hadn't seen the flush creep into his cheeks. "Oh," she murmured.

"You coming from home and all, I thought you were the right person to finally see it with."

Her eyes felt moist and she realized it was because his motives were pure. He'd come up here not to make out with her on a chairlift, but because he liked her and wanted to spend time with her. She couldn't remember the last time a guy had genuinely wanted to get to know her better, with no ulterior motives.

Who was she kidding? It had never happened. Going to a ski-country boarding school and then college, she'd found most guys who pursued her only did so because they wanted a chance to meet her famous ski-coach father. But Brody already knew her father, and he didn't want a thing to do with him. Brody was up here because of *her.*

She pulled off her heavy ski glove and wiped at her eyes.

"What's wrong?" he asked.

She just shook her head. Tomorrow in church with Jeannie would be one of the hardest mornings of her life, if she were honest with herself, but right now was perfect. "Nothing about this day is wrong," she said softly. She held out her hand and he took it. "I like skiing with you."

But the sun was sinking, and soon it would be too dark to ski. She wasn't ready to let him go just yet. She felt comforted by his presence, and she didn't want him to leave. She certainly didn't want to go back to Jeannie's party.

"Do you want to grab some dinner?" he asked, still holding her hand. "I can ask one of the guys on my team to pick up some sandwiches for us. If we take that trail—" he pointed with his chin toward the left fork "—there's a place at the bottom where we can meet him. It's a harder trail, but I know you're capable."

She made a small laugh. "I'll never get over how ironic that sounds."

"Will you stay?" With his free hand, he fumbled inside his jacket pocket for his phone.

"Yes, Brody. I'll stay."

CHAPTER FIVE

AMANDA LOVED THE TINY, QUIRKY Leopardo Hotel. One of the guys who worked for Brody met them there with a grocery bag filled with sandwiches, a bottle of wine, real cutlery and glasses for a mini-picnic in the room Brody rented. As he set it on a table in front of the already-burning fire, Amanda smelled fresh salami, cheeses and yeasty bread fresh from the oven.

"There's a woman in the village we trust," Brody explained, opening up his wallet and pulling out some cash. "She has a clean kitchen and makes great food the way we ask her to."

Amanda's stomach growled. She unzipped Jeannie's ski jacket and then stepped out of the rental boots the way Brody had done.

"Sorry," he said, turning from paying the young guy for the meal. "Amanda, this is Steve. He's my ski tech. Steve, this is Amanda."

"Pleased to meet you." Amanda held out her hand, but Brody's ski tech ducked his head, his shaggy blond hair covering his eyes, and mumbled something she couldn't catch. He was out the door before Amanda could say anything more.

"Don't mind him," Brody said, "he's shy."

There must have been a lot of that going around, because she was suddenly feeling it too. She bit her lip as he pulled out a bottle of wine from the bag and immediately started uncorking it. Maybe this wasn't such a good idea after all.

He passed her a glass of red wine—Barolo, according to the label. "Do you want to toast?"

She looked at the glass for a long time. The wine glittered in the firelight like rubies. "I really shouldn't drink anything." She could feel the flush in her face. What the heck, she might as well state the obvious. "Jeannie's wedding is tomorrow morning, and then I'm flying home afterward."

She gazed at him so he'd know. "To New York City."

"I...YEAH."

Brody got the message, loud and clear. There was no future to this...whatever they were doing. But was it bad that he only cared about now?

He tossed the corkscrew into the grocery bag. They should just eat dinner and then say goodbye. He could take her phone number and call her when he'd accomplished what he needed to.

But he didn't want to eat or to say goodbye. Not yet. He didn't want anything but for Amanda to stay a while longer.

He stabbed the metal poker at a burning log, licking with flames. The wisest thing to do was to end the day on a high note. Escort Amanda back to her hotel and get his head straight for tomorrow, which was packed with training sessions and meetings.

Amanda's soft laugh sounded behind him. He glanced back to see her holding a condom box.

Whoa. The kid had packed *condoms* with their dinner? He shook his head. He needed to have a talk with Steve, pronto.

But she was laughing, her head tilted. "Magnums, huh?"

A roaring sounded in his ears. She wasn't shooting down the idea. "I didn't tell him to do that."

"But he's used to your habits, isn't he?"

"No, I don't have *habits*—he's just a stupid kid who doesn't understand that I don't do this. Not for any reason."

Maybe he was too vehement, because a look flickered across her face—like disappointment or sorrow.

What was happening here?

Touch her. If I don't touch her, she'll leave.

And he didn't want her to leave.

In a moment he was beside her, pressing her to him and pulling off her woolen cap and resting his chin on her soft hair. He gathered it up and inhaled. Her shampoo smelled like summer raspberries. She was the summer to his winter, and it was killing him.

"Brody…" she breathed. And then her sunny gaze settled on his mouth, tempting him.

He exhaled and closed his eyes. He *needed* her to stay. With a guttural moan, he kissed her full on the mouth again, and as before, she made a small sound of need then opened her lips to him. His tongue swept inside, mingling with hers, kissing her like he'd never kissed another woman. She tasted so good, he didn't care if tomorrow never came.

"Please," she whispered, urging him on, and her slight hands were tugging at his waistband. It was so easy to slide his hands down from her silky hair and along the sides of her torso to the edge of her shirt, before pulling it over her breasts and up over her head. He dropped the shirt, heard it whisper to the floor.

Her bra was lace. Peach lace, and he could see even

pinker skin beneath and a beaded, rosy nipple. A feeling of helplessness overtook him, as if he'd jumped into a pool so deep he couldn't escape if he wanted to. "Yes," she murmured, and he slid his thumb beneath the lace and stroked.

She felt so soft, so welcoming to him. He'd never wanted to be anywhere more. His mouth went to her breast. She gasped and pressed her hips against him, against the hardness in his jeans.

"Are you sure you want this?" he asked in a low voice.

"Since the moment we first shook hands in the interview room."

He smiled, his cheek catching against her fullness. During the interview he'd been distracted by the same thought. He lifted his head, smoothing back her hair and gazing into her eyes.

She nodded. And to let him know exactly what she wanted from him, no mistake, she reached under his cotton shirt, dragging it up and across his skin.

He sucked in his breath at the feel of her cool hands touching him—across his chest, his shoulders, down his arms. He had a scar there, from stitches when he'd been a teen and had face-planted at Whistler. Her fingers hesitated and then shook, as if he scared her.

He stood motionless. She could still back out if he wasn't careful.

"Does this hurt?" she whispered.

"No," he said honestly.

With a sigh she raised his arm and pressed kisses across his scar. He lost it and picked her up, carried her to the couch. Something seemed to drop away—the gate he'd been keeping closed, the control he'd been adopting for her sake. But she'd asked for it, and he was here, and yeah, maybe this was truly who he was.

He peeled away her bulky clothing—all of it, every last stitch—and he was glad for the crackling fire. "You, too," she said, and he sat back, letting her undress him, helping her take off his jeans.

Her fingers rested on his erection tenting the cotton boxer briefs, and he hissed out a breath.

He was waiting for her to stop him. He didn't want her to—he was ready for this—but if she was going to change her mind then he needed her to tell him so now, because he no longer could think of any reason he shouldn't—

Her hand edged beneath his boxers and gently stroked him, skin to skin. It took all his concentration not to move. His mouth was so dry he couldn't swallow.

"Brody, it's been so long for me," she whispered, "you have no idea."

Like hell he didn't. It had been two years for him, too, living like a monk in his self-imposed new way of life. "Believe me, I know."

And then he cupped her face in his hands. She'd shown him that what he'd done those two years was right. Just as what he was doing now was right. He wanted her to know that though he'd known her only a short time, in that short time he'd shared a deeper connection with her than he'd had with any other woman. And he wanted to complete that before she left. Because their time together was only temporary.

But their connection didn't have to be.

She blinked and tilted her head to him, questioning. But he couldn't tell her everything he'd been thinking, he could only show her what he meant. He was a physical guy; physical was what he did best. By making love to her, he would be holding on to the moment as long as he could. He pulled her onto his lap. "Will you stay with me tonight?"

She smiled, her cheeks flushing. "Yes, Brody."

"Good."

And then he pushed her hair back from her face and kissed her, deeply, again and again, using her gasps and whispered pleadings as his course markers.

Her hands dropped from his shoulders to his waist, clutching him. And it was a pleasure to stroke her bare skin. To take his thumb and drag it through her beautiful curls. He caressed her, a rhythm she set with him by dragging her hips against his hand. Her skin was dewy and damp and she was smiling at him. It was more than a pleasure to glide his fingers inside her as her body pulsed and contracted around him.

"You're killing me," she whispered.

He drew back his hand.

"No, I mean, I want you to…do everything. I want to feel you inside me…"

The condom packet, he remembered. Cripes, the kid was smarter than he was. And then they were both fumbling for the box.

"Let me do this," she said. He let her take the condom and sheath him with shaky, unpracticed fingers, but he didn't interrupt to help her. It was more erotic to him than anything he could imagine.

When she was done, he took her hand and kicked open a door until he found the bed. It had a thick feather comforter, and he led her to it. She immediately pulled him to her, body to body, skin to skin. Her legs wrapped around the small of his back, and he almost lost it right there. He tasted the sweetness of her skin before he dragged himself to his elbows and cupped her cheeks. He kissed her, gently at first, and then more deeply.

"Brody, please, I can't wait." She arched her hips to him and without hesitation, he stroked inside her. It was as if he were made to fit her. She rose to meet his thrusts, gasping every time his body touched her where she wanted it most, and when his mouth caught her nipple and sucked it.

"I need this so bad," she whispered.

He became intent on loving her, his aim to fill her up, to bring her somewhere with him, to keep her pleasured and content. He could barely take a breath before she was rocking into him, coaxing him higher, better, closer to fulfillment.

With a cry, she gripped his shoulders, shattered and came, a sweet release that went on and on. He caught her cries in his mouth and he came himself, muttering her name as her drove into her body, unable to stop, not for anybody or anything.

"Oh, Brody."

He slumped in her arms, a roaring in his ears. He felt more rooted in his own body than he'd ever known. *What's going on?* he dimly thought. *Is it supposed to be like this?*

And then her eyes met his, so shy and shining with happiness just to be with him, and he thought, *Yeah. Yeah, it is.*

She drew the sole of her beautiful foot up his leg to the small of his back, settling there. Maybe he'd found a little piece of heaven.

This, he would hold on to. This, he would make a place for.

HOURS LATER, AMANDA STRETCHED, her body throbbing. She and Brody lay tangled in the twisted sheets, the scents of their skin intermingled.

Never had she done anything so outrageously out of character as to have sex—and unbelievable sex, at that—with a man she'd only known for a day.

It must be Italy. Smiling to herself, she caressed her fingers over the broad, hard planes of Brody's chest and biceps. He was built like a masterpiece. Thick muscles, masculine, lightly haired skin, a rugged jaw lined with a day's growth of faint, prickly beard.

He stirred, shifting his weight to lay his head across her belly, holding out an apple slice to her, snagged from the picnic basket Steve had brought them. Opening her mouth, she let him feed her, the fresh fruit tart on her tongue, his fingers sweet to her lips.

Amazing how she felt so little embarrassment or self-consciousness in being with him, completely naked and unashamed, not a care in the world.

Sighing, she rolled over and nuzzled her head inside the crook of his arm, as naturally as if she did this sort of thing all the time. Which was funny because it wasn't as though she had a lot of experience with men. Yeah, she'd been with a couple of guys in college. Not during the school year—she'd taken her course work too seriously for that—but during summer breaks. That was before her mother had gotten sick, before the trouble with her father. Back then, she'd been so young, really, so untouched by love and loss.

She looked away, out the window and to the black night beyond. She'd turned off her phone—they both had—but from the darkness outside, she guessed it was midnight. Jeannie's party would soon be over.

"Brody?" she asked.

"Hmm?" The syllable from his chest echoed inside her core, striking a chord deep within her. There was something about him. It was as if she instinctively knew he'd been through the wars, just as she had.

She reached out and pushed a lock of light brown hair from his eyes. He wore his hair short and straight and it felt soft in her fingers. "What was going through your mind in the interview room today?"

He smiled and rolled to his side. With his hand tracing her cheek, he said, "I was thinking there was nowhere else I'd rather be."

Her insides heated. She wanted him again. Reaching for a condom, she rolled it onto his erection.

"Will you say that again?" she whispered.

"There's nowhere else I'd rather be." He lifted her hips to slide inside her. The sweetest sensation filled her; she felt as if she'd never understood what lovemaking was until now.

She would remember this night and this man for the rest of her life. Squeezing her eyes shut to block the emotion, she cupped her hands around Brody's butt. So amazingly muscular and round. A skier's butt. She could hold him there all night.

And much longer than that.

Though she didn't see how.

THE SUN WAS A FAINT BRIGHTNESS on the horizon when Brody woke. He lay on his back, naked, his arms flung over his head. He rolled over and felt the warm indent on the sheets where Amanda had slept. The last he remembered, she'd been curled beside him, her smooth hair fanned over his chest, blanketing him.

He sat up, blinking. But he then heard the water turn off in the bathroom, and he lay back down, stretching, waiting for her to crawl back into bed with him. He didn't know what time it was, but judging from the sun, they didn't need to leave just yet. They'd only slept for about three hours, tops, and he felt lazy. Lazy and sated. Last night had been all about sex, but in his mind, they'd conversed volumes together. It felt as though he'd lived with her months, he'd been that comfortable.

None of which had been in his plan. But he honestly didn't regret it. No, sleeping with Amanda had been perfect.

He glanced over in time to catch her exiting the tiny bathroom, tiptoeing. She was dressed in her ski outfit, with her ski boots in her hands.

Aw, hell.

He sighed. She probably had an earlier morning than he did and couldn't linger. He lowered his lashes to a slit, anticipating a wakeup kiss. Maybe he could coax her into making love one more time, before exchanging numbers.

The door creaked as it opened. His heart dropped into his gut and he bolted upright.

But she was already halfway out the door, not even bothering to look behind her. No kiss, no note. Nothing. It was as clear a ditching as he'd seen.

"Manda?" His voice was hoarse from lack of sleep.

She froze in her tracks like a surprised prowler. "Brody?" she whispered. "I, uh, didn't want to wake you."

"Forget about that." He cut right to the chase. "Can I see you again?"

"I, um, have wedding stuff all day, and then I'm flying home early tomorrow morning, so I don't think…" Her voice trailed off.

He stared at her, dumbfounded. She was really cutting all ties? Her body language telegraphed it; she leaned as far away from him as she could. He knew what that meant from all the times he'd done that himself.

"I have to go," she mumbled.

Yeah, he'd said that, too, way back when. Of anyone, he knew the score.

"Right." He forced out a laugh. "I get it."

Because he already knew all the excuses: the sex was great, but there was no way it could work between them. There were a thousand reasons she couldn't see him again and he couldn't see her, starting with her career and ending with his. She liked her life the way it was and didn't want to change it. She didn't need the complications he gave her. *Agreed.*

How many times had he made up stupid excuses like these? *Just get out the door and run. Say anything and be gone.*

He lay back on the pillows. Suddenly, he couldn't smile anymore. Maybe everything was coming due. *There's more to integrity than winning ski races. Or sleeping with a woman you think you share a connection with.*

"At least kiss me goodbye, sweetheart," he tried to joke.

But she only bit her lip and shook her head.

He knew it was just as well, but it still hurt to watch her walk out the door.

CHAPTER SIX

REGRET. THAT WAS THE FIRST thing Amanda felt when she looked at Jeannie, standing before her in their mother's beautiful white-lace wedding gown.

Her eyes stung and she had to blink, hard, to keep the emotion locked inside. This was the part of the ceremony she'd been dreading. She hadn't wanted to think about it because it didn't serve anybody to bring up the obvious: Mom had desperately wanted to see Jeannie celebrate her marriage vows, but she'd passed away too soon.

"Have you seen Massimo?" Jeannie asked. He was all Jeannie thought of today, and for a moment, Amanda blinked. But for her sister's sake, she swallowed the pain and crossed the side room where she and Jeannie had gathered. At the doorway she peered into the ancient Italian chapel.

There he stood, Jeannie's beloved, grinning from ear to ear beside his long line of groomsmen. The priest stood at the altar behind them, calmly waiting for Amanda and Jeannie to walk down the aisle so the wedding mass could begin. From the choir loft above, an organist solemnly played "Ave Maria." But the church wasn't hushed. Low murmurs filtered throughout. On Jeannie's side of the aisle sat her female ski-team friends and a smattering of aunts and cousins. A sparse turnout, but that was their sparse family.

Amanda's eyes watered. But no, she wasn't going to think about her mother. Instead, she glanced to the groom's side of the church.

It was packed, with everyone from Italian grand-mothers sobbing into their handkerchiefs to children scampering beneath the pews. A line of hard-bodied skiers filled the back row, and, for a moment, Amanda found herself looking for the hottest one of all.

Yeah, right. When I win the Pulitzer Prize. This was a one-night stand, and you knew it going in.

So why was she suddenly wishing with all her heart Brody had come?

Because I've never had a one-night stand before.

Can I see you again? Brody had asked. But all one-night stands said that the next morning, just to be polite. Didn't they?

A tear rolled down her cheek and Amanda swiped at it. Jeannie's arm curled around her waist.

"Mandy, this is a happy day," Jeannie said.

"It is." *I'll get over it,* she thought. The key was to keep her feelings locked inside and let them out only when it was safe.

Now was not safe. She trained her gaze on the gran-ite floor, and felt another tear dripping down her nose.

"Mandy, what's wrong?" The celebrants were get-ting itchy. Heads were turning. Voices rising to open conversation.

"I wish she were here," Amanda whispered.

"I know, sweetie." She felt Jeannie's scratchy lace sleeve slide over her shoulders. "But you have to know you took good care of her. Mom told me so herself. You couldn't do anything more to help her."

"She wanted to make it to this day. She wanted to be here, desperately." The waterworks were flowing harder now. Dammit, she'd promised herself she wouldn't do this to her sister.

"Don't you know?" Jeannie dabbed Amanda's eyes with her "something borrowed, something blue" handkerchief, and then tucked it into Amanda's hand. Who was the big sister and who was the little sister now? "Mom *is* here with us, Mandy. Can't you feel her spirit?"

Amanda hugged her sister. Yes, she could feel her mother's calm presence, because Jeannie *was* her mother's calm presence. They were like twin souls. And Amanda had never understood how they could stay so accepting of life as it was, and not as it should be. "Aren't you mad?" she asked. "Don't you feel cheated? Don't you feel like you deserve more?"

And then Amanda did what she'd been avoiding doing all week—she looked specifically at her baby sister's metal crutches. The crutches that would be part of her life every day for a long time, maybe always. The crutches that were all her father's fault because he'd pushed her and pushed her, even when she wasn't physically ready to race that mountain.

He's not even here, she thought bitterly. *He can't stand for everyone to see what he did to her when she hobbles down that aisle. And he should stand it. Oh, he should.*

But Jeannie just smiled—that same, angelic "mom" smile that used to drive Amanda crazy—and she kissed Amanda on the cheek as she handed her the maid of honor's bouquet of yellow daisies and white baby's breath. "I do deserve more, and I found it. He's standing at the altar waiting for me."

Amanda couldn't help smiling. "Massimo, the Prince of Men."

The gentle Italian was nothing like Dad. He wouldn't hurt Jeannie.

And Jeannie, in the most important way, was nothing like Mom. She had a boatload of accomplishments under her belt. More accomplishments than Massimo, if that was possible. Jeannie would always have the power to fight back and stand up to him if she ever needed to in their relationship. The two of them would always be on equal footing.

"Don't worry, Amanda," Jeannie promised, "we're going to find someone for you, too."

I've already found someone I like, Amanda thought, *and he hates Dad more than I do.*

And for that alone, it was impossible to have anything more with Brody than their stolen one-night stand. She lifted her chin and gripped the handkerchief in her fist.

And then she steadied her other hand against her sister's back and prepared to walk her down the wedding aisle.

BRODY SAT WITH HIS TEAM at a trattoria in the village. The remains of a wolfed-down lunch lay spread over a pockmarked table, though Brody hadn't touched his plate. Franz, fluent in Italian, was turned to the television on the wall and was translating the commentary from a news program about politicians and sex scandals. Hermann and Steve cracked jokes, and even serious Jean-Claude tossed in his X-rated two cents.

Just what Brody needed; he felt like crap as it was. He closed his eyes and held a heavy white porcelain cup, steaming with thick espresso, to his face. He'd dragged himself through two morning meetings followed by a grueling workout and then this lunch meeting, but the whole time his mind had been fixated on the early-morning hours and his last conversation with Amanda.

He'd made a huge mistake with her last night. Taken a risk and been kicked in the teeth for it. Maybe it really was karma, and he had a lot to make up for before he could earn the life he wanted. He wasn't entirely sure he bought into that stuff, but why else would he have fallen for a city-girl reporter who lived six time zones away?

And yeah, he'd had sex with her. Sweet God, had they had sex.

His body still throbbed with it. No amount of weight-lifting or cardio could push away the memory of her skin sliding over his. She was under his skin even now, like an itch he couldn't scratch. And he couldn't start over with her, track her down and ask for her phone number, because MacArthur was attending the wedding reception where she currently was.

That was a sign, if Brody had ever seen one. A sign to get on with it. He put down the espresso and reached for the bill because Harrison had left early to drive to Alto Baglio for a meeting with the Xerxes people. After Brody settled the charges, his guys were loading up the RVs, packing the Alfa, and they were all headed to Alto Baglio, as well.

Chapter closed on Amanda Jensen. It was for the best. Pack up and move on.

So why did he feel so lousy?

His phone buzzed. *Harrison*, was Brody's first thought. He glanced at the phone to be sure.

Massimo Coletti, the caller ID said.

He picked it up, not knowing what to think. "Yeah, this is Brody."

"Brody Jones?" A female voice murmured his name uncertainly. "This is Jeannie Coletti."

He blanked for a minute, but then he remembered: Jeannie Jensen, the wedding, she'd married Massimo. "Congratulations," he said carefully.

"Thank you." Her voice dropped to a whisper. "I'm sorry if I'm out of line, but it's about Amanda."

In a second, he was on his feet. "What's wrong?"

"She's…crying in the bathroom." Jeannie's words came in a rush. Wherever she was, there was noise—conversation in Italian and faint music—so he had to cover his free ear to hear her. "We just got to the reception, and we're lining up to take pictures. She doesn't know I'm calling you. Massimo does though."

He looked over at his guys. They had stopped joking and were staring at him, straining to hear.

"I know she was with you last night, Brody," Jeannie said. "She told me before she left to meet you. And then when she didn't come home…"

He turned to the window, but he wasn't seeing anything. He spoke softly into the phone. "Did she tell you why she's upset?"

"I…no. And it's been a busy day for me, I've been occupied with wedding things. I just thought…well, we want to issue you an invitation to our reception. If you can come, that is."

He heard an intake of breath on the line. "Never mind. *He's* here. I shouldn't have called you. This is a bad idea, for everyone. I need to go."

"Jeannie, don't—"

"Forget I called, Brody, okay?" The line clicked off.

He shoved his phone in his jacket. Jean-Claude, the driver who'd been tailing MacArthur, arched his brow and waited for an update.

Yeah, *he* was there. *He* meant MacArthur Jensen, the bride's father. Who else could it be?

Brody looked around the table. Four pairs of eyes stared back at him, and all he could think was, *What did Jeannie Coletti mean by "bad idea for everyone"?* Did she think it was a bad idea for him to go to the reception? Or a bad idea for Amanda to see him?

It was the latter that ripped him apart more.

THIRTY MINUTES LATER, Brody, dressed in his suit and a white dress shirt, pulled open the door of the hotel ballroom and wondered if he'd ever been such an idiot.

Snowflakes dusted his sleeves, shoulders and hair. One to two inches were forecast to fall on the mountains tonight, and instead of getting the early start he needed, he was standing in the back of a reception hall where he clearly didn't belong.

Find her and make sure she's okay. Then wrestle her phone number from her, and leave.

That was his mission. He'd give himself twenty minutes, tops. And if he could do it in ten minutes, then he was a superstar.

He glanced around the crowded room but didn't see Amanda. None of the wedding party had arrived—no bride in a big white dress, no groom in a tuxedo. Then again, he'd never been to an Italian wedding before, so he didn't know what was supposed to be happening.

In the corner, a bar was open. Liquor flowed freely, and a group of guys he knew waved him over. Normally he'd join them, but his life was far from normal these days. He shook his head at them, and then looked to the rest of the room. Family groups of all ages and sizes were crowded at round dinner tables, staking their places. A plump grandmother poured her grandson a glass of red wine mixed with water, and the boy happily drank it.

He loved this culture. They were out in the open and honest; happy and loud and proud together. Someday he'd love to move to Europe permanently, settle in a mountain town like this one and start a family. He didn't care how many kids he had—or even if he had any—his main requirement was familial closeness.

A commotion sounded from the front of the ballroom. Supported by attendants carrying her aloft in a chair, the bride made her grand entrance. All around him chairs scraped and people jumped to their feet, whistling and chanting in Italian.

He didn't know what they were saying, but he was tall enough that he could see over their heads. Every fiber in his body concentrated on finding Amanda. The bride was set down on a dais. Crouched behind the bride's train, fixing and primping and spreading it over the floor, making sure the bride was the main attraction, he finally spotted Amanda. His heart made a small jump.

He cleared his throat and stepped forward just as she stood. The back of her dress was cut in a V, and from shoulders to waist, all he could see was skin. The same sweet, soft skin he'd kissed and stroked and tasted last night.

His mouth went dry. He wanted her again. He kept his gaze on her, following her movements as she turned. Her dress was made of a silky, clingy fabric that flowed when she walked, and he imagined her dropping it for him. Somewhere in private, smiling at him and wearing nothing but her dark hair up and studded with those tiny silver and white pearls he could pick out to make it all come cascading down again.

"Just what do you think you're doing here?" The unmistakable voice sounded in Brody's ear, and he felt the bottom slide out of his stomach.

MacArthur Jensen, his former coach—now the head director of the skiing federation—was giving Brody a withering look, the look he'd give gum scraped from the bottom of his shoe.

I'm screwed. Brody stared into the eyes of the man he'd told to "go shove it" as many different times and ways as he could over the years, and he knew he'd messed up.

Harrison would pitch a fit if he knew Brody was here. "Like teasing a cobra with a stick," Harrison would say. "What's that going to get you, Brody?"

Not a damn thing but trouble, he silently replied.

And now, he forced himself to breathe. To lower himself and make nice with the king of all snakes.

"I'm attending the wedding of a fellow skier," he said evenly. His mouth tasted brackish and he hated himself for doing it, but he held out his hand in a gesture of conciliation.

"You have a lot of balls." MacArthur's dark eyes hooded to slits. "You cross me, and now you dare to show up at my daughter's wedding?"

Brody dropped his hand. "I was invited."

"And I'm uninviting you."

So MacArthur wouldn't make it easy for him. He probably wouldn't accept Brody back on the circuit, either. The only thing Brody could do now was get the hell out of Dodge, and then hope it was enough to survive the one race he needed to ski.

He stepped back.

And MacArthur smiled. A gloating look, pleased at

the reaction he'd received, at the control he still held over Brody.

"I'm feeling magnanimous because it's my daughter's wedding. Turn around and leave now, and I'll pretend I didn't see you."

MacArthur was giving him a pass? Brody clenched his fists. More than anything he wanted to give him the two-fingered salute MacArthur so hated, but he sucked it up, even though he knew he was a coward for doing so.

"Yeah, I'll be going," Brody said.

MacArthur smirked. "Watch yourself." And then he proceeded down the aisle of the ballroom. Brody should have left right then, but fury was coursing through him—at MacArthur and at himself. MacArthur's entourage of followers surrounded him, one to carry his coat, another to hold his BlackBerry and still one more just to make him look more important—and Brody hadn't done a damn thing to stand up to him.

There was nothing he could do to stop the man who had ruined his life because MacArthur would always hold all the power. One word, one move from MacArthur, and Brody's name was dust.

He unclenched his fists. For some reason, his feet were rooted to the floor. He watched as MacArthur's daughter paused—Massimo was hugging her around her crutches and "dancing" with her to slow music as the crowd sat, eerily silent. Even the bad-ass skiers he knew had frozen in their tracks. They were a superstitious group, and nobody liked to view the aftereffects of a horrific alpine crash.

Brody exhaled. MacArthur himself wavered, and his entourage stopped. For a moment the guests held their collective breath, but then the bride beckoned to her father, a huge smile spreading over her face, which MacArthur didn't deserve. But Brody had to give him credit; MacArthur squared his shoulders and walked onto the dance floor.

Massimo released Jeannie's arms. A flicker of something—physical pain?—crossed her face, but it was quickly replaced by a look of joy as she balanced herself over her crutches again, one hand on her father's shoulder. Then she kissed him on his cheek.

Revulsion kicked Brody. How could she forgive the tyrant who had ruined her life?

Amanda, he noticed, shared his revulsion. But she was wise enough to disappear discreetly into the background during the father-of-the-bride's entrance. Even Massimo stood back as if he was a nervous high-school kid taking out the principal's daughter.

Brody switched his attention back to Amanda. She turned toward him, and then he saw the tears she was blinking away. She was obviously affected by the bride's awkward dance in her metal crutches.

Her metal crutches. He felt as if he'd been smacked in the head by a slalom gate. *This* was why Amanda had been crying in the bathroom when Jeannie had called him. He could see the true reason, and Jeannie couldn't.

He was striding forward before he'd thought anything through. All he could think was what an ass he'd been to so cavalierly make Amanda go skiing with him. Then the band struck into loud, festive Italian music while the band leader announced into the microphone—in both English and Italian—that the family of the bride "will say the words of greeting and then the dancing will begin!"

Obviously, he needed to wait until the "words of greeting" finished. But with any luck he'd have

Amanda spirited out of here soon afterward, before MacArthur noticed he hadn't exactly left the building yet.

Brody's phone beeped, and he glanced at it. A text message from Harrison. Brody had already ignored dozens of them, so he might as well answer this one while he had a minute. Where are u? the message asked.

On my way, Brody typed.

Where r u now?

He thought of Amanda and couldn't help the private joke. Free skiing.

A pause. Then, Good. Stay away from that wedding.

Brody glanced up at "that wedding" and his scalp started to itch. Amanda stood at the podium, staring at him, an expression of horror on her face.

Why was she so upset? And what was she doing standing at the microphone?

"And here I present to you Miss Amanda Jensen," the band leader hollered. "The maid of honor and sister of the bride!"

Sister of the bride? The hand holding his phone dropped to his side. That couldn't be right. Amanda wasn't Jeannie Jensen's sister, because she wasn't Mac-Arthur Jensen's daughter. She had sworn that to him, and on her own voice recorder.

He stuffed his phone in his jacket, his hand shaking. He was getting the bad feeling that he'd been lied to in a way he'd sworn would never happen again, not while he drew breath.

He gritted his jaw and met Amanda's gaze with a burning look. *Tell me the band leader made a mistake.*

But she blinked at him and shook her head, sadness spreading over her face. "I'm sorry, Brody," she mouthed.

She was *sorry?* She'd been lying to him from the moment she'd met him, and she was *sorry?*

Yeah, well, I am, too, sweetheart, he thought.

He turned on his heel and stalked from the room. Then he pulled out his phone and ordered the caravan to gather. Before his shoes hit the pavement, his team would be mobilized with engines started.

Out of here.

CHAPTER SEVEN

THE SOLES OF HER DYED-TO-MATCH shoes made outlines in the snowy parking lot as Amanda raced down the rows of flake-dusted automobiles, searching for Brody.

She'd been so happy to see him at Jeannie's reception. But just as quickly she'd realized what the master of ceremonies would say, and her joy had been swallowed by a horrible, sinking pit of despair.

And why? For a guy she could never be with after the weekend?

Now, she didn't know what she was doing. Chasing after a one-night stand? It had to be the emotions brought on by her little sister getting married. That had to be the reason—she'd officially gone insane.

The below-freezing temperature chilled her to the bone. She'd run out without a coat; she still wore her bridesmaid's dress with nothing to cover her bare arms and back. Though it was late afternoon, the sky was dark with falling snow, a flurry the weather forecasters had predicted would amount to little accumulation. But above the cover of dark clouds, where she couldn't see or feel it, the sun would be present, low and beautiful on the horizon, just as it had been when Brody had kissed her on the mountain yesterday.

How could so much have happened in twenty-four hours? Her emotions would swamp her if she stopped to think about it.

But then she found what she was looking for: over the slope in the lower parking lot, a group of men in ski parkas milled around two motor homes, their engines already running.

Brody! It had to be him and his team leaving for the next race on the circuit. Panic spurred her on, and she sprinted toward them, panting. "Wait!" She windmilled her arms as the last man stepped inside the idling motor home. "Hold up a minute!"

But no one answered. Desperate, she gasped as she ran harder. Her upswept wedding hair came out of its pins, the ends whipped by the wind and blowing into her eyes. She stopped paces away, shivering, aware of how ridiculous she must look.

Please, Brody. Don't leave yet. Not like this.

Beside her, his sexy, languid body unfolded from the driver's seat of a black Italian sports car, parked next to the motor home where she stood.

"Brody?" she asked.

His penetrating eyes focused on her. They were dark now, not heart-stopping baby blue, but cloudy. Angry, hurt, maybe even resigned.

She shivered. His brow rose at her dress, her hair, her presence. "Here." He unzipped his parka and handed it to her. "Put this on and go back inside."

"No." She wasn't leaving until she'd explained herself. She caught the coat in her hand and then held it, waiting for him to face her, not letting him see how cold she was. "I need to talk with you. It's important."

"There's no point."

"Please." She put all her heart into that word.

He seemed to waver, the muscles in his jaw clenching and then releasing. He gave a curt nod, then leaned inside the motor home to speak to the team member. "Do you mind waiting? I'll be ready in a minute."

So he would hear her out, then. She rubbed at her goose-pimpled arms as a big guy, blond, probably German or Scandinavian, lumbered down the RV steps and joined the group in the second, smaller motor home.

"Are those the guys on your personal team?" she asked Brody. Of course they were. Coaches and ski tuners and trainers. Jeannie had told her he'd split from the main team because he couldn't get along with her father. "That's quite an entourage."

Brody crossed his arms and leaned against the motor home his men had left him. "It's expensive fielding my own team, which is the only reason I gave you that interview yesterday."

Okay, so she'd expected him to be angry with her. But there had been more between them than just business, and she needed him to acknowledge that. She licked her lips and stared at her toes, picturing the messed-up pedicure inside her shoes. "You asked me to go skiing with you afterward."

He laughed dryly. "I'm a seat-of-the-pants kind of guy. I follow my intuition. But my intuition hasn't done me any good where you're concerned, has it?"

Humor. That was it; they needed a bit of humor.

She smiled sadly at him. "Brody, your intuition is working just fine. It's my sense of self-preservation that isn't."

He shook his head. "Don't try to charm me, Amanda. This is serious, you lied to me."

"No," she said slowly. "I told you the truth. I don't have a relationship with that man."

"That man is your father."

"Not in his mind he isn't."

He shook his head again. "I know him. He doesn't let anyone go, ever, not for any reason."

"He did with me. He walked away," she insisted.

Brody stared dully at her. "I don't believe you."

"I didn't lie to you yesterday. I said I have no relationship to that man, and I don't." Her chest was heaving from all the running she'd done, and she felt cold from the tips of her fingers to her toes.

But Brody wasn't listening. He'd turned his back to her, and she wanted to make him pay attention.

"Didn't you see him in there?" she shouted, pointing to the hotel. "He hates me! He'd as soon cut off his arm as look at me. I don't exist to him, Brody, don't you get that?"

"How would I get that?" Brody turned furiously. "From where I'm sitting, you conned me. You deliberately conned me." His voice broke.

"I didn't!" Tears burned her eyelids, and she swiped them away. "Jeannie told me there's bad blood between you two, but she didn't tell me why and I didn't ask any questions. Growing up, pretty much everybody in my town thought my father was a pompous jerk, so I'm used to that reaction to him. I get it." Bitter laughter shotgunned from her mouth. "More than anyone, I get it."

"For a journalist, not asking questions about the guy you're interviewing doesn't seem likely."

"Brody, interviewing guys like you isn't my normal job. I don't do celebrity promotional pieces. They only used me for this because I'm already on site for Jeannie's wedding. It was cheaper for them that way." *The bastards.*

"What's your normal job?" he asked coldly.

"I work on corruption investigations back in New York." Or at least she hoped to. She had so little experience in the business, and she needed more. She should be running from Brody Jones and all the complications he brought her.

She looked down at the snowy ground. "Forget it. I need to get back to the wedding."

And all the sadness that stirred up in her heart. Missing her mother. And both hating her father and feeling hurt by him. Tears threatened again, and she shivered uncontrollably.

"Hey," he said softly. His arm was on hers, and he was escorting her up the stairs of his RV. Dimly she felt a soft fleece blanket encircle her bare skin. It smelled like the same kind of fabric softener her mom had used, and that made a sob escape, as though a faucet had burst open.

Oh, God.

He drew her within the circle of his arms. Her face pressed against his coat, cold from the snow, and then closer still, warm with his body heat. As if she could cuddle against him and be blanketed with comfort. She'd felt that for a split second this morning, but she'd pushed it away.

Now…she clung to him.

Outside, a horn tooted.

Brody stepped back. "Sweetheart, wait here. I'm going to tell them to go on without me."

"But…"

He shook his head. "I'll catch up with them later."

Feeling empty without his embrace, she snapped out of the spell. She wiped her eyes, then took off the blanket and with shaking hands attempted to fold it.

"You don't have to do this." But her wavering voice betrayed her.

"Yeah, I do." He gently placed the blanket back around her shoulders. Then he smiled wanly at her. "Maybe it will be good for us to compare notes. When I come back, you're going to tell me everything."

WHILE AMANDA WAITED FOR BRODY, she walked the length of his personal motor home. It smelled comfortable inside, like ski wax and freshly laundered bedding. In the back was a bed, made up, with two pillows and a down comforter similar to the linens in the hotel bed they'd shared last night. She squeezed her eyes shut, blotting out the memory that was too painful to think of.

She sat at the table instead, beside a large window that faced the hotel. On the table was a map printed from the internet, with a route traced in red marker and a handwritten date circled and labeled: Alto Baglio, Sunday.

That was a week from today. Alto Baglio was a stop on the World Cup tour famous for its slalom race. Though still in Italy, the course was hours away on the other side of the Alps at a mountain resort in the Dolomites, closer to Austria.

She propped her chin in her hands, studying the map. She'd been there once. She knew that place.

A door slammed, and she heard the noise of a motor home driving off with a rattle, followed by the crunch of snow beneath the tires of a car.

Brody came inside, bringing winter with him, and stomping the snow from his shoes. His suit jacket was open and he still wore his dark wedding pants and white shirt. His tie was loosened around his neck and the shirt unbuttoned a few inches, as if wearing a suit made him uncomfortable.

"Are you sure you want to do this?" she asked.

"Yeah." He unrolled a bag of coffee, dumping grounds into the bottom of a French press. He was plugging in an electric kettle, setting water to boil.

"Why come back for the wedding?" she asked. "You have a race to prepare for."

His eyes, so electric blue, met hers. "I came back because Jeannie called me about you."

She gasped, feeling the shock to her heart. Her beautiful, injured sister was worried about her, and on her wedding day?

Amanda had to stop this misery. Obviously, she needed to get it out of her system, talk with somebody before she went back into the ballroom and celebrated her sister's wedding the way Jeannie deserved.

But with Brody?

Wrapped up in his blanket she watched him hunting down mugs, making them coffee to taste—his black, hers with milk—and then sitting across from her at the small table. The bed was in his line of vision, but either he didn't notice, or it didn't affect him the way it affected her.

He curled his big hands around his mug of coffee and gave her that quiet look she couldn't resist. "What happened to make your father angry at you?"

She looked down at her own hands. She had willingly pursued this line of questioning by following him in here.

"Manda?" he asked softly.

That made her smile. His personal nickname for her, a reminder of their intimacy last night.

"He's not just angry at me, Brody," she said slowly,

"he disowned me." She inhaled the familiar, welcoming smell of coffee beans. "He told me I'm no longer his daughter, and since last spring he's been true to his word. He looks through me like I don't exist. Like I'm invisible."

Brody swore under his breath.

She looked up from the coffee's curl of steam into Brody's blue eyes. "Why is he mad at you?"

Brody shook his head. "I chafed against his training instructions. It doesn't matter." He stared at her. "Because I'm not related to him. He dotes on Jeannie—why doesn't he dote on you? I trained with that man for a year, and he only ever mentioned one daughter."

Once again, Brody had struck the heart of the matter. Her face heated.

"Manda?" he said in a low voice that made her want to curl up on his lap. "Is it because you didn't win ski races?" he asked gently.

"It…started out that way," she admitted. "When I was young. It got worse in college, when I switched my major from business."

"Is that why you chose journalism? Because he hates journalists?"

"I…no."

Not completely anyway.

Brody was studying her. His brow was creased with the concern of a guy who wanted to help her, but didn't yet know that it was futile. Some conflicts were just too big to solve. All you did was survive them.

"He never really…approved of me, Brody. He just… tolerated me. I could live with that. But the end came when I started advocating for my mother. She was…diagnosed with cancer. She was so sick. They said there wasn't any hope for her, but I found this one doctor who had an experimental treatment he wanted to try. But insurance wouldn't pay for it and she didn't have any money and he—"

Her throat had shuttered and she couldn't go on. Brody's hand closed over hers. "You stood up for her, didn't you?" he asked quietly.

"Y-yes." But she'd failed. Horribly. "I confronted MacArthur and gave him an ultimatum, which only made him angrier."

Brody's breath expelled. "You gave him an ultimatum?"

"I did."

"And this was during his divorce?"

He knew. He understood. She felt so relieved she didn't have to explain the embarrassment of her father to him. Most men…well, who could understand a person like her father? "I'll never know how anyone could be so big a bastard as to divorce their spouse right after a cancer diagnosis," she said bitterly.

He took a drink of coffee, glancing at her over the cup. "You were aware he had a girlfriend he was chasing at the time?"

No. Yes. But her mom had told Amanda not to believe the rumors. That she didn't believe they were true.

Brody would know. "You think that had something to do with it?" she asked in a small voice, sipping her coffee. It was heartening, warm and strong and milky.

He shrugged carefully. "He never talks about his personal life, so who could be sure? But MacArthur is like a chess player. He keeps everything close to the vest. His actions seem inexplicable, until you remember he's always playing ten moves ahead. Only then does he start to make sense."

She was getting a clearer picture. Her father could

have lost his money and his assets in the divorce, with nothing to start again. She didn't know the divorce laws in her state, but maybe this had something to do with his motivation and his timing and why he'd seemed particularly, needlessly cruel.

But she'd never know for sure. She and her father would never talk, not the way she and Brody were talking now.

Her eyes watered.

"It's for the best, Amanda." He leaned forward and gave her an intense stare. "Because now you're off his radar screen. He's not hurting you anymore."

"Just by refusing to talk to me, he's hurting me."

"You *want* a relationship with him?"

"No. I'll never trust him enough for that. I just want..."

What? What did she want?

Brody waited, too.

"I want...to stop feeling like a failure when he looks past me." She glanced up at him. He wasn't smiling.

She faked a smile. "Never mind," she said lightly. "I'll bet you had the most understanding, supportive father in the universe. One who stood behind you and applauded you no matter what you showed a talent for."

He stared dully at her.

"What is he?" she asked. "A teacher? A doctor?"

"A con man," he said coldly. "He's in prison. Fraud, five years."

"I...oh."

"It's the best-kept secret on the tour. And now you know."

HE DIDN'T REGRET TELLING HER. Amanda had been so forlorn and upset, thinking she was the only person in the world who had a rotten father, and feeling ashamed for it, as if it was her fault. Brody knew how that felt, but unlike her he'd gotten over it years ago. He knew there was no sense trying to change someone, no sense trying to get someone to act in a way that was contrary to their nature. His father compulsively lied. Hers compulsively lorded over people.

He accepted that. He stood then and collected the empty coffee cups, dumped out the electric kettle, while she dried out her shoes and wiggled her toes back into them.

So she was returning to the wedding like a trouper. He was willing to bet not too many people in her life accepted her as she was. Maybe her sister, from the way Amanda spoke of her, but that was about it. Amanda probably would never realize it, but she'd shown him a thing or two about hanging tough and standing up for one's self.

While he watched her, she squinted at the small mirror on the wall. She was pulling at her cheek with an expression of "I don't look good enough." But she did. God, she did. And that silky dress was covering her curves, so warm and perfect.

And then the blood was heating through him. He went up behind her and pressed his lips to the nape of her neck. She sighed, arching against him, and it was easy, too easy to reach down and bunch her long skirt, draw the material up, over her bottom and to her waist. He pulled her to him and slid his hand inside the elastic of her panties.

"Don't go." The words seemed hoarse, his breath hot against the snow of her skin.

From somewhere, a phone trilled.

"It's Jeannie," she whispered. "I have to take it."

CHAPTER EIGHT

WITH REGRET PULLING THROUGH his heart, Brody dropped the skirt of her dress, and it fell over her panties with a swish.

Her cheeks flushed, she stepped away from him and answered the phone. "Hi, Jeannie, I'm coming."

Now? He ran his hands through his hair and sat on the bed. He didn't want to eavesdrop, but he couldn't help overhearing Jeannie's voice emanating from the phone.

"Mandy, where are you? It's so crowded in here I can't see you. Can you stand on a chair and wave or something? We're getting ready for the bouquet-tossing and, um, Marco's been asking for you. Should I tell him to forget it?"

Brody stilled. Marco? Who the hell was that?

Amanda's blush deepened. "I, um, I'll be right there," she said into her phone. "Wait for me before you do anything." She disconnected the call and gave Brody an apologetic look.

"Who's Marco?" he asked.

"Nobody." But she was already pinning up her hair. "Look, I really have to go. She's my only sister and I'll regret it forever if I miss any more of her wedding."

He didn't know what to say. Which bothered him most, that another man was intent on meeting her, or that Amanda wasn't turning him down?

She looked sidelong at him and reached for her purse. "I'd like you to stay for the reception, but if you can't, I understand."

"Hell, Amanda, you know that I can't."

She nodded, lifting her chin. "You're right. Have a safe drive then." Swallowing, she stuck out her hand. "Goodbye, Brody Jones. Good luck at Alto Baglio."

SHE HATED TO LEAVE HIM, but it was for the best. He had his training, and she had a flight to catch first thing in the morning. Their schedules didn't match and neither did their lives.

Right, Amanda. Way to rationalize. She huddled against the cold, hurrying across the parking lot and trying not to sniffle. Her chest felt tight but no, she wouldn't let herself break down. This was Jeannie's day. She'd been wrong to leave her sister's wedding in the first place. Now, she needed to make it up to her. She'd miss Brody later, that was for sure, but not here, not until she'd done what she needed to do.

Inside the hotel, she quickly made her way to the ballroom. The noise was deafening, with the band playing an Italian pop song and the strobe lights flashing as if they were in a Milan disco. A group of wedding guests threaded through the wildly dancing crowd and sang the lyrics to something Amanda couldn't catch. The "Chicken Song" in Italian, maybe? The "Electric Slide"? She'd never been to a wedding on this side of the Atlantic, so she wasn't sure what the customs were.

Jeannie, however, seemed happy. Thank goodness. The Colettis had embraced her sister as one of their own, and Amanda was relieved she'd found the big-family harmony she'd always wanted.

Jeannie spotted her in the crowd and waved her over.

"Come up here, Mandy!" She sat on a chair on the dais, clutching the master of ceremony's microphone in both hands to her chest. "Excuse me," Jeannie's hoarse-from-celebrating voice rasped into the microphone. "All the single ladies please come to the front of the room. It's time for the bouquet toss!"

But nobody in the crowd came forward. Most of the guests kept dancing until Massimo borrowed the microphone and translated Jeannie's words into a string of ultra-fast Italian from which Amanda, with only one semester of night-school Italian under her belt, couldn't pick out a familiar word. Why did Italian always take more words and sound so much more romantic than English did?

And then a middle-aged lady and a teen joined Amanda on the dais. Just two women in this whole wedding reception were single? It figured. The teen grinned at Amanda and the middle-aged lady smiled and patted her hand.

My lonely-hearts support crew, Amanda thought.

"Ready, set, and…go!" Jeannie turned around and tossed her bridal bouquet of daisies and English ivy high overhead. Personally, Amanda was rooting for the middle-aged lady to catch it. The teen looked far too young for settling down, and Amanda, well, she had her job to set her heart on, didn't she?

Plop. The bouquet landed on the parquet before them. None of the three of them had made a move to reach for it.

Now this was embarrassing. Jeannie's face looked flushed and distraught. Her beautiful bouquet lay on the dusty floor like a lonely wilted memory.

Amanda stood before it. Wouldn't she be a good sister if she dried the daisies for Jeannie and made an arrangement for her? Maybe she could trim some of the ivy and grow a plant for her, too. Then Jeannie would have something to remember her wedding forever. She'd looked so happy standing there with her new husband.

"Mandy?" Jeannie pleaded. "Will you pick it up, honey, please?"

"Okay." So for sisterly reasons, and for sisterly reasons only, Amanda picked up the bouquet.

BRODY SPENT EXACTLY FIVE minutes behind the wheel of his RV, engine idling, before he turned it off and pocketed the key. *Damn it.*

He had to be out of his mind. He had appointments tomorrow morning he couldn't afford to miss, and a half inch of snow already covered the pavement. With more falling every minute, the driving would be slower than usual.

But he couldn't leave yet. Not after the way he'd felt holding Amanda just now, and not after the visions he was having of her lithe body pressed against a horny Marco dancing with her—which he'd never had the chance to do, by the way—sending daggers of jealousy stabbing through him.

Besides, he thought, slamming the RV's door behind him, there was an even bigger issue niggling at him that he needed to stand up and face: the fact that Amanda had confronted and stared down MacArthur, and MacArthur had left her alone for it.

That was the classic reaction of a bully. Brody hadn't realized it until she'd shown him.

Having MacArthur leave him alone was all Brody needed in order to solve his problems. It was that simple.

He pulled his phone from his pocket and purposely turned it off. He wasn't running with his tail between his legs any longer; he was going back to have his say with his old coach. Locking the RV, he trotted across the parking lot, the snow falling gently, and then marched inside the hotel. As luck would have it, MacArthur stood in the lobby, not ten feet away.

Brody stopped, assessing. MacArthur's back was to him, and he held his black cashmere overcoat slung over his arm. A man and a woman Brody recognized as being from the wedding party—Massimo's parents?—were conversing with him in low tones.

Brody jiggled his keys in his pocket as he slowly let out his breath. Now was a bad time for a confrontation. And worse, down the hall, European pop music poured from the ballroom. Massimo was on the microphone, shouting over the synthesizers in rapid Italian. Brody caught the words *Amanda Jensen.*

His chest clutched with the sense that she was in trouble. He stalked inside the crowded reception, which had doubled in size to about three hundred people. Wedding crashers, he realized. *Hell.* A group of thirty to forty guys milled in the back; they looked like fans left over from the downhill race earlier in the weekend. Brody moved past them, threading his way toward the bride's table, searching for Manda. His shirt was still unbuttoned at the neck and he hadn't bothered to knot his tie, but judging by the rest of the crowd, he fit right in. A woman staggered past looking as if she'd had too many limoncellos. She saw his face and screamed, "Brody Jones!" in the manner he knew so well.

Here we go, he thought, as a chorus of voices picked up his name. He lowered his head like a ram and went plowing through the crowd, figuring if he wasn't anonymous, he could at least be quick. "Excuse me, moving forward."

One of the wedding crashers, a young man of about twenty-five with a scraggly goatee stepped directly into his path. "Can I have your autograph, Brody?"

"Yeah, sure," Brody said by rote. "Got a pen?"

The fan stared blankly at him. "No."

"Then if you don't mind, we'll do it another time."

He moved on, visions of an Italian lothario stalking Amanda onto the dance floor urging him to hurry the hell up, but then the fan grabbed his arm and tugged back on him, hard. "Can you find me a pen?"

Brody had thought he'd seen everything, but the attitudes of some people never ceased to amaze him. He stared pointedly at the fan's claw-like grip on his suit jacket, and then at the fan. "No, I cannot," he said calmly. "Please release my arm."

"No," the fan said.

No?

"I am your biggest supporter," the fan slurred. "I travel to every race you ski, and I will not leave until I have your autograph."

Brody glanced toward the dais but he couldn't see Amanda, he just heard Massimo shouting something in Italian into the microphone.

This didn't bode well. And he didn't understand enough Italian to know how bad it was.

He sighed and stared down at the fan's bony grip on his arm. In the old days, pre-injury, Brody would have shaken off the guy and then laughed about it with his friends. Maybe he would have called hotel security if the fan got persistent enough. But he had too much to lose now. He couldn't afford to tempt the many journalist-fans with blogs and camera phones and grudges to air.

But he also needed to get to Amanda, pronto. He didn't have time to run down a pen and glad-hand this guy and his group of friends who were fast assembling, elbowing through the wedding guests and screaming for "Pen! Pen! Pen!" which none of the guests were offering up because they were too interested in listening to whatever it was Massimo was saying.

"Okay," Brody said to the guy. "Here's what we do." He held up his finger. "Invisible ink." He pointed to the guy. "Tattoo." And he scrawled an imaginary autograph on the guy's forehead. Hard.

"Wow." The guy removed his grip from Brody's arm and instead rubbed his own head. "That was super cool."

"When it wears off, come find me with a marker." Brody stepped aside. "But wait a while, because I need to get to the front of this room, or else I might not make it to Alto Baglio on time. You got it?"

"Okay." The fan nodded. "You are the man, Brody."

Shaking his head, Brody continued to push his way through the maze of bodies to Amanda. He found her sitting on a chair in front of the dais, looking stunned, though she still had the flush of the mountain wind in her cheeks, which made him smile.

Beside her, her sister beamed. Before them was a line of...was that the Italian men's alpine ski team?

They were locking arms and singing drunkenly. It looked like Saturday night after the downhill race in Val D'Isere.

You have got to be kidding me.

His first instinct was to storm the proverbial castle

and save Amanda. But after the shock wore off her face, she gave him a pleading look: *don't do anything rash.*

Yeah, he thought, *do you really think I'm going to let you suffer, sweetheart?* He would have sent her a text message asking her what she wanted him to do, but he didn't have her phone number.

And then came the deal-killer: a skinny, dark-haired guy with glasses that magnified his I'm-a-puppy-dog eyes tugged at Brody's suit jacket and then pushed in front of him, cutting directly into the center of a line of guys that was forming beside the skiers.

What the hell?

"Marco!" Jeannie called to the guy, recognizing him. "This is Amanda!"

Marco? Was this a setup?

And then it all happened in slow motion. First, the ski team stopped singing. Then the band decided to rest between songs. The guests stopped dancing the tarantella and decided to see what the action was up front, so they crowded the dais, pushing him forward.

An itching started on Brody's scalp. Every instinct of foreboding was screaming at him to do something. *Now.*

All eyes were on Amanda. And Marco, in the center of the line of men. The bespectacled runt was the recipient of bawdy backslaps and obscene mutterings.

Brody's teeth slowly began to grind.

"And…here we go!" Massimo Coletti lobbed something fist-sized into the air. The unidentified flying object was light blue and feminine-looking, made of satin and frilly lace. And it was arcing directly toward Marco. No one else even made a pretense at going for it, including the guys on the ski team.

Brody got a bad feeling in his gut this was some kind

of lewd ritual aimed at Amanda. Whatever the game was, she sat on her chair looking like a sacrificial offering to Jeannie's happiness, an expression of pure fear stamped across her face.

His teeth gritted. The decision was simple—he reached out his hand and caught the flying object. *Bam.* Like a fan over the Green Monster wall at Boston's Fenway Park, picking off a home run ball into his glove. Then he scrunched up the silky satin and stuffed it into his jacket pocket.

Marco blinked at him. He still held his empty hand forward, as if to say "That was mine."

"What did you expect?" Brody said to him. "I'm six inches taller than you and I have longer arms. It wasn't a fair contest."

And then a chorus rang out. "Brody Jones!" About three hundred voices comprised of wedding guests and crashers, most with Italian accents, chanted his name. The rest of the instructions they were shouting were unintelligible to him.

He turned to Marco. "What are they saying?"

"You are to put the garter on the thigh of Miss Jensen," Marco explained patiently.

"I'm to do what on the where?" He took the garter out of his pocket and stared at the thing.

"It goes on the thigh of the lady. As high as your hand can reach." Marco mimed the action. Brody felt his blood pressure soar ten points. The twit looked a world-class groper.

This is baloney, he thought. In his mind, weddings were sacred events, not a time for post-race barroom antics. Not that Brody had been to many sacred events. But he could imagine.

So he did what any self-respecting man would do.

He strode forward, picked Amanda up and carried her away from there. Through the crowd, toward the darkest corner of the deserted dance floor, where he set her down, hoping she wasn't mad at him. "Could we, uh, please dance or something?" he asked.

Amanda was laughing. "You never cease to amaze me." She kissed him on his cheek. "Thank you for rescuing me." But still, she shook her head as if he was the funniest guy she'd ever seen.

"What? I don't get it."

"Don't you know about throwing the garter, Brody? It's just a wedding game."

"It seems like a perverted version of Pin the Tail on the Donkey."

She draped her arms around his neck, pulling him closer. The band was on break and somebody had hooked up an iPod. U2 was playing an excellent, bluesy version of "Love Rescue Me."

Brody wasn't a dancer, not by a long shot. But there was something about the way the bass vibrated through his bones, something about the woman who held him so tightly and yet so loosely, too. She was smiling up at him in a way he hadn't seen in a long time, probably never.

She understood him. And she accepted him, even knowing a bit of his crappy background. That was a comforting feeling, he was fast realizing.

He slid his hands around her waist and drew her to him. But they weren't alone for long. A guy dancing in the crowd bumped into her, stepping on her foot. She winced, and he steered her into a corner.

"Pardon!" the guy called.

"I think he's one of the Rome relatives," Amanda explained, bending down as she rubbed her toes. "Massimo's mother comes from a big family down south."

"Maybe so, but that doesn't give them the excuse to put you up on the dais like a piece of meat for their entertainment."

"A piece of meat, huh?" She smiled at him. "Then I'm glad you weren't here earlier for the *buste*."

"What's that?" Or did he even want to know?

She stepped into his arms and put her head on his shoulder. "It's a tradition where the male guests pay to dance with Jeannie. Only in this case, they kissed her on the cheek because it's awkward for her to dance."

"Massimo's friends do this?" He felt incredulous.

"It's a sign of respect. Not everybody thinks in terms of sex like you do," she whispered into his ear.

"Trust me, sweetheart. Every man thinks of sex." He drew back and looked into her eyes. "Amanda, we're in Italy. They invented sex."

"The *buste* is perfectly innocent. It's for fundraising. You know, to pay for the wedding."

"Uh-huh. And I'm a ballroom-dancing expert. Come on."

He clasped her hand and led her out of the crowded room to the quiet corridor beside the coat racks. The place was deserted—even the attendant had decamped in favor of the open bar. Out the window, the snow fell silently down. The only sound was the faint drift of music playing inside the ballroom.

He looked at her, beautiful in her silver dress and upswept hair and shining eyes. He felt like a kid at his first real dance.

"Will you dance with me, Amanda?"

She smiled up at him. "Yes, Brody."

He had all the time in the world to ask for her phone number. For now, he just wanted to enjoy being with her.

So he took her hand and she stepped into his embrace. *I'll never feel like this again,* he thought.

And he couldn't stop himself. He buried his head in Amanda's hair and took a deep, cleansing breath. God help him, he clung to the fantasy, just for a moment, that they were a real couple. Not this summer or next winter or whenever it was they were finished with their goals, but here and now. He imagined he could take her out in public, today, and have people respect their relationship. Nobody assuming he was dogging her because that's what skiers did.

It felt good being with Amanda Jensen. He could get used to this feeling.

She smiled up at him again, her hazel eyes softening, and he knew in his heart she felt the same way.

But like a ghost, she transformed before him. Her face grew pale, her eyes wide. "Brody…"

And then he felt a cold, deliberate tap on his shoulder.

He closed his eyes. Only one person had ever tapped him like that. "Excuse me," he murmured in Amanda's ear. "I'll be back in a minute."

He turned and, as he'd expected, he found the hard, angry face of MacArthur Jensen staring him down.

BRODY STOOD IN THE MEN'S ROOM, manning up the way Amanda had manned up before him. He faced the new head of his country's ski federation, his arms crossed, while MacArthur coolly washed his hands and avoided his gaze.

"Listen, Mac, there's no reason for us to be at odds any longer," Brody said. "I'm back and I'm here to win, which will only help you and your cause of having Americans on the podium."

"Is that so?" MacArthur shook off the water from his hands. "Then come under my organization's umbrella. Rejoin the main team and take my funding."

He couldn't do that. To compete under MacArthur's control was to be destroyed again. "Is that what you really want?" he asked, hedging his bets. "Or wouldn't you rather have the public credit for my successes? Because I'm willing to give you that, in spades, but only if you let my team keep their autonomy. That's non-negotiable."

MacArthur frowned and reached for the paper towels. "Impossible. You need to take my funding." He gave Brody an oily smile.

If Brody took his money, he'd be subject to MacArthur's scrutiny. Brody had spent two years healing injuries caused by this man's games. There was no way he would open himself up to it again. "We won't win that way," he said. "Think of the good of the overall team."

"Do I care?" Mac asked softly, still smiling at him.

His stomach sank. It was true; MacArthur didn't care. He wasn't bluffing. The way MacArthur played, there would be no winners, only losers who had their faces saved.

He felt cold all over. He hadn't expected Mac to be as bad as this. He'd worked with him for just one season, Brody's last, and he'd known him as a control freak. An egomaniac with an insatiable need to win, to be right, to be superior. Mac was easily offended, and he judged himself on the basis of his achievements, which Brody had assumed were the guys on his team who stood on the podium.

But he'd been wrong about that. Mac wanted control. Pure and simple.

"I thought as much," MacArthur said, his smile twisted and his eyes strangely flat in that dead way Brody remembered. "Now get out of my daughter's wedding before I grab the microphone and tell everyone your deep, dark secret."

Brody felt his pulse thudding at the base of his neck. He had to do something to stop this.

He groped for what he'd rehearsed so often, the reasoning, the logic to cover it all. "You can't do that without hurting yourself. Because you were involved in it, too."

"You underestimate me, Brody," MacArthur hissed. "I always win."

"If I fall, then you fall, too."

Brody owned that point, and he saw the doubt forming in Mac's eyes.

But then MacArthur seemed to recover. He smiled and pointed to Brody's chest, his finger stabbing at Brody's breastbone. "Know this, and tell your manager this—I am playing the long game. I may not win tonight. I may not win tomorrow. But I'm smarter than you and I always win the final trophy."

"Mac, drop this, for one last season while I win—"

"You made that impossible when you went over my head to the international organization, Brody."

Harrison had made that decision in order to apply to field their own independent team. Damn it. "So it comes down to that? That in the process of regrouping, we inadvertently disrespected you?"

MacArthur smirked and headed for the door. "I'll see you in Alto Baglio. Watch your back."

"That's it? That's all you have to say?"

"No." He turned to Brody. "Stay the hell away from my daughter."

"Amanda? I thought you disowned her."

MacArthur laughed, his eyes gleaming. "I did."

THE SNOW WAS FALLING LIKE BIG, soft clumps of goose down when Amanda stood in the lobby in her jeans and wool coat, her luggage packed and on the floor beside her.

"I wish you didn't have to leave tonight," Jeannie was saying. "We've arranged for the ballroom to stay open later. Nobody's going anywhere in this weather."

"I'm sorry," Amanda said, "but I really do need to get going."

She felt beyond numb. She'd waited for Brody for an hour, but he'd never come back after he'd left with her father. And yeah, it had stung. As they'd walked away, neither of them had looked back at her once. Brody had to know how much that hurt her. The whole situation felt even worse because she'd taken a chance and confided to him how her father made her feel. Talk about vulnerable. She'd been a fool to trust him.

Clenching her fists inside her pockets, she knew she had to end this silly fantasy she'd been living. It was over. She was never coming back on the ski circuit to see Brody, and he was never going to New York to see her either. Who were they kidding?

Fling is finished, she told herself. *Get over it.*

"Amanda, are you all right? You look pale."

She shook herself and forced out a smile. This was a happy day and she would be happy—if not for herself, then for Jeannie, dammit. "That's because I hate leaving you. But the first staff meeting since the restructuring is tomorrow at four o'clock, and I told Chelsea I'd be in the office by then. If I don't show up, I'm worried about being on the layoff list."

"You wrote a profile on Brody Jones for them yesterday," Jeannie said gently.

Can we not talk about him, please?

"Amanda?" Jeannie peered at her. "I know we haven't had a chance to talk about what happened last night, but have you been upset because of it?"

"No. Really, Jeannie, I'm not upset. I'm just thankful you and I got to spend the week together. We need to do this more often, okay?"

"I'm so glad you said that," Jeannie whispered. She raised her arms and gave Amanda a hug. "And I need to tell you something. I called and invited him here. I'm sorry if it was the wrong thing to do."

Amanda felt the flush creeping up her cheeks. "You don't need to apologize."

"I do, because I want you to be happy. You're important to me, Mandy. That's why I wanted you to come."

Amanda shook her head. "You don't need me here. The Colettis are good people. I'm glad I got to know them better this week."

"Will you visit us this summer?" Jeannie's eyes were watery.

"Every day of vacation time I've got." She clutched Jeannie in a hug again. Oh, great, now her throat was closing up.

"I'm so sorry things didn't work out for you here," Jeannie whispered.

Was *that* it—her sister had wanted her to stay in Italy with her and had tried matchmaking as a way to make that happen? "It's my fault it didn't work out with Marco. I'll try harder next time, Jeannie, I promise."

"I was talking about Brody," Jeannie said miserably.

"We saw you dancing with him after the bouquet toss. It was the happiest you've looked since you got here."

Her sister seemed so distraught, Amanda couldn't help wanting to wipe the concern from her face. "It was just a fling, and now it's over." She tried to laugh it off, but it came out strangled. "One of his many flings, I am sure."

Jeannie shook her head. "Massimo says he isn't like that." Her big eyes blinked up at Amanda. "He thinks Brody's a bigger workaholic than you are."

Amanda faked a smile. "See? Then if I ever bump into him again, there'll be no awkwardness between us." She glanced toward the men's room. "The last time I saw him, he was going off with Dad somewhere, probably to argue with him over racing strategy. I just wish I knew what happened between those two."

Jeannie fiddled with the lace on her sleeve. "I didn't want to say this before, but you've finished writing your profile, so…"

"What, Jeannie? Tell me."

Jeannie hesitated. "I wasn't there—this was before my time on the circuit—but Dad told me that Brody got in trouble once and Dad bailed him out. That's probably why he's having so much trouble dealing with you being Dad's daughter."

Amanda's stomach dropped. Her instincts had been right. Brody was hiding something. "What kind of trouble?" she asked quietly.

Jeannie's gaze slid away. "I wasn't there when Brody skied and I don't know him so I really can't say. You should ask him yourself, Mandy."

"Will you ask Massimo for me?"

Jeannie looked up. "Are you sure this isn't serious between you two?"

If it was, Brody wouldn't have left her standing alone for so long. He would have come back to her. But Amanda didn't feel like explaining everything to Jeannie, so she just shook her head. "I'm sure. I'm driving to an airport hotel tonight and catching a flight home first thing in the morning."

"And he's racing in Europe all season."

"Exactly." Amanda hoisted her carry-on and tossed the strap over her shoulder. This made her more determined to get on with it. "Have you seen my ride? Because I really do need to get going."

"He's with Massimo in the sales office arranging for more hotel rooms. I'll wait here while you go and find him."

Stay the hell away from my daughter.

Amanda thought her father had let her go? Hardly. She was wrong, and he had the proof.

Brody stalked toward the lobby in a foul mood. All he could do was hope he made it through Alto Baglio before the dirt came out. MacArthur didn't know he only really cared about that one race, so maybe that fact would save him.

Then again, maybe not. Like the snake he was, who could predict when or how MacArthur would strike?

This has to stop. He gripped his RV keys and strode down the hotel corridor, looking for Amanda to explain what he could. But he had to be careful. Because he'd take no phone number from her, no email address and certainly no last kiss.

He couldn't. After MacArthur had left, he'd stayed in the men's room and splashed cold water on his face to literally make himself numb. This really was the end of his and Amanda's weekend.

When he arrived in the front lobby, the first person he saw was Jeannie Coletti, still wearing her wedding dress and sitting alone in a chair. On her lap she held a tray of small goblets filled with cream-colored liquid that looked too thick to be milk.

"Hi, Brody." She held the tray forward. "Thanks for coming to the reception. Will you drink a toast to Massimo and me?"

He eyed the liquid in the goblets. It looked like a protein-powder shake.

"It's my mother-in-law's famous almond-amaretto nightcap," Jeannie explained, nodding to the tray. "Almonds are good luck in the Italian tradition. You drink it to one hundred years of happiness. *Per cent'anni,* you say."

One hundred years. He wouldn't have one more minute with Amanda. He suddenly felt sad.

She offered him a goblet.

"No, thanks, I'll pass on the drink."

She blinked up at him. "You're not going to toast us?"

He leaned over and kissed her on the cheek. Massimo's wife seemed like a good egg. He wished the two of them all the happiness. "*Per cent'anni,* Jeannie."

She smiled wistfully. "Thank you, Brody."

"No, thank *you.*" Because inadvertently, by offering him the drink, she'd hinted at the answer to one very big question for him. She didn't seem to know what her father had done to him, and so, likely, neither did Amanda.

He stepped back and studied Amanda's sister. She was solid and strong, a born downhiller, but to him she lacked Amanda's appeal. "Have you seen your sister?"

She shook her head sadly. "Please don't ask me about her. I was wrong to get in the middle of it."

His heart sank. "Did she leave already?"

Jeannie hesitated, glancing over his head. He turned and followed her gaze.

Amanda strode from the direction of the front desk, wheeling a red suitcase. She was dressed in jeans and a wool coat with a laptop case swung over her shoulder.

He straightened. Even now, he was drawn to her.

Get over it, he told himself. *You've got way too much at risk.*

He squared his shoulders and prepared to have his guts ripped out. But he'd survive, he always had. In childhood, there had always been a next town over the horizon.

His folded his arms and faced her. "Do you have a ride out of town?"

She lifted her chin. She knew the score. "Yes, Brody, I do."

"Someone who will get you to the airport safely?"

She raised a brow at him and crossed her arms.

And then, strutting down the hallway toward her, calling out "A-man-da!" and hauling the red overnight bag that obviously matched Amanda's suitcase, was the second-to-last last guy Brody wanted to see. The irrepressible Marco.

CHAPTER NINE

AMANDA STARED AT BRODY. He wasn't going to make their parting easy for either of them. Well, she ached, too. She didn't want to leave him, or Jeannie, but something more important drove her, something she didn't quite understand and didn't want to examine too closely.

She adjusted her carry-on bag and tried not to look at him, his arms rigid at his side, his gorgeous mouth flat-lined. "I'm ready," she said to Marco. "We should get on our way before the weather gets any worse."

Then she strode over to Jeannie and gave her the hardest hug she could. "I don't want to leave you," she whispered. "I really don't."

"Me, neither," Jeannie whispered back. "But what I really want to know is, do you always have two guys chasing after you?"

"Until yesterday, I hadn't so much as kissed a man in over two years. Do not be jealous of me."

"Wow, Amanda, that's rough," Jeannie breathed. Then she grinned. "It never rains but it pours, Mom always said."

Amanda laughed in spite of her mood. She glanced back at Brody, who was watching Marco like a hawk. Marco seemed perfectly normal and good-natured, sipping a glass of Jeannie's mother-in-law's killer amaretto concoction and toasting Massimo. *"Per cent'anni!"*

"How much has he had to drink tonight?" Brody quizzed Massimo.

Amanda squinted and looked more closely at Marco. Maybe he *was* wobbling a bit. And at Brody's question, Marco smacked his lips and staggered up to him. "You are leaving tonight for the next stop on your World Cup tour, yes?"

"Snow's coming down hard," Brody said pointedly to Marco. "Roads will be treacherous. Are you okay to drive, slick?"

Amanda put her hand over her mouth to cover her laughter. *This is not funny.*

"The lady asks me for her favor," Marco insisted. "I am an excellent driver." He rose on the balls of his feet as if Brody had insulted his manhood.

"This is interesting," Jeannie whispered. "Look at the two of them fighting over you."

She *was* looking. A muscle twitched on Brody's jaw, and although he didn't say a word to Marco, the challenge was clear.

"All right, standoff is over," Amanda said, pulling at her luggage. "Goodbye, Jeannie." She gave her sister one last hug, basking in the homey, vanilla scent of her perfume. "I'll call you when I get to New York. You, too, Massimo. Take good care of my sister."

"Yes, I will," Massimo said, kissing her on both cheeks. "Goodbye, sister Amanda."

"Drive safely." Jeannie waved her off, her smile determinedly bright as she watched Marco hustle for Amanda's luggage.

Amanda picked up her laptop bag and followed behind him. For the short time she'd talked with Massimo's friend, he'd seemed like a good guy. They even had shared tastes—he'd looked with interest at the book she'd chosen to read on the plane—but chemistry? It just wasn't there for her. And once Marco got past his competing-with-Brody fixation, he'd see clearly that it wasn't there for him, either.

Unlike with her and Brody. Every time Amanda saw him, she couldn't help remembering how it felt to lie in bed with him.

The flush crept over her until she felt as heated as Jeannie's almond-amaretto surprise. She and Brody naked was a visual she didn't need right now.

Shaking it off, she clung to her bags and strode past the porter into the twilight.

Except…it was no longer twilight. Full darkness had descended.

She stepped onto the sidewalk and nearly slid backward off her boot heels. The snow was slippery. And… abundant. At least two inches covered the roads like a blanket. She wiped her gloved hands over her hair, dusted with a cap of fat snowflakes.

Okay, so the snow was more plentiful than she'd realized. While she'd been picking up bridal bouquets and dancing with Brody, Mother Nature had been deciding to laugh at the weather forecasts. One to two inches? They were past that and heading for three to four…

Marco struggled beside her with her suitcase, the wheels of which didn't turn so easily in the thick snow. "My car waits," he said, pointing to a black, late-model Mercedes which was idling by the valet stand.

"Thank you. I appreciate you warming the engine for us." She picked her way over to it, gingerly now, because there was no way she wanted to fall on her butt under Brody's watchful stare.

And he was staring. Somehow, he'd materialized at

the valet stand, jiggling his RV keys in his suit-jacket pocket and peering at the snowfall.

Marco tugged harder on her suitcase, awkwardly attempting to drag it through the snow to his open automobile trunk. Amanda realized with a sinking heart that he was inadvertently telling Brody that he didn't have the strength to lift it easily.

And sure enough, in one smooth motion Brody took over, elevating her suitcase in one hand and then depositing it in Marco's trunk. "What route are you taking to the airport?" he quizzed Marco, his arms crossed and his hip leaning against the side of the car.

Marco swallowed.

Please don't answer him, she silently ordered.

"We, ah, drive to town first…"

Stop. Do not proceed. Speak no further.

"…where I keep an apartment…"

Brody's jaw clamped shut. His gaze swung to Amanda.

"Oh, for goodness sake, Brody. Marco lives beside the office where I'm picking up my rental car."

"Rental car office?" Brody exclaimed. "Why isn't he driving you to the airport?"

Marco tilted his head and smiled angelically at her. Or, he was attempting to smile angelically.

"Because I'm perfectly capable of driving myself to the airport," she said hotly to Brody.

"You're planning to drive in this storm?" Brody demanded.

She crossed her arms. Now his interference was personal. He was criticizing her driving skills. "This is nothing. I grew up in New Hampshire, remember? The day I passed my driver's test we were in the middle of a blizzard."

"The airport is almost a hundred kilometers through a series of mountain passes, Amanda," he said through gritted teeth.

"And? You were going to drive to Alto Baglio, which is *several* hundred kilometers through *several* mountain passes, as I recall."

Yeah, smarty pants. I've been on the World Cup tour, too. Once, with her mother, the year Brody was gone, following along after her father those last, desperate weeks when her mother was still trying to cobble things together with him.

Without a word, Brody unloaded her suitcase. Then he spun on the heel of his dress loafers and trudged through two inches of unplowed snow in the parking lot, carrying her regulation fifty pounds of suitcase by its handle.

"Where are you going?" She had no choice but to run after him. Or rather, tiptoe after him. Two-inch-heeled booties didn't have the best of traction on icy mountain snow. "I didn't say you could drive me to the rental car office!"

"I'm taking you to the airport. It's on my way."

"Brody, do not presume to order me!"

He stopped in his tracks, his suit glistening with snowflakes. Those blue eyes were churning with thought. "You're right," he said finally. "You do have a choice. You can drive by yourself in the mountains during a snowstorm, which, since you've lived in snow country, you should know is a dangerous, stupid undertaking, or you can drive with me in my motor home where at least we can look out for each other if we get stuck."

Was this some kind of trick? Was he being reasonable just to throw her off guard?

She paused, her shoulder aching, and adjusted her laptop strap to a more comfortable angle. What if she turned around and walked in the other direction? That would show Brody the importance of her need to make her own decisions. But did she want to leave her suitcase? Was there anything in there more important than clothes, and shoes and toiletries?

Well, she would like to have a clean change of underwear in the morning. And she needed her mouth guard for sleeping. She had a bad tooth-grinding problem. It would cost hundreds of dollars on a dental plan she didn't have anymore—thanks, *Paradigm,* for the cost-cutting—to replace it.

She sighed. "Fine," she called after his retreating back. "But I'm driving."

He snorted. And she heard him, because it turned out that snowfall wasn't quite the damper of sound he assumed it was.

"Amanda!" Marco pulled beside her in his warmed-up Mercedes. "You are cold. Please come inside."

She leaned into the passenger window he'd opened for her, feeling the welcoming blast of the heating vents. "As much as I'd like to go with you and rent my own car, Brody's probably right. It's not such a good idea. Thank you for offering me a ride to town, though, and for going out of your way to help me."

Marco slowly nodded. He seemed resigned to her decision. "Would you like for me to drive you to Brody's camper?"

She smiled at him. "That's kind of you. But under the circumstances, I'll pass. Goodbye, Marco. Take care."

He waved goodbye to her, and then after he'd driven away, she gritted her teeth and followed Brody across the parking lot, wondering if she'd made a huge mistake in yielding so easily to his will.

So when they both got to the RV, she stepped in front of Brody and said, "You touch that steering wheel, buster, and I'm calling my father directly. And don't think I won't do it."

THAT WAS A LOW BLOW, bringing her father into it. If Amanda had any idea of the hell she was threatening him with, Brody would have turned on his heel and dumped her suitcase into the first snowbank he saw.

But she didn't. And he knew she'd been upset when he'd left her to confront her father, though he couldn't tell her why he'd left. Harrison's accusations to the contrary, he did have a shred of self-preservation left in him.

Bottom line, he'd cut her some slack. He opened the door to the motor home and heaved her suitcase inside. He turned, but she was blocking the door, her hands on her hips.

"Sleep in the back," she snapped. "I know you haven't slept since I left your room this morning. At least I had a three-hour nap."

At the reminder of the sex they'd shared, her body naked beneath his, he got an immediate hard-on. Great. "Amanda—"

"I said *relax,* Brody."

Easy for her to say—she could concentrate on driving.

She opened her bag and pulled out a container of bottled water and tossed it at him. And because it was factory-sealed, he pulled it open and drank. "Thanks," he said grudgingly. He looked at the snow that drifted over his windshield and roof, making the motor home resemble an igloo.

"Look, we're adults," she continued, as if he didn't know that. "I know this whole thing sucks. I know there's too much baggage between my father and you, and my father and me, and I know our lives are never going to mesh, even if we wish they could."

She didn't know the half of it, but she was pretty much on the money. He took another pull from the water bottle and didn't say anything.

She propped her hands on her hips again. "Do you think we can coexist peacefully for one more hour?" she asked, exasperated and still angry with him. "Just one more hour, and then we'll never have to see each other again?"

He stared at her. Was she planning to drive the same way she made love, full of passion and fire? "In this snow, the trip will take from two to three hours."

She blinked. "Fine. Two to three hours, then."

He searched for any sign of doubt in her face, but she looked confident of her snow-driving abilities. She'd have made a great ski racer if she'd put her mind to it. Equal parts reckless, ambitious and crazy. He shook his head.

She crossed her arms. "After we get to the airport, we'll part ways. You'll go back to your life, and I'll go back to mine. Are we understood, Brody?"

Completely. He nodded curtly at her.

For a second, he hoped she might kiss him.

But she kept her arms glued to her sides. "Sleep, Brody. You look like hell."

Yeah, and I feel like hell, too.

He'd lost races scores of times before, he thought, leaning against the bench seat and watching her as she maneuvered his motor home down the twisting exit. He knew how to accept defeat. He was lucky one of his first coaches had taught him early on that it was as important to know how to lose as it was to know how to win.

Not that he ever played to lose. He always raced to win. He always assumed he was going to win—right up until the moment his time flashed across the scoreboard. But if he didn't win, then he aimed to do better the next time. Because there was always the next race. Always the final season standings.

Great racers aren't affected by what other people think of them.

Another piece of wisdom from that same old coach. They didn't make coaches like him anymore.

He shrugged. So he'd lost this contest with Amanda. Move on, there would be another, more important contest ahead: this Sunday at Alto Baglio. That was where he should concentrate his focus.

He leaned back, silent, as she slowly wheeled his creaking RV down the narrow mountain road. He watched, muscles tensed, as she downshifted to avoid skidding in the snow.

Not bad. "Have you driven in the Alps before?" he asked.

"Yes. With my mother." But before he could process her answer, she muttered, "Go to sleep, Brody."

Just as well. He didn't need to learn more about Amanda. What he needed was to erase her from his mind.

Gradually, his clenched fists relaxed. Amanda turned the RV onto the main highway without any problem. A Range Rover roared past them, but she didn't lose her cool. She simply pulled to the right in order to let the jackass pass safely.

Smooth driving. She knew what she was doing.

She's MacArthur Jensen's daughter, his inner voice told him. *She doesn't need you to rescue her from anything.*

Letting out his breath, he lay down on his bed. He was tired, and it didn't take long for his eyes to drift closed. The motor home puttered along as evenly as if it were Jean-Claude or Franz driving him through the treacherous mountain passes, ferrying him from one World Cup mountain course to another.

Still, I wish she could go with me to Alto Baglio.

It was the last thought he had before dropping into a deep sleep.

AMANDA WAS ACTUALLY SURPRISED that Brody hadn't fought her desire to drive. She couldn't help thinking about her father. He never tolerated anyone else driving while he was in the car. He also never let Amanda's mother make her own choices. In this situation, he would either have ignored her, leaving her to Marco and the drop-off at the rental car office, or he would have thrown her luggage into the RV and told her to stop acting like such a baby.

Her chest ached. Despite the silent treatment from her father these past months, she could still hear his voice in her head. Even after all her small successes and her increasing independence, he still weighed heavily on her life.

She blinked and focused on following the snowy ruts left in the road from an earlier vehicle. The snow was falling faster and faster. Her spine stiffened as she kept her senses on alert. She monitored the shadows on the sides of the road for deer and other wildlife that might suddenly dart in front of her headlights, causing her hands to jerk on the steering wheel, a reaction that could prove deadly.

She glanced at the rearview mirror, watching for hotdogging drivers while she kept a steady foot on the gas pedal. Not too slow and certainly not too fast. Just enough power to the engine to urge it up the steep slope, but not so little power they would stall out.

She checked the gas gauge: full. Excellent. Brody had cultivated a top-notch team. All the equipment worked efficiently, even in the ancient motor home. The GPS was set up, the lights glowing from the palm-sized device attached to the dashboard, showing the route she needed to follow. The headlights were strong, too. The beams shone steadily on the falling snow, the flakes as big as euro coins.

Was it her imagination or was the snow falling harder? There had to be over three inches now. Maybe four?

Her phone buzzed, playing the low tune she used to alert herself to her boss's calls. She glanced at the clock on the dash. Ten o'clock. That was four o'clock New York time.

On a Sunday? But of course. The management team was meeting with the cost-cutting consultants. It was layoff time, and this was a test. For all Amanda knew, the editorial team was discussing her contributions and reviewing her résumé round-robin style. Heck, they probably had her on speakerphone.

No matter the weather conditions, she needed to take this call. Her heart pounding, she eased the vehicle to a stop and picked up the call. "Amanda Jensen here."

BRODY WOKE. SOMETHING FELT different. It took him a moment to remember where he was, but he smelled perfume in the darkness and it came to him. *Amanda. RV. She's leaving.*

He sat up and realized the motor home had stopped moving. Wiping the sleep from his eyes, he peered through the window.

She was standing outside in the rapid snowfall, talking on her cell phone. One hand was pressed to her forehead and she was listening intently, as if to the announcement of impending doom. Something wasn't going well.

On a hunch, he turned on his own phone. Immediately it rang, a low chirp that reminded him of a nagging bird.

He rolled over and wearily held the receiver to his ear. "What, Harrison?"

"Dammit, Brody, where the hell have you been?"

"Out of reception," he said.

"Yeah, well now that you're in reception, answer this question—do you know who she is?"

"Who *who* is?" He gazed at Amanda outside, pacing up and down beside the van. She looked as if she was arguing.

"That reporter," Harrison spat out. "Do you have any idea?"

Yeah, she was MacArthur Jensen's daughter. Got it. She was also a beautiful woman he was leaving in a few hours because he couldn't risk having her in his life, that's who she was. "I'm not in the mood for this," he warned. Because he really wasn't.

"MacArthur Jensen called me. He says you're to stay away from her."

"Yeah, I already got the message."

"Have you? Because it gets worse, Brody."

"How can it possibly get worse?"

"Does this sound familiar? Last year, Amanda Jensen wrote an article about the cover-up scandal of positive steroid tests in baseball. Did you know that?"

Brody's blood went cold.

"She's an investigative reporter," Harrison said. "And she specializes in smear-jobs."

He hadn't seen this coming. Not at all.

"Brody, are you there?"

"You're wrong. She hates sports and is more interested in city corruption."

"The truth hurts, Brody, doesn't it?" Harrison's voice crackled over the phone. "She writes whatever her editors tell her to write. Whatever will sell them magazines. Whatever will give her a juicy byline."

"Sounds like a woman after your own heart, Harrison. The art of the deal, and all that."

The muffled sounds of swearing came through Brody's phone. "Just tell me you're not with her now."

"I'm not with her now."

"Dammit, Brody, I talked with your team. They saw her go into your motor home with you. Tell me you sent her on her way."

He looked into the wintry night and saw Amanda. *She's gone,* he thought. *We're leaving. We can't be together.*

I want to be together.

That was his body talking. His body betraying him.

"What does it matter?" he said tiredly. "It's done. Her piece is filed. She won't be interviewing me anymore."

"You couldn't have foreseen this," Harrison said wearily.

"Foreseen what?"

"She's going to dig and dig, and she won't stop digging."

"What are you talking about?"

"Listen to me!" Harrison's voice was shrill with fear, which wasn't like him. In his years, he'd been around, he'd seen everything. "You don't think she'll uncover your secret, Brody? You don't think she'll blame you for testing positive on those steroid tests?"

His heart stopped beating in his chest. Harrison never said that aloud. The thought was always there, just below the surface, but they had an unspoken agreement that they would never mention it.

He held his head, which suddenly throbbed. First MacArthur threatening him, and now this? He looked out the windshield just as Amanda punched her phone off. The headlights of the RV illuminated her back, tense and shaking. The snowflakes clung to her wool jacket.

"What are you saying, Harrison, they want her to write more about me?" He felt tired and sick. Not even being in his own bed in his own motor home on his way to the race he'd dreamed about for the past two years could make him feel better.

"That's not what I'm saying," Harrison said, "it's what the money is saying. *Paradigm* wants her to feature you for a longer piece, and Xerxes Energy Drink is beside themselves with joy because they want inroads into the U.S. market."

"Tell them no," he said flatly. "No more interviews."

"I told them yes, Brody. I had to."

"Forget it. We'll get the money elsewhere."

"We don't have money!" Harrison yelled. "We can't even make payroll!"

What? His hand shook. "You never told me this."

"That's because up until now, your job was to ski. But things have changed because you've changed them. You got yourself involved in the business end."

"That wasn't my intent."

"What's the matter?" Harrison laughed sharply. "Don't you want to spend another two days with your lady reporter? Because it's beginning to look like that's all you care about."

"Is that so? Then maybe I should be looking for another agent."

"Show me you still care about the integrity of your record and I'll pretend you never said that to me."

"I made the mistake and I'm working to fix it," Brody said through clenched teeth.

"No one will forgive you for your mistake, and that's why you need to make sure it never gets out. Think of the baseball players who regret saying anything to her about their mistakes."

"I said I'll fix it."

"If it gets out, there is no fixing it. Period. Don't you get it, there is no forgiveness in sport, Brody. Do you see what you're risking?"

His hand shook on the phone. Uncontrollably, like a spasm.

"Brody?"

He sucked in his breath. He'd never had a panic attack before, but he was pretty sure he was experiencing one now.

"Don't say a word to her until I get there," Harrison said. "Do you hear me, Brody?"

He had to get up. He had to get out of here. "I won't tell her anything."

CHAPTER TEN

AMANDA LAUGHED HOARSELY as she shoved her phone into her pocket. Earlier, she'd wished that she and Brody could stay together for a few more days.

While the snow had been falling she'd daydreamed about being kidnapped by pirates and left on a deserted Caribbean island, just the two of them. Now, she had her wish. Except, as in all tales with genies and Ali Baba, the wish had been twisted until the result was the worst thing that could have happened to her.

We want you to stay in Europe with Brody Jones for two more days. All expenses paid.

It was heaven, and it was hell. The expense-account, holed-up-in-a-hotel-room-with-him part would be heaven. The fighting-with-him-to-get-the-story part would be hell.

Not to mention, she'd already slept with him. Her journalism advisor—God rest his soul—would be rolling in his grave. "Journalism has ethics." Yeah, and sleeping with a future interview subject was pretty much near the top of the list of no-nos.

She paced in the drifting, ankle-high snow. On Amanda's first day of work at *Paradigm,* Chelsea had been very clear about her own ethics and those of the magazine.

"Look, hon," Chelsea had explained in her Brooklyn-tough accent, "reporters have been schtupping their subjects since the beginning of time. I myself have been known to indulge. So believe me when I say that the key is to always act like a grownup and a professional—and to keep your extracurricular activities to yourself. In short, don't be stupid and announce to anyone what you're doing. For God's sake, if you want to work here, keep it to yourself. Do you got that?"

Loud and clear, Amanda had thought. The funny thing was, at the time, Chelsea's speech had mortified her. Never could she have imagined sleeping with an interviewee. She'd actually shuddered at the thought.

And now? Amanda laughed aloud. She really was getting New York City–jaded, because she had no regrets about having slept with Brody. None.

Instead, she'd attempted what would have been inconceivable to her before now: she'd tried to talk Chelsea out of assigning her the story of the year.

"Why me?" she'd asked her editor. "And why us? This story doesn't fit our demographic. We're not a sports magazine. Our readers won't care about a skier."

"But they care about scandal. And celebrity. And sex appeal. And your profile, Amanda, touched on all these things. The team has talked it over and we agree. He's hiding something. Some reason he's come back to compete, something that drives him, something about his past, and he doesn't want anyone to know what it is. You're just the person to find it. All the skills are there, the connections are there, and he seems to trust you. Look how he opened up to you! Amanda, don't you see how the stars are aligned?"

Amanda threw back her head. There were no stars in this sky. She didn't believe in stars, or in planets, or in alignments.

No, through long, hard battle, she believed in herself. And the great irony was, she'd been duped by her own ambition. If she'd let the profile be the puff piece it was meant to be—if she hadn't written such an intriguing piece, hinting at the chaos and angst beneath the surface of his celebrity—then Chelsea and the rest of them wouldn't be interested in Brody Jones's deep, dark secrets.

Way to go, Amanda.

She turned and saw Brody standing in the glow from the headlights, his arms crossed, his head tilted toward her, and through no will of her own, her heart leaped. The man was heart-stopping, six feet plus of pure sex appeal. His body called to her, no matter where they were or what emotions flowed between them.

Even when they'd sworn to leave each other in the morning.

What's stopping you, anyway? the devil in her whispered. *Why not shack up with him for two days, enjoy an all-expenses-paid fantasy in a love nest in the mountains, and then write some garbage for Chelsea. Make stuff up. And never mind the ethics of it, because Chelsea herself said that you shouldn't.*

Right. As if Amanda could do that. As much as she was itching to pull Brody to her and beg him to hold her in his arms again, she couldn't. He was hot and he turned her gooey inside, but she needed her job. His job wasn't more important than her job. *He* wasn't more important than *her*. She couldn't pull punches with her career just because she had enjoyed the inexplicable connection with him. She hadn't given in with her profile and she couldn't give in now. If anything, this article had to be more seriously and objectively written than her profile had been. And he wasn't going to like it. He was going to push back as hard as he could.

Yes, maybe this assignment *was* about power. Maybe Brody would always be more powerful than her. But after she'd picked up the pieces when her mother had fallen apart, Amanda had learned her lesson well.

Don't let yourself be in the position of weakness. Never, ever, ever.

She stood tall, watching her breath make puffs of steam in the cold mountain air. With resolve, she clicked open her phone one more time. The reception was waning and she had one slim bar of power. They were heading farther from civilization, farther into the uninhabited, wild reaches of the mountains, so it was now or never.

Chelsea picked up her call on the first ring. "You've made up your mind? Because if you don't do this, Amanda, I need to tell you that I can't save your job from being cut—"

"I want a promotion," Amanda said firmly into the phone. "To staff reporter. I want on the masthead. And I want a contract for three solid years."

She held her breath, counting on Chelsea's pride at having already sold her story idea to the rest of the team. And there were precedents for such a contract at *Paradigm.* For someone her age it was rare, but maybe that was because older people were better at playing hardball. Well, she'd learned a lot already. Power isn't given. Power is taken.

"I'm proud of you, Amanda," Chelsea cooed.

Amanda eyed Brody, standing silently beside the RV, listening to her end of the conversation. It was nice Chelsea was proud of her, because Brody looked as cold as stone. Obviously, Harrison had informed him about his participation in the matter.

She turned away, shaking. "Is that a yes or a no?" she asked Chelsea.

"We discussed this," Chelsea answered. "I was just waiting to see what you came up with."

"You know what I'm capable of." *I get you the truth,* she added silently.

Chelsea gave a low laugh. "It's a yes. But for a two-year contract, not three."

Amanda had been aiming for one year. Her heart pounded furiously. *I won. I really did it this time.* "Fine. You'll get your story."

Brody made a small noise beside her. *Yeah, hon, I share your pain,* she thought.

"Five thousand words," Chelsea insisted.

Wow, a long piece. "Right. Five thousand words."

"With photos."

Oh, God. No way was she repeating that aloud.

"Fine," Amanda said. "I'll type up the terms and email them to you. Send me confirmation." She clicked off her phone and holstered it as if she were some sort of old-world gunslinger. Brody leaned against the motor home, his eyes hooded, his cap low, looking like John Wayne assessing his opponent before a gunfight.

She took two steps toward him, her boots crunching in the snow. "There's a way out of this, Brody. If we get it over with quickly, it'll be less painful."

He laughed, but the mirth didn't reach his eyes. The light from the headlamps spilled over his body, showing his snug jeans, his cotton shirt open at the neck, his big arms crossed across his chest.

He'd tossed on a pair of boots, but hadn't tied the laces. He was without a parka or a coat, and it was well below freezing. Icicles covered the windshield wipers, which she'd forgotten to turn off, and they click-click-clicked with the thump of ice against glass and metal.

He held out his hand, palm up. "Give me the keys, sweetheart."

"Not on your life." She pushed past him and opened the driver's door, easing herself into the now-familiar worn seat, adjusted to her height and style. She rummaged quickly through her purse before Brody had time to enter the van.

She had to get the interview done now. Something told her Brody would be out of here before the two days were up. She had to make time. Get her quotes. Get her hunches straight.

He opened the passenger door and sat beside her. He looked pointedly at the voice recorder she'd set on the dashboard.

There was no time for dickering between plan A and plan B. This time she was all hardball, right out of the gate:

"Why don't you start by telling me the truth about why you came back this year." She gave him her best reporter's stare. "You already have Olympic medals. You already have more placements and trophies than anyone else competing. What is it that you're trying to prove, Brody, and what does it have to do with my father?"

With a determined look, Brody leaned over and closed his hand atop hers, pressed against the ignition switch.

And God help her, at his touch, a thrill went through her. This was not good.

"Drive, Amanda," Brody said, his voice rough. "If you don't, I swear to you I will."

The snow *was* piling up. The tracks the motor home

had left behind them were covering quickly, now nearly indistinguishable from the white field that spread up the slope in the rearview mirror. She swallowed and swatted his hand away, shifting into Drive.

Brody was so big and so strong, he could toss her out of the way like a ski pole if he wanted. But she had to trust he wouldn't. And the way to make sure was to continue to assert herself.

She pressed her foot onto the gas pedal. The RV was nestled in a shallow ditch of snow, and like any good north-country girl, she rocked the van out of the rut by first easing the transmission into Drive, then Reverse, then Drive again—until they were back on solid traction.

Brody gave a grunt of approval.

She gripped the steering wheel, hard, the moisture from her palms making it slick. She couldn't see well— she should have thought to wipe down the headlights while they were parked. Man, it was dark. The snow was flying fast and furious and the windshield wipers beat a fast tempo. But at least they were no longer on a hill; a level lane stretched in front of them.

She dared to relax. Turning in her seat, she gave him her best stare. "Tell me what happened the race before you quit, Brody."

"Tell me why a promotion at *Paradigm* magazine is so frigging important to you."

"You were injured in that last race, weren't you? Only you weren't telling anybody."

"I don't see you telling me anything about your job."

"Nobody cares about me, Brody. The world cares about you, and that's why people like me have to interview spoiled arrogant guys like you."

"Why don't you tell me how you really feel, Amanda?"

"This isn't about me, it's about you."

"Is it?"

"Why did you turn down my father's funding?"

"Why do you care about him disowning you?"

"I don't have to take this."

"Now you know why I shut down in interviews."

"You should shut down now. You've lost all goodwill I felt for you."

"That's just great. You know what? You *are* a reporter. Congratulations." He set his cap over his face and leaned back his head in an I'm-finished-with-you pose.

Argh!

She pounded her fist on the steering wheel and gave a little scream. He'd pushed every one of her buttons. And worse, she'd let him.

"Brody?"

Nothing. No answer.

She sucked in a long, deep breath and then blew it out. "You won't put me off finding out about you. Because I *will* find out. Uncovering secrets and bringing them to light is what I do. And yes, if I do my job well, it brings me promotions. And power. And a position from which to bargain. And it *will* put me on the same importance level as you, the celebrity skier. So don't go lecturing me about what I do. Think about the irony in what it is *you* do, Mr. Integrity."

She hadn't meant it, but her voice was raised and she was yelling at him. Her fists were clenched. Brody roused from his shut-down pose and stared at her, and then, his eyes widening, at the passing road before them.

"Amanda, slow down."

She swiveled her head forward. In a flash she saw the baby deer dart out, a gentle Bambi, his eyes wide in fright, and without thinking, she slammed down her foot on the brake.

"Amanda, no! He'll get out of the way—"

But it was too late. As Bambi scampered safely to the side of the road, they went into a long, heart-wrenching skid, the van squealing sideways down the snow-covered mountain road.

Amanda screamed, but Brody's hands were already on the wheel, fighting to control the skid. He threw his body beside hers and was frantically using his boot-clad foot to pump the brakes.

Yes, that was what you were supposed to do in a fishtail skid. But everything seemed upside down...

Items started flying from the back of the van, smacking against the side of the RV. But Brody managed to straighten the motor home, and they were windshield first again. Amanda's recorder smacked into her forehead, hard. She felt a searing pain, and for a moment she saw stars. She moaned and then her head jerked toward the steering wheel, and then back, past her neck.

Everything hurt. Everything swam. Everything was in a fog.

It was as if she was inside a dream, floating in water. They must have stopped, because Brody was shouting her name (*Manda*, he called her, *Manda*), lifting and carrying her to a spot beneath a pine tree on the side of the road.

Dimly she felt a streak of warmth roll down her nose. Blood. It smelled like blood. And then she felt cold where the warmth had been. She blinked her eyes open, and Brody was holding a packed ball of snow to the bump on her forehead while he wiped away her blood with his shirt.

"God, Manda, I am so sorry. I am so, so sorry."

He curled her up in his strong arms, on his warm lap. He rocked her. He sounded anguished in a way she'd never heard.

She guided his hand with the lump of cold snow away from her face so she had a clear line of vision to him. "I'm okay. It's just a bruise from my voice recorder. Nothing lasting."

He shook his head. His eyes were a desolate, burning blue. "I should have driven. I should have insisted. I shouldn't have argued with you about the interview."

"It's okay, Brody."

"No, it's not." He shook his head harder. "It was my fault. It'll never be okay."

"Hey." She touched his cheek. It was fevered and moist. "Why are you blaming yourself? I'm the one who was driving. I'm the one who wasn't watching the road."

"Don't let me off the hook, Amanda," he said brokenly. "It's my vehicle. It's my responsibility. I should have been paying attention."

"You *are* paying attention," she whispered. She slid her hand inside his shirt, feeling his bare skin. He flinched at her touch. But when she felt his heartbeat beneath her palm, she kept it there. "I forgive you," she said calmly, gazing into his eyes. "And if I can forgive you, then you can, too."

She didn't know why she'd said it, but she knew it was the right thing when he crushed her to his chest and held her there.

She leaned her cheek against his heart and felt it beat, rapid-fire, against her. Her own heart felt as though it was bursting open. Something had just happened with him, here in the snow and cold, though she wasn't exactly sure what. This feeling was more intimate than when they'd slept together, if that was possible.

She closed her eyes. If only she could change the awful situation their jobs put them in. It sucked. Ten minutes ago, she'd been counting on the comfortable force of her drive and her anger to get them through it. But obviously that wasn't working anymore. It could have gotten them killed, in fact. Brody was still shaking from the near miss. She wasn't, but maybe that was because she needed to stay emotionally strong for him. Or maybe she was in shock. Either way, it was obvious she needed to find a new approach to their impasse, something beyond the anger and fury of her helplessness.

He cradled the back of her head in his palm, and a flood of emotion overcame her. This wasn't going to be easy. But maybe if she held on to the compassion she felt for him—for both of them—then she could find a way to make this work.

Because she needed to make it work. Desperately.

BRODY WAS STILL SHAKEN when he tucked Amanda into the passenger seat of the motor home. He wanted to be gentle with her. He didn't want to risk putting her in the back because he needed to keep watch on her, even though she would be more comfortable in his bed. He couldn't tell if she'd hit her head hard enough to have a concussion. They were many kilometers from the nearest hospital, and neither of their cell phones was working. The storm must have knocked out the communications towers.

He leaned on the motor home, briefly stretching the cramps from his arms and shoulders and looking up at the snow that was still falling. One thing was certain, he didn't deserve Amanda's forgiveness. He should have been stronger, more assertive from the beginning, and because he wasn't, she could have been seriously hurt. Forgive himself? Not likely.

Then again, he knew that feeling and, as before, all he could do was move on, so he pulled the blanket from his bed and tucked it around her. Then he buckled her in. He wished he had time to make her something hot to drink—tea, cocoa, anything—but the storm was getting worse. He needed to get her to warm shelter, and soon.

As he shut her door, he saw her observing him through the side window. Thankfully she was conscious and not in pain. He shivered, glancing at the road they'd fishtailed down. One long, scarred trail of broken snowdrifts marked their trail. Now they were in the middle of nowhere at midnight. Snow blanketed the pine trees and firs surrounding them in a silent, white chapel, except for the cove where she'd bled in his arms.

Shaking the image out of his head, he went inside and put on a maroon-colored chamois shirt. His old shirt was shredded, stripped into a makeshift bandage that he'd pressed to the cut on Amanda's forehead. He hadn't felt safe enough to risk leaving her to raid his first aid kit, but once he'd realized she wouldn't bleed to death, he'd applied a proper bandage to her wound. He'd also studied her pupils, and they weren't dilated. Even now, she gave him her normal intelligent, if amused look. Though what was funny, he would never understand.

He cleaned up everything inside the RV, made sure there was nothing loose that could harm her if he needed to brake suddenly. And then he climbed into his seat, adjusted it and turned the key in the ignition.

The engine gave a low whine, but then revved to life. His shoulders relaxed. Their next move was simple: they needed to find a more stable location to ride out the storm than his RV. The snow came more quickly and he had no idea of current weather forecasts—the radio gave nothing but static—but several more inches had accumulated since they'd set off. They were at the capability limits of the aging motor home's snow tires.

Holding his breath, he turned on the GPS unit mounted to the dashboard. The satellite access was working, because it keyed in their location. Yeah, pretty much the middle of nowhere, still in Italy but not far from the Swiss border. He knocked at his teeth. Thought back through ten years on the World Cup circuit. Who did he know who lived nearby?

Of course. He pulled up an address he hadn't used in years.

"Can I help navigate, Brody?"

"No. Don't worry about anything." He spoke with reassurance he didn't feel. "I'm taking you someplace close where you can rest and I can watch over you."

"Guess we're not making it to the airport hotel *Paradigm* paid for, huh?" She winked at him as if making a joke.

He felt her cheek. Her skin was cool and clammy. Alarm threaded through him; he blasted the heat dial up another notch, then wove his fingers through hers and squeezed.

Warm up, Manda. She needed to raise her body temperature. "How's your vision? Is it blurred? Or can you see straight?"

She leaned back and smiled at him as he pulled forward into the storm, the windshield wipers clicking, the snow groaning under the tires. "I see you, Brody."

"I'm serious, Amanda."

"So am I."

He sighed and squinted into the circles of light the headlights threw onto the narrow road. Three more kilometers. He had to backtrack up the mountain, past where they'd slid. Beyond that was a side road. He only hoped it was passable. He could always hike, carrying Manda if he had to, but he hoped it wouldn't come to that. Her clothing wasn't warm enough, and he didn't have his cross country skis or his snowshoes.

She shifted beneath the blanket, then took his hand and drew it to her pulse at the base of her neck. Here, she was warm. He flexed his palm, covering her skin, and she sighed in response.

What was it with her and him? He snatched his hand away. "I want you to be safe."

"I am safe. You're with me."

"No, I'm worried about your head wound." He glanced at her. No blood showing through the bandage—that was good.

"I bet you've been through worse in your day," she said cheerily. "Haven't you?"

And then she looked sideways at him. That expectant pause; she was waiting for him to say something leading. A reporter's look, questioning him.

He must have bristled, because she burst out laughing. "Got you, Brody."

"It's not funny. When I wipe out on the slopes I have a team of experts poking, prodding and x-raying everything. Hell, one time I—" He caught himself. "Don't try to make me feel better by changing the subject. You hit your head. You could have a concussion. I need to watch you, and I don't want to be distracted from that."

"Are we supposed to, like, stay up all night together while you watch me?" Her tone was gently mocking.

"Stop it." He knew she was trying to keep him from being concerned, but he wouldn't let down his guard with her again. Nor would he take his gaze from the road. He was gunning it in second gear up a too-steep, too-slick hill. The RV shuddered from side to side. Any moment the side road would be coming up...

Now. He eased up on the gas as the GPS device cooed an instruction for him to turn.

"I'll bet you purposely chose a woman's voice for your GPS, didn't you?" she teased.

"If someone has to tell me what to do," he said, turning the wheel carefully in a near U-turn through the storm that was starting to blow sideways, blizzard-style, "I'd rather it be a woman than a man."

She burst out laughing, as if they weren't in a life-or-death situation. He couldn't tell if it was intentional, to relax him. "Can I quote you on that?" she teased again.

"Absolutely not." And that wasn't a joke. Though he looked with relief at the outlines of a driveway where a driveway should be. He could almost let himself celebrate. "There will be no interview and no quotes, and that's the last I'll say on the matter."

"Hmm." He heard the smile in her voice. "You know, I've been thinking about that."

"Now you're really making me worry about your head." With his fingers crossed, Brody turned the RV toward the driveway. Beyond the curtain of blowing snow, he saw it: a small, two-story snow-covered chalet at the top of the steep hill.

"Is this it?" she asked.

"Thank God, yes." He gunned the engine, and the motor home made it ten feet up the driveway before the wheels lost traction and spun. He stepped on the brake. The RV would go no farther tonight. Blowing out his breath, he slid the transmission into Park.

"When we get inside, I really would like to stay up for a while and talk," she said.

Only now did he turn away from the windshield. Amanda was curled up casually in the passenger seat, her knees tucked up beneath her, her chin tilted back. The white bandage was pale in the glow of the headlights.

"What will happen now, Amanda, is that you will sleep and I will wake you periodically to check on your head. And that's all." He swung out the door, the cold wind and snow blasting him in the face.

"I suppose this involves us sharing a bed," she called matter-of-factly.

"Of course not."

But then he looked at the empty driveway and the dark windows, and he realized that it probably did.

He grabbed a flashlight from his toolbox and headed out to face the bigger hole he'd dug for himself.

CHAPTER ELEVEN

AMANDA HELD ON TO BRODY'S shoulders as he carried her to the chalet set off the road and nestled into a hollow.

His flashlight shone brightly in front of them, illuminating the snow that drifted over the pathway. Wind whipped and blew into every exposed crevice.

She shivered, shielding her face inside his warm parka. Brody was nothing if not capable. She was glad she'd driven with him and that he'd found a safe place for them to ride out the storm. He'd been right to insist they stay together; if she'd traveled alone, who knows what could have happened to her?

Swallowing, she clung onto him as he trudged through snowbanks higher than his knees. Because he stepped carefully, he never once jostled her. She felt his even breathing against her hair, and he barely seemed bothered with her weight.

The benefits of an athlete, she thought, grateful for his strength. It was flattering to know he was worried for her, and reassuring, too. Maybe he hadn't followed her back to the wedding just because of the sex, or left with her in his RV because of it either. But still, she needed to remember it wouldn't help either of them to sleep together, ever again. Not when their lives and their goals were so permanently at odds.

She stepped back as he set her down before the front door, the stoop bare because of an overhead awning and a wind tunnel whistling past them. "Who lives here?" she asked.

"A friend of mine and his wife."

"Do you think they're home?"

He shone his flashlight inside a small window, then shook his head. "Hans's Audi is gone, so it looks like they've already left for Alto Baglio." He knelt, scooping and clearing snow from a partially hidden rock with his bare hands.

They really would be alone together tonight? "Won't your friends mind us staying here without them?"

"Why? It's the skier's code, and I'd do the same for them. Come to think of it, I already have." He stood, triumphantly holding a small house key. "Here it is, the key to the castle."

Amanda couldn't help smiling. He looked so adorable—tall and strong and wearing his baseball cap covered with snowflakes. "Remind me never to put my apartment key under my front doormat."

"You don't like house-crashers?" He shoved open the door with a grunt, glancing at her sideways. "Then you must really dislike skiers."

Funny how she'd been adjusting her opinion, and in just twenty-four hours. "I think they might be growing on me."

He darted a look at her. "This is only for one night, Amanda."

She bit her tongue. If she could help it, their stay would last as long as she needed to get him to talk to her. As far as she was concerned, he had an interview to give, and she could never let that go.

But this time, she didn't push it with him. She simply smiled. She'd learned that much from the accident. He frowned, then bent and picked her up again—his hands on her jeans cold from the snow—to carry her over the stoop.

"What is this, a honeymoon?" she quipped.

"Don't make light of it." But his voice wavered, betraying him. "I told you I'm taking care of your head wound tonight. Get used to it."

"I don't have a head wound, just a slight cut. And I'm not shaken. See?" She flashed him a grin.

"Stop thinking about your interview," he growled, carrying her into the house. "Because it isn't going to happen."

He knew her too well, and it *was* going to happen. She shifted to help him grope for the light switch, though the electricity was obviously out. Then he fumbled with the wall phone, but from his look, that didn't work either.

She gave him an innocent smile. "Tough luck, Brody?"

Grunting, he pulled the flashlight from his back pocket, the beam splaying across the homey, peach-painted walls as he carried her upstairs and around the corner of an upper-level hallway that smelled inviting, like dried herbs from the alpine countryside.

"This is the guest bedroom where you'll be staying tonight," he said gruffly, setting her down on a quilt-covered twin bed that squeaked uncomfortably under her weight. "No argument, you need your sleep."

"Sorry, but that's impossible right now. It's too cold to sleep here alone. You'll need to stay and talk with me."

He pressed his hand to her forehead. "Damn it, we need to get you warm."

With the help of the flashlight he explored the room, fiddling with the thermostat and inspecting the heater.

Then he straightened and sighed. "Wait here, all right? I'd leave you with the flashlight, but I need to check out the water heater. I'm pretty sure it runs on propane."

"Why, are you planning on dunking me in a hot shower?" She laughed.

When he didn't smile, she sat up.

IT WAS A STEAMING HOT BATH. Amanda climbed into an oversize soaking tub set into a tiled platform, and big enough for two adults.

Not that Brody made a move to join her. On the contrary, he'd turned his back as she'd stripped off her panties and her T-shirt. She slumped inside, watching him, the flickering light from four pillar candles on the platform's ledge illuminating the pull of the fabric across his shoulders. She coughed, then stretched out her legs in the water, but neither noise made Brody budge.

She leaned back, unsettled. Hadn't he felt anything making love to her last night? Because she certainly had. Didn't he…miss her?

She sighed heavily into the Epsom-salt-and-lavender-oil-scented room.

Cautiously, he turned his neck. Too late, it dawned on her that beneath the clear water she was completely naked, and that maybe it wasn't such a good idea to bait him.

His stare burned as he drank in the outline of her breasts and bare legs, then blinked hard and dragged his gaze to her face. A vein throbbed in his neck and a tortured look heated his intense blue eyes.

She had her answer; he did miss her.

"Damn it, Amanda," he growled. "I'll wait outside."

"You don't have to leave."

"Yeah, I do."

"Brody…" She wanted him to stay, but she couldn't admit that when it was so one-sided. "Don't you want to…?"

Don't you want to come in with me, she almost said. But that was impossible. And from the pained look on his face, he knew it too.

Grinding his jaw, he faced the wall again—white tile, shadows bouncing across it from the flickering candlelight.

Now what? She dug her fingernails into her palms. The small room was heating with steam, and in response, he pushed up his sleeves past his elbows. From her position in the tub, she could see the deep red scar marring the muscular beauty of his right forearm. Last night she'd kissed him there, but he hadn't told her what it meant. She knew only the bare-bones particulars about his past, really.

"Is that scar left from your injury two years ago?" she asked.

"I said no questions," he snapped.

Sadness enveloped her. Ever since the call from Chelsea, he'd put up such a wall around himself. And that was a mistake, because she and Brody *had* shared something this weekend that went far beyond sex.

From the sunset on the mountain, to the aftermath of lovemaking in the lodge. The comfort he'd given her in the RV when she'd followed him out of the wedding, and then, returning inside so he could dance with her in private.

She missed that emotional closeness. She lifted her hand, letting the water run through her fingers. Yes, on a practical level she could cobble together an article without Brody's cooperation, but it wouldn't be a good one, and it certainly wouldn't be enough to earn her promotion. Regardless of the promotion though, shouldn't she and Brody at least be able to talk out their differences?

"You don't want me to write about you," she said sadly, "and yet I have to. How do you propose we fix this?"

"*Fix* this?" He turned to stare at her. "You don't have a clue what's going on, do you?"

"Then give me one, Brody."

His lips clenched, conveying his seriousness. "What if you're a tool he's using to destroy me? Have you considered that scenario?"

She gasped. "I would never destroy you!"

"No?" he said between his teeth. "Think about the facts. You filed your profile yesterday, a puff piece— and for the sake of this discussion I'll believe you when you say that's all it was."

"That *is* all it was!" Why was he being so suspicious?

"Then why," he asked, "after I have a confrontation with your father, do your bosses suddenly want the full, in-depth, investigative-reporter-treatment sicced on me?"

She gaped at him. "You think there's a connection?"

He snorted. "Can't you smell the setup? Because I can. Can't you see your father's fingers all over this?"

"Maybe I could, if you'd been honest with me at the wedding and told me what it was he said to you!"

Brody crossed his arms and faced the wall again.

"Talk to me," she said, her voice shaking, "because *I* want to be honest with *you*. And I am honest. I told you everything that went down between my father and me, and why. I told you exactly who I am and what I do. I have no more secrets from you."

"This is different," he said in a guttural whisper.

"How is it different?" She sat up, the water sloshing in the tub. "Brody, do you know what my boss said to me? She thinks you're hiding something. You have to be—you try too hard to keep yourself under wraps."

"Why would she think that?" He turned, his nostrils flaring. "Is there anyone on that magazine staff who has a connection to your father, besides you?"

"What? No! Chelsea has never met him and she doesn't want to either. She hates sports. Same with her boss who runs *Paradigm*." Amanda leaned her head back and stared into the flames. "Though in full disclosure, my father does sit on a golfing charity with Vernon Trowel, the industrialist who owns the holding company that owns the media corporation, about twenty levels above me. Trust me, though, that's not how I got the job. My father doesn't even know or care that I work there."

"Damn it, Amanda!"

"You don't believe me?" she asked.

"Haven't you ever heard of a long con?"

"A…what?"

"A long con. A scam that uses a long setup designed to get your trust and then abuse it so the perpetrator can get what they want out of you. It's what con men do."

What was he talking about? Her father was many things, but he wasn't a con man. He was straight and aboveboard when he ruthlessly manipulated a person or stabbed them in the chest. There was nothing charming or sneaky about her father. So why would Brody think that way?

Of course. Brody's father was a con man. That was

the key to his psyche. The answer to how she could solve this interview problem for both of them, equally.

She lifted her foot to the rim of the tub, watching the warm water trickle down her calf. What if she focused her article on Brody's father? He was Brody's deeper secret, after all, the core vulnerability she'd sensed in him from the beginning. *The best-kept secret on the tour,* he'd joked to her.

But it wasn't a joke. Not to Brody. He didn't want anybody to know about his father being in prison, just as she didn't want anybody to know about her father disowning her.

But she had to approach the idea carefully with him. "Brody, you need to give this interview so your sponsor will fund you for the season, am I right? So, what if we were to spotlight your charity? The paradox of the tough, competitive skier putting as much into a charitable foundation as he does into his training." Because why else would a guy who had issues with his father start a program to help kids? "This can only help you," she said. "You can't object to that."

He gave a dry laugh. "Nice try. But you and I both know your readers don't give a rat's ass about my foundation."

"Maybe not specifically," she said calmly, "but like everyone, they love a good story. And what else is conflict but fuel for a satisfying ending?" Yes, that was the answer. "Think about it, if we bring out the 'why' of your foundation, some background about life with your father when you were a kid, then that could go a long way toward bringing interest and maybe even funding to your work."

He stared at her. "Don't try to con a conner's kid."

"You see, you look at everything through that lens. You can't help it. Who could, in your shoes?"

He rolled his eyes. "Following that train of thought, you look at life as an ego contest to win."

Her breath sucked in. "That wasn't nice."

"Yeah, I didn't think you'd want to make that comparison."

She swallowed, determined to go on. "I *have* to write something. And I *will* write something. Sleep on it, Brody. Because you know it's a good idea for both of us. Your father is the revelation that readers will care to know about."

"It's none of their business."

She looked him in the eye. "Have you *ever* talked about it? To your siblings, say?"

He stared blankly at her.

"You don't have any siblings? How about your mother?"

"She's dead," he said flatly.

"Oh, Brody."

"I was a toddler," he mumbled. "I don't even remember her."

That was awful. She couldn't imagine growing up without her sister or her mother. Despite all his success, his followers and his tour buddies, Brody must live a lonely life.

She drew her knees to her chin and hugged herself. "Have you told any friends about him?"

"No." His voice was softer now. She hadn't been wrong—he was a very private person.

"Have you ever told…a girlfriend?" she asked.

Brody shook his head and looked at her bleakly. "Just you, Manda."

Her heart clutched. She felt dizzy, and maybe she

was a little jolted from the accident. But she needed to keep him with her, now, before he walked away for good.

"Brody, if you tell me more about him, I promise I'll keep your confidence. I'll write your story in a way that serves your dignity. And I'll make sure people see the true nature of your charity and why it's important to you."

He swallowed and his jaw went tight. "I don't want those kids interviewed," he said in a raw voice.

Did she dare hope? She kept her tone calm. "Okay."

"And I sure as hell don't want you to see *him* or even say where he is."

Was he talking about his father? If he was, she couldn't promise that. "Brody…"

"And don't assume the guys on my team know anything about this," he said harshly. "I don't talk to them about it and they don't want to know, so don't be thinking it would be productive to call them. I'm telling you up front, that's a no-go with me. Leave them out of this or I won't do it. I'm serious, Amanda."

She slowly let out her breath. The important thing was, he was considering giving her the interview. This was their first step, talking about the conditions. Later, they could negotiate the details, because she *would* have to fact-check him at some point. For now, though, it was smartest to keep the deal as simple as possible.

"Okay," she said, sitting up in the tub. "I understand completely."

He looked down at the floor and nodded shortly. "Good."

"We're agreed, then?"

"No. Like you said, I need to sleep on it." He glanced at her. "And if I were to agree to a sit-down, I'd want this done in one day. I'd give you an hour tomorrow morning, and only if your head is okay, but then we're leaving. I'll drop you wherever you need to go. Then I have training to get to, and an on-site meeting with my ski manufacturers."

"May I attend?"

"No." He looked her in the eye. "And I'd need to see your copy before you file it."

"That is not copacetic, Brody!"

"No?" He was shouting back at her. "Amanda, I don't think about my childhood. I don't go there. I've locked it away and I want it kept locked away. How would you like to spill your guts about your father to a national tabloid? How would you take it?"

"I'm not a tabloid writer," she said coolly, "and if the only way you'll believe me is to see my copy before I file it, then fine, I will make a journalistic exception. But only because I was stupid enough to sleep with an interview subject, so maybe I deserve it."

That vein pulsed in his neck. "We won't be sleeping together again. I can't have sex with you during this thing."

"No kidding!" She was shouting again.

But he was just as angry. "*I'm* the one who has more to lose," he said, his voice barely controlled. "You could change your mind about showing me the copy, and you could still write whatever you want and I'd have no recourse. The words would be out there, the skis out of the gate so to speak, and it would be too late for me to take back anything I said."

He was right. The stakes *were* high for him. But, like it or not, he was the public figure, and that was the price a public figure paid—the entry fee for all the fame and glory and sponsor money.

"I won't betray you," she said softly. "I swear to you I won't."

And then she looked at him, pale and shivering— he was visibly shaking even in the steaming room. He looked as if he'd been the one hit on the head, not her.

She held out her hand to him. "Brody, will you come into the tub with me? I want you to be warm again."

HE WAS IN HELL.

Brody stood at the end of the tub, and despite everything Amanda threatened him with, he couldn't tear his gaze from her.

Her hair was pinned up and the water sluiced over her breasts, the nipples just edging the surface. She'd drawn up her knee, and there was nothing he wanted more than to strip off his clothes and join her, kissing her deeply as she wrapped her legs around him.

He groaned, curling his hands into fists. He had an erection under his boxer shorts and the last thing he needed was to want her and remember the feeling of being buried inside her. When they'd made love, he'd thought it had been the most intense sex he'd ever experienced, but nothing topped the raw emotions he faced now.

He'd never felt his own scars more. He'd never felt anyone else's scars more. He was too protective of her, and it terrified him. All he wanted was to stop thinking about the decision at hand and lose himself in her body again, as if that would make the agony disappear.

It easily could, for the moment, anyway. Until he woke up beside her in the cold morning light with reality stretched before him in the form of her red-blinking voice recorder.

She sighed and climbed out of the tub. With her body

glistening from the hot bath, she dripped across the tiles and fluffed open a bath towel from a low shelf. He hadn't even noticed their surroundings, he'd been so wrapped in their soul-racking test. But she came back to him, wrapping the towel around her shoulders.

"Come on, honey," she said, her skin smelling of the lavender oil she'd poured into the tub. "We need to go to bed."

She really wanted to climb into bed with him? She was crazy. He'd nail her in her sleep. He could not be trusted.

"You're taking care of me, remember?" she murmured. "You need to watch for my head injury. We need to keep warm together."

Yeah, the indoor temperature was about forty or fifty degrees Fahrenheit and they were stuck in a snowstorm together, in a house with no electricity or working telephone service. She'd turned the tables back so neatly on him, hadn't she?

"Right," he said. "I'm in charge."

"At least I know you don't snore." She winked at him. She never lost her good humor, no matter how bad it got, and he did love that about her.

He set to work. He found her dry clothes to sleep in, a pair of warm sweatpants and a long-sleeved shirt from a drawer of clothes that looked as if they belonged to Sarah—Hans's wife—and yeah, he would have to call and thank them tomorrow. There was a fireplace in the master bedroom, so he had no choice but to settle her there, under a down comforter and a pile of blankets. The fire was quick to start, since dry logs, kindling and a box of matches were already set out.

Now there was nothing left but for him to climb into bed beside her. A tight queen-size bed that sagged in the center of the mattress, where Hans and his wife cuddled together, rather than in two separate furrows the way he would have preferred to sleep with Amanda.

He couldn't sleep with her. It was impossible. They had barely slept last night, and he wouldn't close his eyes tonight either, though for a very different reason. Now that he was forbidden from tasting and touching her body, there was a rift between them. A huge red stop sign.

He was scared as hell of the decision he had to make. She was right—her story angle was the perfect solution, though not for the reasons she realized. If he told her that truth, he wouldn't have to tell her the other, more critical thing that must never be named.

Hell, he couldn't even *voice* the words in his own conscience. Harrison had to do it for him.

And as Harrison said, Amanda could never know. No one could. Instead, if he let her follow this other path, the one that lay with his father, then she would lead everyone else there as well.

Problem solved.

And yet, he couldn't imagine taking this path. He pictured his father's face in his mind, and bile rose in his throat. It came to a choice of purgatory versus hell, and Brody wanted nothing to do with either one.

I can't do it. I won't do it.

He could never show her his angst or the truth of the decision he had to make. That was probably the worst of the bargain.

"Good night, Brody," she whispered, the crown of her head snuggled against his shoulder—they'd fallen into the well together, into Hans and Sarah's cozy little pit. "Everything will be better in the morning, you'll see."

He felt a laugh shotgun out of him and into the cold darkness. "How can you say that?"

"My mother always said it to me, and though I didn't realize it at the time, she was essentially right." He felt her arm snake hesitantly around his waist. Thankfully they had no skin touching, but this was bad enough.

"No offense to your mother, but things keep getting worse and worse for us. Haven't you noticed that?"

"If we trust each other, we can't go wrong," she said, her voice muffled against his shirt.

But that was exactly what they couldn't do.

Her sigh was quiet in the darkness. "You've been good to me, Brody. I appreciate it."

"I don't know about tomorrow."

"Hmm." She stifled a yawn. "Then think of the now. Just the now."

A spark crackled in the fireplace and he turned his attention toward the glow. Something lit within his heart and he could feel a small part of the joy of the moment.

A woman in his arms. A woman who'd promised to be careful with him.

BUT SOMETIME BEFORE DAWN, a nightmare woke Brody in a cold sweat. He'd been standing on a mountaintop cliff, terrified of the sheer drop below him, when he'd lost his footing and slipped. The weightless feeling of falling had rushed up to hit him, so real his stomach dipped and then slammed. He woke with a start, moisture on his brow.

The embers from the fire had died out and the room was cold. He and Amanda clung to each other, her dark hair spread over his pillow.

He inhaled her scent. So like her. As unique as any perfume.

He slept again for a while and didn't leave the bed until the sun rose, then crawled out from beneath the covers and soundlessly zipped into his jacket. She murmured and stirred, but was so exhausted from yesterday's accident that she didn't fully wake. He was glad. He'd checked on her hourly, but now he would let her rest. This morning would be their last time together and then they would part ways. He couldn't do this with her anymore.

Sick with regret, he made his way downstairs. The only thing left was to make her remember him as fondly as possible. He stepped into his boots and fought his way through the snowdrifts. He would bring up her luggage and her carry-on bag. Then he would feed her, tell her as gently as possible there could be no interview—not now and not ever—and then usher her to the airport and New York.

And then suck it up and never think about her again, or about what could have been between them, just as he never thought about his father, or the places they'd lived and the times they'd had to leave. He would lock those feelings away in their compartment where there was no reason to ever bring out a key.

He wrestled open the RV with a lump in his throat.

The whine of an engine appeared from the direction of the road. He stared, and two uniformed men roared up the driveway on snowmobiles.

Italian Carabinieri?

His heart sped up. But maybe they were officials assisting with the road being cleared.

"Hello!" he called in clear English. "How is the pass?"

"Closed, sir," the younger official answered, with just a slight accent. "We are under avalanche warning. No traffic allowed through. None at all."

What? "For how long?"

"Three days. And then we will see."

CHAPTER TWELVE

AMANDA SAT UP, STRETCHING. Outside, a few flakes drifted from overcast skies, though the flurry was gentler.

Safe, was her first thought. *Brody kept me safe through the storm.*

Turning away from the window, she rested her palm on the indent beside her. The space where he'd slept was still warm. She'd loved sleeping beside him, falling asleep to the rise and fall of his breathing and the heat of his body. It felt good not to have to sneak away from him because she needed to get to Jeannie. It felt good to actually stay.

And now she smelled coffee brewing downstairs. She hoped it was a sign he was ready to agree to work with her.

Go easy on him until he does, her instincts said.

She climbed out of bed and found that Brody had lugged in her suitcase from the RV. Smiling, she quickly showered and dressed. By daylight, she could better see the cozy mountain bungalow Brody's friends owned. In addition to the deep soaking tub, there was also a European-style shower stall with water jets at foot, midsection and over-the-head levels. All the amenities to treat a skier with post-workout muscle soreness.

Or a driver who'd survived a frightening blizzard accident.

She felt remarkably fine, considering. The mirror showed just a small cut and a slight bump on her forehead. Not even a bruise to speak of.

She opened Brody's tube of antibiotic ointment and applied that to her already-healing cut, then rummaged in his first-aid kit, carried in from the RV, and tore open the smallest bandage strip. She rearranged her wet hair around it so Brody wouldn't be alarmed.

Patting herself dry, she turned to examine the contents of her suitcase, thankful that her clothes had been laundered by the hotel before she'd packed. She pulled out a comfortable pair of jeans, thick woolen socks and a soft gray cashmere turtleneck. With any luck she'd be interviewing Brody this morning by a blazing fire. Then they could scrounge up a late brunch before getting on their way.

She opened the door and was hit by the aroma of frying bacon.

All this and he cooks, too, she thought, padding down the carpeted staircase to the kitchen.

When she rounded the corner, Brody was using a spatula to flip something onto a propane-fired griddle. She stopped short. Were those…pancakes?

"Oh, my God, I love pancakes," she moaned, sliding into one of the seats in the small eat-in kitchen table, and giving him a smile.

His blue eyes raked her from the bandage on her forehead to her pupils and back again. "How does your head feel?"

"I'm fine, Brody."

He grunted, putting down the spatula. "We don't know that yet."

So he was still uncomfortable with the accident. His hair was in his eyes and he smelled of man and snow. His boots were beside the door, clumped with more snow, and by his windblown hair and red cheeks, she could guess he'd been outside shoveling them an exit path.

"I have no pain, and no dizziness." She pointed to her forehead. "All that's left is a slight cut. Not even a bruise."

"Let me see."

She sighed, sitting still as he peeled back the bandage. The closeness of his body to hers and the brush of his fingers against her skin reminded her of the intimacy they'd shared. She found herself gazing into his eyes:

He didn't notice. He inspected the cut, tilting her head first to one side, then the other. Tension seemed to seep from his shoulders.

"Happy?" she asked.

"No. After we eat breakfast, we need to get you evacuated."

"Why would we do that?"

He frowned, dishing out two plates of pancakes and bacon, and then sat across from her. "Because an official stopped by to tell us we're under avalanche warning. The roads are closed for three days. Nobody's allowed in or out."

"There could be an avalanche?"

He smiled faintly. "It's a safety precaution, standard procedure." He sighed and passed her a bottle of maple syrup. "Though I should have anticipated the road closure. I wasn't thinking."

Amanda tried to wrap her mind around the situation. She opened the syrup—real maple syrup, from Vermont—and poured it over the hot pancakes Brody had cooked for her. They were delicious, fluffy and light. He'd also coddled some eggs in a pan of boiling water. If she had to be trapped by a snowstorm with anyone, she was glad it was him.

"Are you saying we have three days alone together until the avalanche ban lifts?" she asked. "Just you and me?"

"You're not staying here with me, Amanda."

"Of course I am. Imagine what would've happened to me if you'd let me drive into the snowstorm alone. The same goes for you staying here alone."

He stared at her. He wasn't happy, but he couldn't argue with her logic.

They ate without talking. Surely he was realizing that he would have to give her the interview now that they were trapped together. What else would they do? She looked up and found him gazing at her, his expression thoughtful.

"Are we okay with supplies for three days?" she asked politely. "Food, water, fuel?"

She glanced through the kitchen doorway into the sitting room. Brody had fired up the woodstove, but how long would it last?

"I've already taken care of that." He stood and fished out the eggs from the pan, offering her one. She shook her head, so he piled both onto a piece of toast for himself, then sat again. "My RV is stocked with food and water. Hans has gasoline for twelve hours on the generator, and firewood for weeks on the woodstove and fireplace."

She thought of the romantic fireplace in the bedroom last night and knew she was blushing.

Quickly, she wiped her mouth with a napkin. "Are, uh, Hans and his wife okay with us being here?"

Brody swallowed, nodding to his phone lying on the counter. "I sent him a message. He said to make ourselves at home."

"Oh." She thought for a minute. "So we have cell reception?"

"No, but the Wi-Fi is up. I hooked up the generator to run electricity for the morning, anyway."

Wow. She licked the maple syrup from her fingers. If the Wi-Fi was up, she could do some background research. Read more about Brody and see what was on the internet, if anything, about his foundation and his father.

He put down his fork. "But it's a moot point, Amanda, because you're leaving after breakfast. And I'll be fine here alone."

"*I* won't be fine."

He blinked, and she was treated to the sight of his powerful forearms flexing as he crossed them. The slow rise and fall of his Adam's apple as he swallowed.

She looked down at her plate. "Will you go with me if I'm evacuated?"

He shook his head. "I've got race equipment in the RV," he said gently, "plus all my food. I can't abandon it."

His race was the most important thing to him; she knew that. Just as her job was the most important thing to her.

They ate the rest of their breakfast in silence. He'd made another pot of coffee, so she sipped at a cup. He joined her, seemingly relaxed on the surface, but beneath it, there was an undercurrent of tension at what was being left unsaid.

She wanted to stay. He didn't want her to stay.

And yet, what if she did spend the next three days here with him? Sleeping next to him, eating with him and pretending there hadn't once been something physical between them?

He made a sudden intake of breath, and all she could do was stare at his broad chest, remembering how it had felt against her.

She stopped chewing and just…looked at him. He wore jeans and a checked flannel shirt, open over a light blue T-shirt that matched his eyes. Even after everything, he made her want to crawl into his lap and make out with him like a teenager.

"Don't you want to go back to New York?" he asked quietly, setting down his coffee.

"No!" Her vehemence embarrassed her, and her hand shot to her mouth.

His lips tightened. "Three days is a long time."

She shrugged, doing her best to look noncommittal even though her heart was pounding. "I'd enjoy spending them with you."

"For your article?" he asked sharply.

"I wasn't talking about that, but you're right, we do need to discuss it. Set some boundaries, since we're going to be here together for so long."

"Boundaries, huh?"

He stood, and at first she thought he was reaching for something in the cupboard, but when he unzipped a duffel bag and brought out a jumble of small white bottles, placing them one by one on the table, she sat up straighter. "What are those?"

He glanced at her, his intense blue eyes showing his naked caution. "Off the record?"

What was wrong with him? "Of course, we discussed that last night. I have an angle to my story, and I'll stick to it. We agreed."

"We haven't agreed to anything yet." He laid his palms on the table and stared at her.

You were going to decide this morning. But she clamped her lips together and shifted her gaze to the remains of the breakfast he'd made. He was spooked and the worst thing she could do was call up his defenses. "Why don't we talk about your concerns?"

"Concerns?" His brows shot up. "Amanda, don't insult me—we've shared a bed together. Twice." His voice shook with emotion. "You think I want to wake up one day and find you've used what's happening now…everything…for a million people to read as entertainment?"

"Oh, Brody, no!"

"And the accident…and the…fight with your father at the wedding…and the…supplements I take…" He pointed to the bottles lined up on the table. "Will that be fair game for your article, too?"

"No! I said it wouldn't, didn't I?"

"Even if it's in line with your interview angle?" He stared at her. "You tell me to trust you, but if you don't leave now, then we're going to be on top of each other for the next three days. And frankly, I don't think I can take it if I let down my guard and then find out that everything's fair game for your assignment."

"I said I wouldn't do that to you!"

"Yeah, you keep saying that. You come down here, all chipper and happy to see me, and it's easy to be fooled. But I need to know, is that part of an act?" He stared at her, his eyes desolate. "I used to be good at reading people, but with you, my instincts have been proven wrong. Constantly. You've already faked me out once for a story."

"I am not acting." Her voice shook. *Not anymore.* "I don't want anything to be fake between us. Not since…" *Not since I took a risk and slept with you.* She felt her face heating.

She looked down, and her hands were trembling.

"Not since when?" he asked quietly.

"Th-this is more than a job assignment to me." *I'm into territory I don't understand.* She stood, her throat raw, and busied herself with carrying her dirty plate to the sink. "You've affected me, Brody," she said to the running water. "I care about you way more than I should."

He didn't say anything. Not one word.

Blinking, she cleared the rest of the table, taking his plate from him, too. He needed to say something. She wasn't going to gloss over this and then forget about it.

He joined her, picking up a dish towel and drying the plate she'd left in the wooden rack. For long minutes they worked together, saying nothing. She felt bruised inside, exposed and hurt. She didn't know what to think, so she focused on sponging the plates with soapy water and then rinsing them. The silverware. One movement at a time.

She put the last knife in the drying rack, but he moved to block her from walking away. "I've never put myself in this position before," he said in a broken voice.

The heat from his body swamped her. He did care about her, too, and this was the closest she'd get to him saying so.

Intimacy is dangerous for him. He doesn't know who to trust. "You've been betrayed before, haven't you?"

He stepped back. "No. I'm careful to avoid it, and you should be, too."

She nodded, turning to leave, but to do so she needed to squeeze past him in the narrow passage. Her hips brushed his. Their longing for each other was almost tangible, like the air after a dark rain.

"I think," she said, her voice shaking, "that we need to take one evening. Just one evening and dedicate it to this interview we need to do." She swallowed and dared to look at him. "Because we both need it, Brody. And if we find we can't be…friends afterward, then we'll stay away from each other. I'll find a quiet corner and write my assignment. You can…ski. God knows there's enough snow here." She laughed shortly. "Beyond that, we'll share meals and chores. We don't need to talk again if you don't want to."

"That's it? That's your guarantee?" He stalked to the table, agitated, and unscrewed the bottles he'd taken from the duffel bag. His gaze rose to meet hers, and she saw the fury on his face. "You know," he said, pointing at her, "it would help if you showed any awareness of the power you have to ruin people's lives."

"What are you talking about? I've never ruined anybody's life!"

"Let me tell you what these bottles are, and you can guess again."

"The supplements?" Blinking, she scanned the labels on his bottles: A multi-vitamin. Extra vitamin C. Magnesium. Omega 3 capsules. Probiotics. Something called MSM. "Why are you showing me your vitamin pills?"

"Because athletes need them for their *jobs*." He stared at her, his blue eyes bright. "Because what we do is a job, no different from yours, and we need to stay healthy for it."

"I know that. Don't you take other stuff, too?" She remembered all the protein powders from her youth when she lived with her father.

"Like what?" Brody asked flatly.

"What do you call them…?" She snapped her fingers. "Performance-enhancing supplements. Powders and shakes."

"No." He spread his hand over the table. "And this is important. What you see is what you get."

"Why are you being so touchy about this?"

"Because we have to be. And *you* need to understand that. We're poked and prodded and asked to piss in a cup at every turn. Back in the day, some of the over-the-counter stuff had banned substances in them, and guys were unfairly accused."

"Whoa, I never accused anybody of anything."

"You wrote about it." He crossed his arms. "Did you ever consider your allegations from the athletes' point of view?"

Was he talking about her baseball article last year? About steroid use in major-league sports and the effect it had on kids who were emulating their heroes?

"Of course. I covered every point of view in that story," she said, picking up the box of eggs he'd used and setting it down again. The label read Certified Organic. She glanced at the maple syrup bottle. Certified Organic, too. And the coffee beans, nestled in the bag he'd brought from his motor home kitchen. Brody wasn't taking any chances on illegal chemicals getting into his system. He even traveled with his own food and drink. "Isn't this excessive?"

"I can name good people in every sport affected,"

he said, an edge to his voice. "All you have to do is use that word…" He seemed to choke on it. "…*steroids,* and everything they've worked for is over. It's a modern-day witch hunt."

"Are you sure you're not buying into the stereotype of the bastard reporter who just wants the scoop?" she asked, trying to stay calm.

"Manda, those baseball players you wrote about only did what the fans demanded of them." He leaned forward on the counter, passionate about the subject. "Have you ever seen a fan demand an autograph from an athlete? Have you ever seen how fast they turn on them when they're in a slump? Or when they're injured?"

"Yes," she said calmly again, "and if you'd *read* my article on steroids in baseball, then you'd see I did the players justice."

"Do the players think so?" he demanded.

"Have you read my article, Brody?" she pressed. "Or are you just believing what Harrison told you to think about me?"

He paused, obviously taken aback.

Touché, she thought. "Give me your email address, and I'll send you my article."

"Harrison sent it this morning," he said in a low voice. "It's on my phone."

So *this* is what the inquisition was about. "And have you read it yet?"

He made a slow shake of his head.

"Then go and read it. Before we discuss anything else, read it."

He nodded shortly. "You're right. I need to think." He sighed. "And since you're staying, I need to get some wood cut and brought in from the shed before the light fades. The generator needs work, too."

Mr. Integrity. That was Brody. "In the meantime, I'll find a quiet place to work."

"Then you'll need this." He crossed the kitchen and returned carrying her laptop bag.

Her jaw dropped. "You brought in my *laptop?*"

He shrugged, averting his gaze from hers. "I, uh, texted Sarah, and she said you could use her office." His blue eyes met hers, and as they did, her throat tightened.

"Thank you, Brody," she whispered.

"It should be set up for you." He paused. "She's a writer, too."

Amanda felt her eyes bug out. "Your skier friend is married to a writer?"

He looked at her sharply. "To my knowledge, she's never, ever written an article about him, either now or before they were dating."

"Of course," she murmured. "And believe me, I wouldn't write an article about you, either, if I didn't have to. Just like you wouldn't give me an interview if you didn't have to."

They stared at each other for a long time. And then, he simply nodded. "We'll talk later."

She nodded, too. The important thing was, he had brought in her laptop. There were a dozen small actions he could have taken to sabotage her project, and he hadn't taken any of them. Instead, he was staying with her in this hideaway chalet, and talking to her. Listening to her point of view.

She swallowed. Maybe it was finally sinking in to him that she really was going to write this article. It certainly had sunk in to her that he was going to push back and protect his interests fiercely.

But she would protect his interests, too. And in time, he would see that.

"Thank you, Brody," she whispered again.

"I'm not a total bastard," he said in a low voice.

She didn't think he was a bastard at all. She took the laptop bag from him, their fingers lightly brushing. All the wonder over being able to negotiate with a man, to show him her feelings and her values, however guardedly, and not having him dismiss her out of hand—it was new to her.

Emotion welled within her. It seemed to build to one big font of hope that everything could work out okay between them. That they could figure this out somehow.

TWENTY MINUTES LATER, Amanda swiveled in the best writing chair she'd ever sat in. Sarah's attic studio was a little piece of heaven.

In a corner nook were shelves holding all kinds of books in several languages, but predominantly English. A bank of windows overlooked the back of the house and the most beautiful natural scenery outside her home state's White Mountains: the majestic Italian Alps. A working fireplace made of mountain stone was set along the opposite wall, and a comfortable couch with cashmere throws beckoned.

Amanda could envision herself perfectly, editing copy with pen in hand before a roaring fire. Maybe even a glass of brandy. What a far cry from her doorless and ceilingless cubicle in *Paradigm*'s Manhattan offices, noisy and without privacy—certainly without an inspirational view. With internet and telecommunications being what they were, why couldn't she live and work like this always?

She leaned her chin on her fists and gazed down at the yard. Brody was bringing in firewood he'd chopped, judging from an ax stuck in a block of wood. Then he rummaged inside a shed, emerging with a shovel. He paused to check his cell phone, that miracle of modern technology. Really, what stopped people from living the lives they wanted, wherever life may take them?

She ran her hands over Sarah's funky-cool writing desk, a door that had been painted orange. Out of respect for her host, she left Sarah's computer dark and instead set up her own laptop.

While she was searching for an outlet to plug in her adapter, she couldn't help glancing at Sarah's bulletin boards. From the photos and cards, Hans appeared to be a retired local skier, and Sarah an English-speaking writer who published a newsletter with skiing news. She also wrote novels, judging from a second bulletin board dedicated to the checkerboard placement of brightly colored index cards with jotted notes. A list of scenes on a storyboard, Amanda realized.

There were all kinds of writers in the world. And one great thing about being a writer was that she wasn't tied to one spot. Unlike skiing, where a person needed snow to practice, Amanda could write anywhere she wanted to.

She turned on her laptop, then buckled down and cranked out the one piece of writing required for the day: a message to Jeannie letting her know she was okay. That she was snowbound with Brody and riding out the avalanche warning.

While Amanda was online, she checked her email. True to form, Chelsea had come through. Amanda clicked open her short and sweet note: *Enjoy the snow-storm hideaway with your hot skier. When your article hits my inbox, here's what you can look forward to. Chelsea*

Attached was a contract. With everything Amanda had asked for: promotion, job security, status.

She leaned back in the chair and imagined having it all. But no sooner had she closed her eyes than her videophone connection sounded. It was Jeannie.

Amanda toggled the buttons, but she couldn't get the video to work, just the sound. "Honey, I didn't want to bother you on your honeymoon," she chided into the computer speakers.

"I was going to call you anyway," Jeannie's soft voice answered. "I want to thank you. Massimo's sister came and boxed up my wedding bouquet for the dried flower arranger, and the ivy cuttings you put in water for me are making me very happy."

"Good," Amanda said. "That's exactly what I intended."

"Remember how Mom used to make clippings with her houseplants?" Jeannie sighed with nostalgia. "'Giving them sisters' is how she described it to me once. I think what you did for me is very appropriate."

Amanda's eyes misted. She'd never known that about their mom. And until Jeannie had said so, she hadn't made the connection that she was continuing one of her family traditions.

Bittersweet warmth filled her chest. Their mother had touched them in many more positive ways than she'd realized. She was only beginning to see that.

"So tell me," Jeannie chattered on, making Amanda grateful the video connection on the monitor wasn't working, "how is my big sister doing with Brody Jones?"

"I'm…good." She paused, fiddling with her laptop cord. Should she tell Jeannie she was having fantasies that she could write for her magazine and build a relationship with Brody at the same time?

She felt her face heat.

"Is he treating you well?" Jeannie demanded. "Because Massimo will go down there and rescue you if he isn't."

"No need." She laughed. "I definitely want to be here. And…I'm making headway with Brody. I'm just wondering if it's a good idea to want to pursue anything with him. Practically, I mean."

Jeannie giggled. "Are you asking my matchmaking opinion?"

"Strangely, it appears so."

"In that case, I think you should keep yourself open to him. It's obvious he's interested, or else he wouldn't be risking any of this."

"You think so?"

"He came back for you even after he knew about you being Dad's daughter, didn't he?"

Yes. Yes, he had.

"He's stuck with you this far, Mandy, there has to be something there. Besides, Massimo gives him his stamp of approval, and that's as strong an endorsement for his character there is, if you ask me."

Brody *was* proving himself a decent guy. Amanda curled the laptop cord around her fingers, thinking of their talk in the kitchen. "We're negotiating a compromise. And he seems to respect me. He's promised to read one of my old articles."

"He *should* respect you. You have a lot to offer, and I'm not talking about your job."

That's where Jeannie was wrong. Without her position at *Paradigm,* she wasn't anything special. Her job was what had first made Brody notice her—and was the only reason he kept noticing.

Amanda glanced at Chelsea's email. "I need to interview him again. You see, they want another story about him, a longer piece this time. Do you remember the rumor you told me about the trouble between him and Dad? I need to know what that was about, Jeannie."

There was a slight hesitation on Jeannie's end. "I don't know if it's true, really. It's just a hint Dad made. A feeling I got."

"What did he say, exactly?"

Jeannie sighed. "Mandy, you've got to understand where Dad is coming from. Brody is a guy who's had effortless success in the sport. And Dad, not at all. You know how he wanted to be a great skier when he was young, don't you? I swear, sometimes I can see the envy pouring from him in waves. Massimo says you should have seen him when Brody got injured and they weren't telling anybody—I think Dad secretly loved it when journalists started trash-talking Brody. Dad couldn't help rubbing it in to him. Just the snarky things he said about it, you know?"

"Brody would hate that."

"He and Dad are like oil and water."

"I thought you said Dad and I are like oil and water?"

Jeannie laughed. "This is the first I've heard you make light of it. Brody is good for you, isn't he?"

"I...wouldn't say that just yet." Whether he gave her the interview would be the true test.

"He *is* good for you. I've always known when you were happy, and I can feel it now. Don't fight it, Mandy."

If only it were that easy. She thought of what he'd said about never putting himself in this position before. "Has…Brody ever had relationships when he was on the circuit before, and he had to dump the women, say?"

"Never," Jeannie said firmly. "Brody is all business about his skiing. He doesn't get sidetracked."

"Even with one-night stands?"

"Lately?" Jeannie laughed again. "Ah, you're the exception, Amanda."

How embarrassing. She couldn't help smiling.

"So where is Romeo now?" Jeannie asked.

"He's, um, downstairs in Hans somebody's gym."

"Are you at Hans Zimmerman's house?"

"Do you know him?"

"Of course! He's only one of skiing's biggest legends, even though he's retired. His wife Sarah is Canadian—she's really funny. They're both good people, Amanda. You absolutely should get to know them."

"When I come back this summer, maybe you can introduce us and I'll take them out to dinner or something as a thank-you?"

"Awesome! I can't wait to tell Massimo. He's a good friend of Hans's." Jeannie sighed again, happily this time. "Do you know you've given me the best possible wedding present?"

Another verification of how much Jeannie wanted to bring her into her world. The longer Amanda stayed in it, the more she saw the attraction.

"Well, I should let you get back to your love nest, Mandy."

"Jeannie, it's not like that!"

"Why not? Use your time wisely! What are you and I doing talking to each other?"

"I can't sleep with him. Not as long as I have to treat him like an interview subject."

"You work too hard," Jeannie said.

Not hard enough. Brody hadn't agreed to talk to her yet. "I'll let you get back to your honeymoon."

"Tell Brody I said hi."

"And give Massimo my continued regards."

Jeannie's laugh was contagious. "I will."

BRODY PAUSED IN THE THIRD SET of reps in his squats routine. Music pulsed from his iPod and his muscles hummed. He should have felt better than he did.

In the mirror he caught a glimpse of Hans's sweet workout room, designed for storm days like these. If he wasn't so messed up over what to do about Amanda, he might enjoy the day, because this was his kind of life: relaxing in the downtime and enjoying a break from the World Cup tour in a house containing everything a guy could desire.

He peeled off his shirt and wiped down his chest with a dry towel. The woman twisted him inside-out. How often had he vowed never to let himself get distracted? But Amanda was different. He couldn't help trusting her, and he'd already trusted her way more than he should have. She'd uttered the word *steroids,* careless of what that could do to an athlete's record. But how could he expect her to understand when he could never tell her his story?

He picked up a set of Hans's dumbbells. Say he did agree to the interview as she'd outlined it. Problem solved, right? No, because with Amanda, anything could happen. Where she was concerned, he needed to more objectively think through her motivations and how they affected him. Going with his heart would be like skiing toward an inviting section of a course—until he came too close and realized how the mountain shadows hid the treachery.

She didn't even *see* her own treachery. And he was too far engaged with her to have the heart to rip off her scabs to show it to her. He'd tried, down in the kitchen this morning, but at the end he couldn't go for the jugular.

He hadn't wanted to hurt her, and that was his problem.

His phone vibrated on the bench and he stared at it. The email with the attachment for Amanda's article was on that phone, though he hadn't brought himself to read it yet. Harrison had sent it this morning along with a message demanding to know where the hell Brody was.

Brody had sent Harrison exactly one message back: *Avalanche warning, pass is closed, staying at H. Zimmerman's place.*

He hadn't mentioned that Hans wasn't present and Brody was, in fact, alone with "that reporter." But Harrison wasn't stupid; he would figure it out soon enough.

Bzzzt. The phone jumped on the bench.

He'd be damned if Harrison added his smarmy presence to another meeting with him and Amanda. What they decided was between him and her, personal. It was no longer Harrison's call. He shut off the phone.

And he would keep it shut off, for the duration. Because it was time he made his own calls. He hadn't come back to the tour to be jerked around, not by his agent, and certainly not by the woman he was beginning to care for. If he wanted to know what she hoped to accomplish with him, both short-term and long, then an article about baseball players wasn't going to tell him anything.

She was.

He was taking her to the top of the black diamond slope and making her show him her intentions. Now.

CHAPTER THIRTEEN

AMANDA LINGERED IN THE DOORWAY, watching Brody toss his phone into a duffel bag. She hoped he'd read her article and was ready to finish their business together. She didn't think she could take this tension between what she needed in her professional life and what she wanted in her personal life much longer. After sifting through everything Jeannie had said, she was ready to take a chance.

With butterflies in her stomach, Amanda entered Brody's domain, a small gym with mirrored walls and a bank of windows overlooking the mountains. Brody sat on a workout bench wearing only his gym shorts, his chest glistening with sweat and power. No wonder she couldn't concentrate on her internet search upstairs.

She tapped his knee to get his attention from the iPod he wore. She ached to drift her fingers over his smooth, well-built thighs, but that was forbidden fruit.

Pulling off his earphones, Brody stood. One look at her and his eyes burned. He smelled so good, like himself and those powerful, unique pheromones of his that constantly drew her to him. "I'm glad you're here," he said, his voice sounding gritty, "because there's something I need to say to you."

"Y-yeah. Me, too."

He stalked forward and she backed up, two slow, stuttering steps that ended with her behind pressed against the mirror. While her whole body seemed to tingle with anticipation, he leaned over her, one hand splayed above her head, the other dangling at his side. "Are you finished digging into whatever dirt you can find about me?"

"I…" Did he mean researching him? "Y-you're mistaken, that's not what I was doing in Sarah's office." She glanced down, swallowing, at his bare washboard stomach just inches from hers. Unable to resist, she stroked her fingertips to the muscles that ridged it.

Bad move. He clasped her hand and snapped it against the mirror, holding it there like a handcuff.

Her heart beat wildly. They really weren't supposed to be doing this. Yet, she couldn't stop. She pressed closer to him, almost touching.

"What do you want from me, Amanda?"

"I…want us to get our interview out of the way."

"This is my interview now. And I want to know what will happen if your article never gets written?"

She blinked as if he'd thrown cold water on her. "What?"

He made a guttural laugh. "Answer my question."

"You're not serious."

"I am, and this is the last time I'll ask you."

What was he doing? Did he mean to seduce her from her goal?

She pushed at him, trying to understand, but he dropped his hand from the mirror and slid both hands under her sweater, his palms flat on her abdomen. She gasped, but she didn't pull away.

"What will happen to you if I don't give you what you need?" he demanded.

The breath shuddered out of her. In a way, with his hands touching her like that, he *was* giving her what she needed. More than anything, she wanted to lose herself in lovemaking and closeness with him again, but she couldn't. Not yet.

"I need this interview with you. We should do it tonight, before we both explode."

"If it's the money…" He wet his lips and placed them on the sensitive pulse point beside her ear. "…tell me, sweetheart, and I'll get you a check for any amount you want."

He thought he could *buy* her? She sidestepped his grasp. "You know this isn't about money!"

"What's it about, then?" He dogged her, nibbling gently at her ear with his teeth until she leaned back against the mirror and let herself enjoy it. "Tell me why it's so important to you."

"I…oh," she moaned, surrendering to the wave of pleasure that swept from his mouth on her neck to her breasts. When he nuzzled her like that, he made her forget everything else, and her resolve melted like snow. "Please, I need to do this," she whispered, her eyes drifting closed. "Like you need to ski."

He took his lips away, and she felt cool air. All she wanted was for him to kiss her again.

"Not good enough," he said, his voice rumbling deep in his chest. "If it was only the writing that mattered, you'd be like Sarah. You'd write blogs and newsletters and books."

She gasped. "Is *that* why you sent me to her office? To *influence* me?"

"No." His gaze bored into hers. "And I'm the one conducting this interview, sweetheart, not you. So answer my question."

She turned away, but his big hands caught her. Physically caught her by the waist and pulled her to him.

There was sensual power in him, and he wasn't afraid to use it. And yet...

His eyes betrayed him. They were full of pain at what he was doing to her.

"I can walk out of here now," she said quietly. "You don't hold me captive."

He nodded. "Same with me. There's a village and a *pensione* a mile down the road. I could leave and you would never see me for the duration." He laid his forehead against the mirror. "But I haven't done that because you said...in the kitchen this morning...that this has gone beyond a job assignment for you." He lifted his head and looked at her. "If that's true, I need to know what *Paradigm* gives you." His eyes were bleak. "What do they give you that I can't?"

Her mouth dropped open. He was hurt that she sought validation from her job instead of from him?

His hands released her waist and fell to his side, giving her the answer.

"Security," she whispered, knowing she owed him honesty, at least. "Working for *Paradigm* gives me security."

"So does love," he ground out. "So does money."

He wasn't offering her love. She knew this. "Status," she whispered again. "It brings me status."

He looked disgusted with her. "Do you mean fame?"

"No! That doesn't draw me."

"You want to be put on a pedestal? Treated well?" His face pained, he lowered his forehead to touch hers. "Because believe me, sweetheart, I can treat you well."

Didn't she know it? Her mouth was so dry, she couldn't speak. She wished she could rely solely on him. If only she could trust he would never turn on her the way others had.

"What will happen if you lose this interview, Manda? I need to know."

She stepped away again, because she needed distance to make her point. "You know what I'll lose because you already have it." Though maybe he was so used to it by now, he took it for granted. "Look at you, Mr. Hot Skier. Look at everything you have."

"This isn't about me, it's about you." He pointed at her. "You interview people and expect them to be honest with you. Well, I expect the same in return."

"I've been nothing but honest with you!"

"It's hard to be interviewed, isn't it?" He grasped her by the arms. "Tell me, sweetheart. Take a risk and spill it. What can this job give you that's so important that you go crazy at the thought of it being taken away?"

"Fine!" she nearly shouted. But she looked him straight in the eye. "Here's what's important to me—when you belong to something substantial—something big like *Paradigm* or the ski team or the record books—then people take you seriously. Other people—people like you—know you're an equal to them. They can't mess with you. They have to think twice because you have power, too. If they hurt you, you could hurt them right back."

He stared at her. "You would destroy me with your writing?"

"No! I would never do that. Not to *you*."

"To who then? To your father?" At the face she made, he laughed bitterly. "It always comes down to him, doesn't it? You want him to notice you and react to you, and this is the way you make him face you—"

"No! Stop, that isn't my goal!"

"What *is* your goal? What kind of relationship do you expect from him?"

She hugged her arms to her chest, suddenly feeling chilly. "Nothing this article can give."

He snorted. "Do you want him to call you up to chat? Ask you how your day was?"

"No!"

"Then what? Some people don't have relationships with their parents. I don't. It was my choice, and I'm fine with it. Why aren't you fine with it?"

"Because I have a sister!"

"Jeannie?" He paused. "What does she have to do with it?"

"*She* has a relationship with him," Amanda cried. "She's figured out a way to manage it! And I'd like that level of politeness, too. I'd like to be able to pick up the phone and call him if I need to. Is that so bad? I want to be able to sit at a table during a wedding reception with him and Jeannie and Massimo and Massimo's family, and not have to run away and hide in embarrassment because my own father can't be civil to me. I want him to be civil with me, too, Brody."

"And *Paradigm* will give you that?" Brody asked quietly.

"No, *Paradigm* will not give me that. Only *he* can give me that, and it'll never happen. Do you think I'm stupid? I know it's impossible. The only thing *Paradigm* can give me is a bit of power to use against him so he can't hurt me more. Hurt me, Brody, do you get that? If my mother had had something like that, then he wouldn't have left her. He wouldn't have refused her medical bills. Don't you see? He wouldn't have dared to."

Brody slowly nodded. "Your promotion is an insurance policy for you."

"Yes! You understand!"

"And you need it?" he asked. "You need this insurance policy?"

"Yes!" She nodded, blinking away the emotion that sat heavy on her, and hugging her arms to her chest even tighter. It was so cold in this room without a fireplace. So cold without Brody standing close to her. "Yes, I need it."

He reached down and retrieved his sweat jacket. "Then I'm sorry I can't give it to you."

"What?" She blinked at him, but he had turned to load his duffel bag with his gear.

"I can't help you, Amanda." His voice was sadder this time.

Her mouth fell open. For a moment she had trouble digesting what he was saying. "I don't understand."

His face was kind as he hauled the duffel bag over his shoulder. "You didn't think I could give it all up and stop giving a damn about my career, did you? Well, I've always known it would end someday. And I know what I'll do next. The question is, what will you do when you have to find something besides your *Paradigm* insurance policy to keep you company at night?"

She gaped at him. "You would do this to me?" she whispered.

And from his face, she saw that he already had. To underscore the point, he turned his back on her and headed for the threshold. "Goodbye, Amanda."

"Wait!"

But he didn't turn around. Not this time.

The weight of everything she'd just revealed to him seemed to strike her all at once. These were truths she never even admitted to herself. She'd been honest and raw to the point that she felt stripped and beaten—and she'd been the one to do it, not him. She'd wanted this promotion so badly that she'd blown away all the barriers between them, even the ones that kept her safe.

She sank to her knees, her body shaking. A wave of terror, as powerful as an avalanche, swamped her.

Don't leave me alone! something primal within her screamed.

But he *had* left her alone. And he wasn't coming back.

Slowly, she began to rock. A strange wail hiccupped from her. It didn't sound like anything that could come from her. It sounded like a little kid crying.

And then she felt Brody's arms surround her and heard the thump of his duffel bag dropping to the floor. "Shhh, Manda," he murmured, scooping her into his arms. "Don't cry, it's gonna be okay."

But *how* could it be okay? Like her mother being gone, it was simply too final.

She lowered her head and sobbed into her hands, unable to talk or feel anything but this hole in her life. For her there was no alternative if she didn't at least have her job. Even Jeannie would be an ocean away, nurturing her new family. The job was all Amanda had left.

Guiding her to her feet, Brody drew her on the bench beside him. "Honey, I'm sorry. Please don't cry."

He tried to hold her, but she pushed him away. How could she have believed in him when she should have known not to trust anyone but herself?

He tugged her close and she didn't fight him this time, just because it felt better to be held by him, even temporarily.

He cleared her hair from her eyes and wiped her tears with his thumb. "Shhh, it's okay, we have a plan."

He nudged her chin to look at him. "We'll take your angle. We'll do your interview tonight."

It took a moment for his words to register. Then she froze inside. "You were b-bluffing me?"

He shook his head. "This isn't a game to me. It's deadly serious."

"Then you are…s-such a jerk."

"Yeah." He nodded dully. "I know."

She tried to smile because she was so pathetic and relieved he wasn't leaving her.

Because even if he'd refused to give her the interview, she'd still wanted him to stay.

He smiled back at her sadly. "Will you do me a favor tonight, sweetheart?"

"Wh-what?"

"Remember how you felt just now. Because that's how it's gonna be for me when I have to sit and tell you things I don't want to think about."

She let his words sink in. What she had just gone through *had* hurt, horribly. She didn't want anyone to suffer through that pain, most especially him.

Amanda leaned her forehead against his chest. Brody's skin felt cool and clammy. He was emotionally torn up inside, too.

And he was letting her see it. How many people did she know who were brave enough to expose their vulnerabilities to another person, let alone a national magazine?

Not one.

Pulling away from her, he seemed to withdraw inside himself. She tried to make eye contact, to give him reassurance, but he wouldn't meet her gaze.

"There's a price to this," he said, staring at a spot on

the floor. "I don't know how I'm gonna be afterward. I might have to leave."

Numbness filled her chest. But what did she expect?

"I need to take a shower." He seemed embarrassed that she'd seen him so cut up. As she was embarrassed at having cried in front of him. "Why don't you go figure out a place to do this? Open some wine, pour us a glass."

"Brody, I am sorry."

"Yeah." He smiled tightly. "Me, too." But he stood without touching her. "We both need what we need. In the end, I guess neither of us can escape that."

A HALF HOUR LATER, Amanda slumped against the hard edge of the kitchen counter and struggled to open a bottle of red wine.

The corkscrew slipped and fell to the tile. How could she compose herself? The interview wasn't just hard for Brody, it was hard for her, too. It had fully struck her that tonight would be the most difficult thing she'd had to do in her professional career: interview a man she'd come to care about, deeply, on topics that were emotionally loaded to him.

One misstep on her part, and he would shut down and walk away. By insisting he do the interview, she was stripping him bare.

They were stripping each other bare. But the alternative was worse. She couldn't contemplate having nothing left when she flew back to New York.

Putting the wine bottle aside, she laid out the first step to her insurance policy, a neutral area in which to interview him, one that felt safe. She chose the sitting room off the kitchen. It had huge windows that faced the mountain, and Brody loved mountains. Plus, there was no door to the outside world through which he could impulsively leave.

She rearranged the furniture, moving a couch to face the windows and propping fleece blankets at either end to cocoon him in case it got cold. She dragged away the coffee table and placed a hassock at one end so he could stretch his legs. Like a shrink's office. God, this was awful.

She checked the time: hours to kill, because he was taking a walk alone. Now what?

Cook, Mandy. This was her mom's voice. Amanda felt calm radiate through her. That was what Mom would do—she would create something nurturing for herself and the people she loved.

It was so unfair. Why did Amanda's needs have to butt square against what Brody needed? At any other time, in any other place, he might be the best man in the world for her. If he allowed himself to, maybe he could give her the love she needed. Maybe she could love him back, the way she'd been dreaming about.

I'm going to make him sauce. Her mom was Italian-American, and that was what they called tomato-based spaghetti sauce in her house. She picked up the bottle of Brody's jewel-toned Barolo, opened it, and poured herself a glass. Just to ease her nerves while she cooked.

She opened the cabinets, but her absent hosts didn't share Brody's organic fetish. So Amanda pulled on her boots and trudged outside to the motor home, following the shoveled-out path Brody had made.

Mother Nature had dumped close to three feet of snow on them. The frigid air was cold to her bones. Inside the motor home she blew on her hands and rummaged through his cupboards. Bingo. She sat back on her haunches and stared at Brody's stockpile: cans of organic tomato paste, organic tomato sauce, organic stewed tomatoes. A head of organic garlic. A bottle of organic olive oil.

Back in the kitchen, she was relieved to find that the organic tomato paste looked and tasted exactly like the tomato paste her family used. Mom would be so proud. Her heart cried a little more, so Amanda sipped some wine. *To Mom,* she thought, sniffling as she downed the Barolo. *To all the good stuff she taught me.*

She was standing over the stove, frying the garlic, plus an onion and a pepper she'd found in Sarah's pantry, trying not to bawl her eyes out on account of the stinging onion fumes, when Brody walked into the kitchen, hours earlier than she'd expected.

He'd dressed up for her interview as though he was attending an important press event and the consideration touched her. Her eyes teared, and this time not from the onion. His hair was damp and combed. He'd shaved. He wore a preppy dress shirt and corduroys.

She wanted to hug him, but held back. "What about your walk?" she asked.

"This smells too good. I couldn't leave."

She put down the spoon she'd been stirring the sauce with. "It's far from ready."

"Can I help?"

She rubbed her arms and tried not to cry. "Yes, please."

He gazed at her, those gorgeous blue eyes drinking her in. Then he poured himself a glass of wine and topped hers. "Just when I have you pegged, you surprise me," he said, passing her the glass.

But he avoided touching her. He leaned toward her slightly as if he was going to kiss her, but then caught himself as if he could never do it again.

An ache swirled in her chest. But she couldn't dwell there.

Still cradling her glass, she turned to flick the light switch. Nothing happened. "Why isn't this working, Brody?"

His low rumble of a laugh sounded so sexy. "Did you forget the electricity is out?"

"It's not out. My laptop is charging upstairs, remember?"

His gaze never left hers. "Because I set up the generator to power Sarah's office for you."

"You…?"

He smiled sadly. "There's only one circuit on the generator, Manda. I needed to make a choice."

Her heart felt as if it was about to pound its way out of her chest. *Do you see how good he is for you? Why are you doing this to him?*

Oh, God.

She took a deep drink of her wine.

Without a word, as if he could read her mind, he pulled open a drawer and rummaged until he found a box of matches. Lighting two beeswax candles on the table, he motioned for her to sit.

She wanted this pre-meal time with him, the calm before the storm. Proof they could enjoy everyday rituals other couples took for granted. Even if it never happened for them again.

Over the glow of the candles, he told her about his friend Hans. "I met him on my rookie downhill race, when he was beside me doing course inspection. I was completely in awe of him, because I'd been watching him on TV for years. But he ended up taking me under his wing, teaching me what it meant to be a professional."

"I wish I knew someone like that in my business," she said wistfully.

He nodded. "It's hard to find in any business."

"Do you talk with him out of season, too?"

"Yeah, two summers ago he helped me buy a house." He smiled, remembering. "I've been thinking of remodeling it after this one. Building a bathtub and shower like his."

Oh, Brody. "I do love that bathroom."

"I visited him here once, right after he got together with Sarah." Brody looked at his hands. "They were as different as fire and ice, and I didn't understand it at the time. To tell the truth, I figured it had to be sex that bound them, you know? What else could it be, unless there's a big cosmic joke. And sometimes I'm sure there is."

They were veering into dangerous territory. She should have known their peace couldn't last.

He sighed and stared into his wineglass. "I'm beginning to see that in spite of the surface differences, they had bedrock beneath the relationship—an understanding that their commitment to each other is more important than anything else." He looked up at her. "The stuff with our fathers—what if none of it matters?"

She suddenly couldn't breathe.

He shook his head. "Take out the tape recorder. You know what, let's just get the interview over with."

"But what about dinner?"

"We'll put it on hold. I don't want to eat anything right now anyway."

Amanda laughed, trying not to let the tears leak through. "You're not on some crazy race diet, are you?"

He raised a mock brow at her. "I'm a downhill skier,

Amanda. We drink, we eat. Do we look like figure skaters?"

Impulsively she leaned forward and brushed the hair from his eyes.

Brody stiffened at her touch. "Don't."

"Sorry." She forced herself to smile weakly at him. "I'm going straight to hell, aren't I?"

"No." And then he lifted a hand to curl her hair behind her ear. "You're just prolonging the pain, is all."

"Then let's end it." Because the real pain was knowing she could never make love to him again. She wanted that almost as much as she wanted her interview.

"All right," he said. And stood.

CHAPTER FOURTEEN

BRODY FOLLOWED AMANDA to a sitting room overlooking the dark, snowy mountain. A full moon shone overhead, so close he felt he could almost touch it. With a fire blazing in the woodstove, she sat on a cushioned chair. He dropped onto a couch facing the windows and stretched out, fully prepared for the inquisition.

He'd brought in the wine bottle. Now he tilted it to his lips and took a long draw.

In vino veritas.

Tell her the damn truth, Brody.

His background. He'd spent so much time blocking it, it was like taking a blowtorch to a sealed steel wall.

"You want to know about my father?" he said, as a way of setting her on track. No more tiptoeing around it, no more harmless half truths. "Well, he's sitting in a federal prison in Pennsylvania, locked up for income tax evasion." He let out a dry laugh. "All the cheating and conning he's done, and this is what they convict him on. Tax violations. He's a regular Al Capone."

"Have you ever visited him?" Amanda asked softly from across the room.

He was aware of her digital voice recorder, its red light shining like a steady beacon on the edge of the coffee table. This wasn't a conversation between them, not like they'd had in the kitchen—it was a formal interview. It would always be a formal interview. He closed his eyes and let in the anger that suddenly engulfed him.

"No," he answered, his voice sounding flat even to his own ears. "I do not visit him. You could say I even disowned him." He snorted at the absurdity of it, and he glanced at Amanda. But she, who really had been disowned, wasn't laughing. She'd curled up her legs beneath her body and was gripping herself tightly by the elbows. From what he could see of her expression in the flickering firelight, it looked pained.

He jerked his gaze to the moon. And the mountain silhouetted in the glass.

She'll never see you again after this, he thought. *She's like every girl growing up who held his crimes against you.*

But Amanda wanted his taped confession—had cooked for it and fought for it and cried for it—so he would give it to her. He would talk until he got it all out of his system and there was nothing left for her to ask him.

And then she could leave him, or he would leave her. Either way, there would be no future for them. He didn't see how they'd make it out of this interview without her recoiling when she looked at him. In preparation, he'd already packed his bags and put them in the RV. He'd walk to the village from here. He'd...

"Brody," Amanda said gently. "I'm listening."

He tore back his hair. *Say it. Screw the voice recorder. Don't think.*

"After my mother died it was just me and him, moving from town to town until I got to sixth grade and won a scholarship to a boarding school in New Hampshire," he said, all in a rush. "A skiing scholarship, all expenses paid."

This was the good part of his childhood and he smiled, remembering it. "During that year, I saw a whole new world." He stretched out his legs, feeling his shoulders relax. She didn't speak, just nodded her encouragement, so he took that as a sign to go on. Maybe he did want to tell her this part.

"There were counselors at that school—men mostly, because it was an all-boys academy—and they were intent on teaching character and integrity." Until this moment, he hadn't realized how much they'd affected him. How their influence had come full circle with his career.

"I guess you could say that what they taught stuck with me. After the first year it was like a thirst. I wanted to get away from my past, from the embarrassment of having a father who couldn't tell the truth, who always had an angle to run."

He pulled again at his hair. He wouldn't look at Amanda through this part. *Just say it.* Say it and get it over with and let her leave if she had to. "Yeah, I had to go home to him during summers and holidays until I graduated and went to high school." He shook his head at the wonder of his escape. "That place cost almost forty thousand dollars a year, even back then, and it had all these rich kids. Boys from upper-class families— industrialists, bankers, foreign ambassadors' kids…"

Was she listening? She hadn't said a word. Maybe that was a reporter's trick.

He sucked back another swig of wine. Tasted the sweet mellowness of the eleven-year-old wine. This vintage was fantastic, the best of the Barolos, but it was wasted on this story. For this, he'd be better off with a bottle of rotgut.

"Our graduation ceremony was a big deal." He

tilted the bottle, let the wine slosh back and forth like a melody. "I must have been feeling heady, because I made the mistake of inviting him for the weekend." The memory still burned, and he took a breath to shake it off. "At that point, I hadn't seen him in a while. But I was getting a President's Award for character and citizenship—" he let out a snort "—and I was so pumped up about it, I didn't stop to consider. I just wanted *somebody* there to see, you know? Somebody to support me, to be proud of how far I'd come."

He glanced at her, sitting in the shadows cast by the glow of the fire, the smell of clean smoke permeating the room. How could he expect her to understand anything he was talking about? She'd had a relatively normal childhood, MacArthur notwithstanding, and an intact family. She'd had her mother and her sister to balance difficulties with her father.

But this exercise wasn't about her, it was about him. And he would never have said a word about it if she hadn't demanded it of him. And since she'd asked, since she wasn't saying anything to stop him, he would push away the shame and keep talking. He was only going to relive this once. Never again.

He gazed back at the moon. "I already told you my mother died before I could remember her. She was killed in a car accident." He closed his eyes. "I never knew anyone from her family, and my father was estranged from his, so he was all I had. Everybody around me, my buddies, my roommate—they were filling out address cards for the school to send invitations to their relatives. I was so excited about my award—so stupid— I didn't think it through. I invited him on impulse."

He was tensing again, his words coming faster because he was getting to the crappy part—just one day in a string of crappy days he never revisited in his memories, except if he was having a nightmare. But who could help nightmares?

"He showed up, of course," he said dully. "Dressed all wrong, but I'm not big on exteriors, so I put that out of my head. He sat beside my roommate's parents. They were Korean, very proper. They owned a tire company." He plunked the bottle on a side table and forced himself to look back at the moon. "At the reception before the ceremony, I noticed my father pitching them an investment idea. A total lie, but he didn't care, he always talked his way out of things if he got caught. And because he chose his marks well, he was fearless about it. Not a conscience on him."

He squeezed his eyes shut, the shame stabbing through his own conscience. "Once, he even stole from a church treasury. Here I am, eleven years old, going to church for the first time in my life and my father steals ten thousand dollars from the damn missionary fund."

"Brody, I'm—"

"Don't, Amanda. Let me finish." He stood and paced. Pacing helped get rid of the bad energy the confession stirred up. "Did he need the money? No. He had a job, with decent people, better than he deserved. When I confronted him about it, he got self-righteous that those funds were for poor people, and we were poor because he couldn't afford fancy coaching for me or a pair of racing boots that fit."

Right. He tossed a pillow at the couch. "But that was all bull. Even when I was eleven I knew he had a sickness, a compulsion that nobody ever called him on. They—the religious people, the kind people—they were all so forgiving of him. It just grew and grew, because that was how he picked his marks."

Amanda made a small noise but he couldn't move, couldn't turn. *She's going to leave me. She's going to leave, but I have to tell her anyway.*

"So I washed my hands of him." He wiped his palms, sweaty and hot, on his corduroys. "After my graduation when he embarrassed me for the last time, I told him to go away. That I was done with him. That he'd dumped on me and the life I was trying to build for the last time. In my heart I cut him off, but not in the dramatic way your father did. I just turned around and focused harder on my own life. Created my new family, so to speak. I earned a spot on the national ski team. Achieved what I could." He rubbed at his roiling stomach. He felt like throwing up.

"Brody, I'm sorry," Amanda whispered.

"I said *don't*. You're interviewing me, remember? Keep it professional. Ask your questions. I'm only doing this once."

There was a silence, and then he heard her soft intake of breath. "Why did you start your charity?"

"It was...an accident." He whirled on her. "And don't connect the two, because it has *nothing* to do with my father," he said vehemently. *"Nothing."*

"Okay," she said.

"When I train at home, I have all these teen boys who come up to me in lodges and after races, wanting to talk about skiing. That's the thing about this sport, Amanda, it isn't like other pro sports where you're separated from the amateurs who play it. Pro baseball and football players have their own facilities, but who could corral a mountain for us? So we'll get teens hanging around while we train. Kids like I used to be, boys hungry for role models."

"What do you do for them, Brody?"

He'd promised her honesty, so he would answer every foolish and painful thing she asked. He sat on the edge of the couch, staring at the backs of his hands. There wasn't a sound in the room but the crackling of the logs in the woodstove. "My foundation grants ski academy scholarships," he said finally, "and coaching and mentoring grants. I keep it anonymous and local to New England because that's all I can handle right now."

He stared over at her, but he might as well have been talking to a shadow, for all he could see of her face. "I want to keep this low-key, okay, so don't write too much about it." He stared at his hands again. "Because if I'm honest, the whole thing helps me more than it helps anybody else."

She made a small noise in her throat. "What about funding?"

He shook his head. "What do you mean?"

"Where does the money come from?"

"Me, of course." Where else? "Back when I earned more in sponsorships, I used to twist my sponsors' arms, and quietly ask for donations from private individuals, people who knew me, whenever I could. But that's all changed."

"Brody, what did you mean when you said the foundation helps you more than it helps the kids?"

He laughed. "I sleep at night. I figure I'm doing *something*. I've been given influence, money—God willing—and even if I don't have time to administer it as well as I'd like, I can still spread the good around. Maybe one guy will…" He stopped. He'd actually forgotten the voice recorder was rolling.

"Did you have your own male role model?" she asked.

Was this for her, or for her article? "Yeah, sure, guys on the tour. Older guys who took an interest in me." He smacked the cushion beside him. "Hans, like I told you. He's showing me now how I'd like to live once I'm retired from competing."

There was a silence. And then: "Y-you mentioned a family you created. Are they the guys on your team? The guys who travel with your RVs?"

She was perceptive. No one had ever asked him that. "I went to high school with Jean-Claude, my trainer. Steve was a teen my foundation gave a scholarship to." He chuckled. "He's a real ski bum. I wanted to find something for him to do around the tour, so I made him my ski tuner. Hermann and Franz are pros who worked on the team with your father, but quit because they weren't happy with his direction. They were friends of mine, and they came with me when I regrouped."

"That must have upset him," she murmured.

"Yeah. Harrison wasn't happy with my decision, either. But they approached me, and I wasn't about to say no to them."

"You dropped off the tour for two years. What did you do then? Did you know you weren't done with the sport? What will you do when you *are* done?"

Brody leaned his head back. These were questions he'd spent hours thinking about. But he had to tread carefully. "I...rehabbed during those years. The truth was, when I left the tour I was injured...my ankle and my knee. I didn't want anyone to know, so I didn't talk about it." His heart was pounding. *Get it together.* He sat up straight and stared at that gorgeous full moon. "Back home, I even went to college for a semester because I thought I'd never get back to form, that I'd never fully heal. But school taught me my life will always have something to do with skiing. It's in my blood. I don't ever want to leave it completely."

He gazed over at the mountains. "It will always be in my blood."

"What did you study?"

He smiled at the irony. "Sports psychology. I was interested in applying motivational theories to coaching other people, but all it taught me is that it's impossible to even think of coaching as long as MacArthur heads up the federation. Besides, I wasn't ready to retire."

And then, because she deserved it, he turned and teased her by laughing at her questions. "You know, I learned enough basic psychology to know you're tossing me real softballs, Amanda."

She reached over and turned off the voice recorder.

"What are you doing?" he asked.

She stood and walked over to the woodstove, hugging herself and huddling over the glowing embers as if she couldn't get warm enough.

"Manda?" He went to her. Maybe she was sick. Maybe her head was bothering her.

He pressed close to her back and wrapped his arms around her waist. She was shaking from the cold. But as he lowered his head and rested his cheek against hers, he felt the dampness of her skin.

She was *crying?* Why?

"Manda, what—?"

"I hate this," she whispered. "This is so personal to you and I feel dirty having to write about it."

He stared at her, stunned. She hadn't given him the impression it hurt her to question him. And the questions she was asking him…wasn't that what she did every day? Wasn't that her job?

Tears were streaming down her cheeks. "Do you

know what I have to do now? Of course you don't, because you don't understand basic journalism. These aren't softballs, Brody, I have to work with facts. And the fact is, I *do* have to call that prison. I *do* have to verify your father is there. And that school question… that wasn't a softball, everything is a fact to check, to see if you're telling me the truth, but I know you're telling the truth—"

She broke down crying.

"Holy hell, you're crying about me," he whispered.

"Who else would I be crying about?" she shouted.

And he could only shake his head. She didn't get it. Nobody cried about him. Nobody ever had, not for real anyway, not for the guy he was beneath the skiing trophies and the world championship globes.

That guy was nothing more than a con artist's son.

And now she knew it.

SHE HAD TO PACK HER BAGS and get out. She would write her article elsewhere. She couldn't face Brody anymore. Couldn't look him in the eye because she was so sorry and sick of what she had to do. Of what they had to do to each other, just to do their jobs.

There was no sugarcoating the pain she felt over opening up this very private man.

But Brody's hands were touching her, running over her cheeks and smoothing her hair. "Manda," he was whispering. "It's okay."

It wasn't okay, and it never would be okay. "It's not fair to you," she insisted. "Don't you see? Who could stand to have someone poke through their childhood pain—I couldn't. What if you had to ask me about the difficulties and the shame with my father and then write it up for the world to see?"

He clasped her tighter, and a laugh rang in his throat. "I love that you really do understand me."

"I didn't before tonight!"

He just smiled, as if she was the most beautiful thing on earth to him, and he would indulge her to the moon and back.

Because, of course, how could she have been expected to understand any of this before tonight?

Not before she'd had to ask him these questions, sitting and pretending that he wasn't who he was to her. That she hadn't spent the past three days immersed in him, and he in her. That he hadn't pushed and challenged her to understand what drove her own actions. That she hadn't enjoyed and been fascinated by him, getting to know his heart and to appreciate him as she'd never appreciated another person.

To want him as she'd never wanted another person.

He touched his forehead to hers. "I'm glad you know these things about me, sweetheart. I'm glad I told you."

"Was it for m-me, or for the article?" She needed to know.

"For you." He grinned at her. "No one else would've gotten any of this, and you know it."

Yes, she did. To any other reporter, he would have stubbornly said nothing, no matter what Harrison told him to do. The way he had in their very first interview. She started crying again, big, wrenching sobs. "I w-wish it had been just for m-me. Not as a r-reporter."

"It *is* just for you. You're the only person who has ever lived, who will ever live, who I trust to tell my story."

She couldn't help it, she flung her arms around him. "I bet you say that to all your reporter groupies."

He buried his face in her hair, sifting it between his

fingers. "You've never been a groupie to me, Manda. Not for one minute. Not even on that first day."

The honesty of his admission made her stop sniffling and just stare at him.

"You were the only woman I never wanted to walk out on me," he said, his voice low. "That's why I made love to you that night, even though it went against my intentions. I didn't want to rush things and make it seem like my interest was casual. Because it wasn't." He stroked his hand against her cheek. "And then when you walked out on me anyway, I knew I'd messed up."

"You...wanted me to stay?"

"I still want you to stay." The words came out clear as a bell, no stumbling, no hesitation. He'd apparently made his decision. He picked her up and carried her to the couch. Turned out the interview area she'd so carefully arranged also managed nicely as a cozy place for love.

Love she craved. It was part of her, the person she was and the career she wanted. Love with him didn't have to be either/or. She felt as though he was showing that to her by bringing her here, to this place, and that touched her heart.

With the moonlight bathing his features, he sat and drew her on top of him, and she melted into his heat. He cupped her chin and brought her close to his face, where he caught her lips in his and kissed her thoroughly.

She moaned and felt her body taking over, letting her feelings be rushed along and merged with his. But a small part of her mind stood out. *You are a journalist and he is your subject,* it said in a firm, authoritarian voice that sounded suspiciously like her father's.

She jerked back from kissing him. "I'm a journal-ist," she repeated dumbly.

"Yes," he said, gazing into her eyes.

"You're…my subject."

"Yes." Again, that patient voice.

Why shouldn't she make love to him? He accepted the situation, and he accepted her. She knew that, she was grateful and humbled, but to the world around them?

"I can't," she whispered, drawing away from him. "After I file the article, people will find out I slept with you and they'll judge me for it."

"They won't know," he said, putting his finger to her lips. "Because I won't tell your story. I'll never tell it. Never. To anybody."

He wouldn't. She knew he wouldn't. Because he was a man of his word and he'd shown that to her.

And this time, she was the one who was crush-ing him to her, kissing him and tearing into his cloth-ing. Tugging at his buttons and fumbling with his belt buckle.

And then his hand was on hers, steady and firm, as he pulled the belt away and stripped off their clothes. They were naked, skin to skin with the fleece blanket beneath them and the stoked fire roaring beside them and the moonlight bathing them in a golden-white glow.

She needed to be close to him. Body and soul. She needed to feel his body join with hers.

He brushed back her hair and stared into her eyes. A slight smile lit his features, and she gazed back at him, drawing her end of their connection tight. She felt as if they were joining their lives together, and it made her shiver.

In the warm comfort of his embrace, as she wrapped

her arms around his neck, she said a prayer that she'd be okay.

That she could trust Brody Jones not to hurt her.

CHAPTER FIFTEEN

Two days later, Harrison Rice drove his rental Mercedes up the winding mountain road leading to Hans Zimmerman's chalet. Brody heard the engine before he saw the rooster-tail of slush spraying from the tires. He paused with his hand on Amanda's shoulder while his agent wheeled the snow-splattered sedan into the shoveled-out space behind Brody's RV.

Amanda stood from the toboggan cushion and frowned, staring at Harrison. She and Brody had been sledding down the back hill on an old-fashioned wooden toboggan he'd found in Hans's woodshed. Before that they'd made love. All morning. Several times, in fact. He'd never felt more satisfied or more ready to race.

"Brody!" Harrison stepped out of the Mercedes and slammed the door, then trudged down the path. "Party's over. Are you ready for a World Cup race in two days?"

He felt Amanda stiffen beside him, so he squeezed her waist in reassurance. "Don't worry," he murmured. "I'll tell him you're with me, and he can follow us down the mountain in his car if he wants."

"You haven't told him yet?" she whispered.

"I haven't turned on my phone in three days."

"Me, neither. Not since I got permission from Chelsea to stay in Italy through the end of your race."

She smiled sheepishly at him, and he took the opportunity to kiss her. He could kiss her all day, and it was going to be difficult to cut back now that they were in public again.

From the corner of his eye, he saw Harrison stop with a shudder. *Negligent!* he could almost hear his agent berating himself.

Welcome to reality, Brody thought.

"Hello, Harrison." Amanda waved at him. "How are you doing?"

Harrison looked as though he was choking, but after a moment he got hold of himself, pasting on a smile and waving back. He bounced another step down the slope but then halted, his wet loafers and suit pants causing him to reassess.

Brody bit the inside of his cheek as Amanda chuckled beside him. He counted to ten, letting his agent suffer for the obnoxious comment about the party being over. Then he figured there was no way around it. He had to face the music sometime, so he ambled up the hill, pulling down his shades to shield him from the bright morning sun.

When he came to Harrison, he crossed his arms. "They only lifted the avalanche ban an hour ago. You must have driven like hell to get here as fast as you did."

"I beg your pardon," Harrison said. "But we have a meeting with your ski sponsor's representative this afternoon, and *she* cannot be present."

Wrong attitude, pal. Brody took off his shades and let Harrison know how it was going to be from now on. "I already told Amanda she could come. I want her there. She's going on with us to the race, too."

Harrison's eyes widened. He wasn't happy, but

Brody hadn't expected him to be. "Brody, there are special circumstances that need to be discussed first."

"Fine. The motor home is packed and we're on our way. You and I can talk about it when we get to the factory."

"What's going on?" Amanda joined them. He slid his arm around her and pulled her closer. Yeah, he was making a clear signal. His life had changed, and Harrison needed to get used to that.

"May I speak with you alone, please?" Harrison asked Brody.

He shrugged. "Speak away. Amanda is writing an article, which you directed me to cooperate with, as I recall."

Harrison glowered at him. "I also told you to wait for me before you said anything to her." He turned to Amanda. "This conversation involves aspects of my agency contract that I don't feel comfortable discussing before a third party not on my payroll or my client list."

"He's speaking legalese, this can't be good," Amanda said to Brody with a smile. "It's okay. I don't mind waiting in the RV."

His heart welled up. She really was one in a million. "You don't have to do that."

"Sure I do, just this once, until he's used to me." She winked at Harrison. "I'm not a spy, you know. I won't telegraph Brody's race plans to the competition."

"Of course you won't," Harrison said. "The journalistic community is inherently fair-minded."

But Amanda simply laughed in good humor. "I'll be warming up your seat," she said to Brody. He watched her cute behind as she climbed into the RV.

"Don't ever be rude like that to her again," he said

when she was out of earshot. "I'm giving you fair notice."

"When is her story due to be filed?" Harrison demanded.

"She has a few facts to check and she needs some quotes from the guys. She's writing the bulk of the article this weekend while I prepare for the race."

Harrison blinked at him in disbelief. "You *gave* her the interview?"

"Yeah, I gave her the interview. Now it's done and out of the way. Don't be a jerk about it."

Harrison let loose a string of obscenities. Then he held out the screen of his phone. "You had better read this."

"Is this Amanda's article on major league baseball? Because you already sent it to me, remember?"

"And you don't see the problem with it?" Harrison looked apoplectic. "This article has destroyed at least one career that I know of. Are you telling me you told her the *truth* about you?"

Brody looked at the jumble of words on the phone, and then he looked at Harrison. He felt the blood draining from his face.

"Brody, I'm asking you. Did you trust this woman with the secret that will end your life, my life and the life of every guy on your team as we know it?"

He sucked in the cold mountain air. There wasn't a coherent thought in his head.

"Brody?"

"No," he spat out. "No, of course I didn't tell her that."

Harrison relaxed. "You had me worried."

But Brody needed to sit. His world was spinning. He looked to Harrison, but there was nothing Harrison could say or do that would ever help him accept *that word* in connection with himself.

To his horror, Harrison grinned from ear to ear. "That's my boy. You conned her."

"I did *not*. I told her everything about me. I told her stuff *you* don't even know."

Harrison winked at him. "Yup. You conned her."

"You son of a bitch. I don't con anybody, ever, and that's my girlfriend you're talking about."

"And thank God smart men keep secrets from their women." Harrison slapped his back, but Brody jerked away.

"You're wrong. That's not me," he said. Because he wasn't the con artist; his father was.

"We all do it," Harrison said, shrugging. "You, me, everyone. We con people when we need to, including ourselves sometimes. Just ask yourself this question— can you ever tell her, under any circumstance?"

Brody fought to find an answer, but he couldn't. He felt his eyes glazing over, he felt his chest turning numb.

I did not con her.

But hadn't he? He'd deliberately talked about his childhood in exchange for keeping her off the trail of the other, worse thing.

How badly had he been fooling himself? Who was he?

"The answer," Harrison said, "is that you can't tell her. Plain and simple, you never can."

He put his arm around Brody, and this time Brody was too sick and destroyed to shrug him away.

"Believe me," Harrison said, walking Brody toward the Mercedes—frog-marching him, really, "if you follow my lead, then you'll be okay this weekend. We'll handle it together. You have your priorities straight now, and that's the most important thing."

It wasn't. Brody couldn't speak.

"You have guys on your team who rely on you, Brody. *I* rely on you. Those kids who get your scholarships rely on you. Think of everyone you'll be letting down if the truth comes out. You think it's just you with something at risk? It isn't. We're all in the same boat, supporting each other. Aren't we your family?"

The bottom seemed to be falling out of his life. That word...it could never be associated with him. Not at any cost. Not for any reason.

"Don't think any more about it," Harrison said, patting his shoulder and opening the passenger door of the Mercedes. "I've got your back. You'll be okay."

Amanda. Brody glanced to the RV where she waited.

And that's when Harrison shoved it into his arms. His World Cup trophy from two seasons ago. The one he'd never felt he'd earned.

"Alto Baglio, Brody," Harrison reminded him. He looked pointedly from the trophy to the RV. Then he stared back at Brody. "If she cares about you at all, don't you think she'll understand that proving yourself in your next race is the most important thing?"

CHAPTER SIXTEEN

THE FARTHER THEY DROVE from the chalet, the more Amanda realized that whatever had happened these past three days between her and Brody was changing, as surely as the landscape shifted from mountain villages to town life.

Brody drove the RV, subdued, distracted and barely speaking. He looked as if he'd been run over by a truck. Harrison sat in the passenger seat, talking loudly on his cell phone. Every time Amanda tried to talk with either of them, Harrison shut the conversation down. She'd known the moment he'd proclaimed he was leaving his rental car in Hans's driveway "to be picked up later," that something big had gone down, but for the life of her, she couldn't figure out what it was.

For now, she lapsed into silence, riding in the back, holding Brody's World Cup trophy, which Harrison had transferred from his rental car like another inside message she wasn't meant to understand. She wasn't even sure what she was supposed to be doing with it, but when Brody had climbed inside the RV he'd passed it to her wordlessly. Now, an hour later, she still held it in her lap, feeling as if the truck had run over her, too.

"We're here," Harrison said as the RV pulled into the parking lot at a small factory outside a mountain town. A green logo on the building read Vivere Skis.

Amanda stood, determined to stretch her legs after

the long drive and to finally get to the bottom of the mystery treatment. She had one foot on the ground when Harrison blocked her. "You wait in the RV."

She glanced at Brody, striding across the parking lot in the cold winter air. She was through being shut out by Harrison. "Brody said I could go inside with him."

"My client wants you to know there's been a change of plans," Harrison said. "He'll meet you afterward, when he's finished with his meeting."

Nope, sorry. Irritated, she stepped past Harrison. "I need to hear that from him, if you don't mind." Without waiting for a response, she stalked toward the show-room, pulling open the heavy wooden doors.

Behind her, the agent huffed at her heels. "Ms. Jensen! Wait!"

She kept going. Luckily for her, Harrison's cell phone trilled, stopping him as he fumbled to see who was calling. He gave a muffled curse, then stayed out-side to take the call in the better reception.

Good. Inside the sales area, a group of guys with huge ski racers' builds and stances were conferring with Brody. Amanda recognized his team members from the night of her sister's wedding.

Blowing into her hands to warm them, she waited beside Brody, outside their circle so as not to be rude. "Hi," she said. But instead of greeting her and introduc-ing her to the others the way he'd said he would, Brody blanched.

Something was very wrong. Her pulse quickened, and she stepped back.

Swallowing, his Adam's apple lifting and falling, Brody turned to his men. "This is Amanda Jensen," he said, his tone strangely flat. "She's the reporter who's writing an article about me for *Paradigm* magazine."

Amanda felt paralyzed. Though his words were technically true, if she hadn't heard the unhappiness in his voice, she wouldn't have believed it. His introduction was a clear message that she was not to be trusted.

She stood rooted in the awkward silence, her mind swimming. What had Harrison told him that could have changed Brody's opinion of her? She couldn't think of anything.

"I…hello…" was all she could choke out.

No one said a word in return, not even Brody. In her worst nightmares she had never expected him to act as if he neither liked nor respected her.

Somewhere in the midst of her misery, a man jumped forward. "I am pleased to meet you, Ms. Jensen!" A short man with a moustache, holding out his hand and a business card. "I am Carlo, please allow me to show you a tour of our factory, yes?"

She waited to see if Brody would escort her back to the RV as Harrison had requested, but Brody wasn't moving. He seemed as shattered as she was.

Eyes watering, she fumbled in her purse. She'd never been a quitter, and she wouldn't run away now. Somehow, she found a business card with her name on it and passed it to Carlo. "Thank you, I would like a tour very much."

Brody's men glanced at one another. There had to be a specific reason they didn't want her on the tour. But nothing jumped out.

Wasn't it her *job* to figure out why?

"Please, come this way," Carlo said. He stayed close to her elbow and guided her ahead of the men to the factory proper. "We are the ski makers who build all the skis Brody Jones wears for his races. We are a family company since 1960."

As her legs moved, she felt the numbness wearing off. She had a concrete goal now. *Pay attention.* Automatically, she reached for her notebook and a pen. The smell of heated fiberglass and resins jogged her. Calling up all of her journalistic objectivity, she jotted down notes.

The former warehouse was stacked from floor to ceiling with every size and color of ski imaginable. Band saws droned in a high pitch on one side of the factory, sanders and planers the other. The tang of adhesives and burning plastic hung in the air. Carlo handed out protective eyewear, explaining to Brody and his team how Vivere had incorporated their ideas into a design custom made for Brody's technique and body mechanics.

I should be taking photos. Chelsea wants photos. The whisper came from her subconscious, and she reached for her camera phone. Maybe she should reconsider the angle of her article because nothing about Brody's past—his father or his foundation—explained his sudden change of attitude, his fear about her presence.

She thought back to Harrison's arrival. To his team's concern over Brody. To their anxiety over the upcoming race.

She watched Brody. Studied him like a subject. His distraction had lifted and now he focused on business, paying close attention to Carlo, inspecting the curve of the skis they'd made for him and asking pointed questions. These were to be his slalom skis, she gathered. One of the four disciplines he'd been known to race, and the only one he chose to race this season.

Why? She tucked that thought away.

One of his teammates muttered something to Brody. They glanced at her, then held a quiet sidebar.

What is the most logical explanation for their behavior? the reporter in her asked. She clicked her pen shut and rubbed her eyes.

"Okay, are we all set?" Harrison stalked into the group, pocketing the phone he'd been glued to. "We need to wrap this up and head to lunch." He blinked at Amanda, surprise and irritation showing plainly in his face. "Ms. Jensen, you'll have to leave now. Brody, say goodbye to the reporter, give her the keys to the Alfa Romeo, and she can drive herself to the hotel."

That was it?

Brody shook Carlo's hand. Then he strode over to her, keys ready, and stood stiffly before her. He'd touched and kissed her a hundred times this week, and now he couldn't even bring himself to shake her hand?

"May I speak with you privately, please?" she murmured.

He took an audible breath, then gave her a quick nod. Leading her a few paces away, nearer the factory with the drone of band saws behind them, he crossed his arms as if he didn't want to be having this conversation.

"What's going on?" she asked.

He gave her a sad, slight smile. "There's been a change of plans. I need to have a meeting with my team before I can say anything else about it."

"What did Harrison say to you? Why has everything changed?"

"Nothing. He said nothing." His gaze shifted back to the group, filing through the doors to the parking lot. "Look, Amanda, I'm sorry I need you to drive yourself, but I can't get away just yet. I wouldn't ask you to do it if I didn't think you were capable."

"What aren't you telling me, Brody?"

"Nothing. There's nothing you don't know." But his eyes didn't meet hers.

"Brody, why are you only skiing one discipline?"

He blinked at her, startled. "Don't you have facts to check about my foundation?" He seemed angry. "Because I thought I was doing you a favor in clearing free time for you to work this afternoon."

Shock went through her, and a chill of recognition. *He doesn't want me to pry.* Something was definitely off with him. He was deliberately hiding something from her.

In her shock, anger built. "I can't leave your team yet. You know I need to talk to them about my article. I need one or two benign quotes, at least. We've discussed this, Brody."

His Adam's apple moved up and down. "Harrison made the decision. They're not going to talk to you. Nobody's going to talk to you, and there's nothing more I can do about it."

Everything within her froze. "That's not what we agreed. I have an article to write and a deadline to meet."

He slowly shook his head. "I'm not happy either. But we'll talk more at the hotel tonight, and I'll do what I can to help you before you leave."

No. She had misjudged the situation, badly. She shouldn't have been so quick to trust him.

"I need to get through this next race," he said. "I need to concentrate on that, above all."

"And then?"

He stared at the floor. "I can't think beyond that

right now." He looked at her, his eyes nakedly pleading. "Manda, the next few days are everything to me. Please understand."

Yes, she realized he had a race to prepare for. She understood it was his comeback and therefore critical to him. But why did he have to lie to her about it?

She put her hand to her throat. She needed to get out of this place; she needed to breathe again.

Except she needed her story more than she needed to breathe. Her job was what *made* her breathe.

By instinct, she scanned the group for the most vulnerable man, the person most likely to weaken under pressure. Because as Brody had said, after today, she would no longer have access to any of them. She zeroed in on Steve, the young ski tech who'd brought them the picnic dinner that night at the Leopardo hotel. And the condom box.

Steve had sad puppy-dog eyes and an expression that seemed more worried for Brody than for himself. Yes, he was the right one. She would latch on to him like a lifeline.

Glancing back to Brody, she steeled herself. "I need a ride to the hotel. I don't feel well enough to drive myself."

Concern flickered in his eyes. "Is your head injury bothering you?"

"No." And because he'd been lying to her ever since Harrison had shown up—she could feel it—she gave him a fake smile and told a complete whopper of her own: "It's my stomach. Breakfast didn't agree with me. I need to lie down for a while."

Brody's brow creased. But if he offered to drive her to the hotel, Harrison would be all over him. They both knew it.

"Maybe you can spare Steve to give me a lift?" she suggested. Brody would never suspect him. Steve was so shy, how could he be expected to talk with her?

Still, Brody hesitated. But finally he nodded.

In the parking lot, she smiled at Steve and settled into the front passenger seat of one of the smaller vehicles Brody's team had arrived in. She needed to crack this problem of what was staring her in the eye.

Brody closed her door and then pressed his palm to the glass, a regretful look on his face. She was sorry, too, but she didn't have time to nurse her hurt or think about her mistakes. As Brody's image receded in the side mirror, she turned to Steve, calling up every ounce of friendliness and cheer she could muster. "Brody looks good, doesn't he?"

Steve cast her a wary glance. He didn't say a word in return.

That was okay, she hadn't expected him to.

She leaned back in the seat and stretched, as if it was the most natural thing in the world to relax in front of Brody's friends. "Harrison sure is paranoid," she said. Then she rolled her eyes and laughed as if she thought Brody's agent was being left out of a joke that everyone else was privy to. "Thank goodness I can finally let down my hair. I know Harrison told you guys you're not supposed to talk to me, and Brody knows it, too. That's why he's playing along with this silly charade, for the sake of keeping Harrison calm."

Steve's brow wrinkled. He was listening to her, clearly interested.

She smiled at him. "Brody told me how he met you at one of his first summer camps. He said he's really proud of you for what you've overcome in your life just to be on tour with him. He says you've already helped him more than you know."

Steve glanced over. "He said that?"

"Yep." She flipped down the mirror and casually touched up her hair. "He also said he didn't know what he'd do without you on his team. Not just for the technical side, but for the interference you run on all the random things he trusts you with. Like bringing us sandwiches that night." She lowered her eyes and twisted her hands in her lap. "He says he can't trust the other guys with that kind of stuff. They might tell Harrison instead of keeping Brody's confidence. But you wouldn't do that."

Steve's breath expelled. He seemed to be thinking.

"Anyway," she said, shrugging, "I know it's not easy for him now. I'm just grateful you're looking out for his interests."

Steve's foot slowed on the gas pedal. "Brody took some bad hits that last season," he muttered.

Her heart rate sped up, but she tried to keep calm. "I know. I hate that, too."

"Everyone's worried about how he'll handle the media this week."

"Yes. I've been trying to help him, but my hands are tied, because Harrison won't trust me." She made a big sigh. "He thinks I'm going to betray Brody—as if I could ever do that."

Steve glanced at her sidelong. "Aren't you going to write about his injury in your article? That's what Harrison said."

She was on the right track. Something was wrong with the injury. "No, though Brody told me all about it, of course." She leaned in closer and lowered her voice, confiding. "I do know everything."

"Everything?"

As Steve's expression wavered, she went for the kill. "Yes." She nodded seriously, adding, "Even the part that's supposed to be secret."

Steve's face went pale. His knuckles tightened on the steering wheel.

She held her breath, waiting for him to talk. There was more, and she was finally going to discover what it was.

"Wow." Brody's ski tech looked at her with his eyes wide. "You really are his girlfriend, aren't you?"

No, I'm not. Her heart hammered and she wished she could stop. Because Brody didn't deserve her as his girlfriend, not as long as he lied to her, and she didn't deserve him as long as she went behind his back to get answers, but she couldn't think about that now. She needed to protect her job, and for that she needed Steve's response. She had to push him to open up. Now was not the time to give in to her emotions about Brody.

"He hasn't told any of this to Harrison yet," she said, licking her dry lips, "because he's waiting to tell him at this afternoon's meeting. That's why he's so freaked out. He was acting strange at the factory, wasn't he?"

"What…what is he going to say?"

"That he's ready to come clean, of course. That's why he's so nervous."

"Come *clean?*" Steve's voice was a wail.

Her heart sank, even as she did her best to nod sagely. "Yes. I told him it's for the best, for himself and for his career. And for all of you."

Steve stared at her. Then he shifted the gear into Park. They idled before the hotel where she and Brody were to have stayed together, a cozy inn with a bright awning and an attached restaurant that smelled fantastic even from here, like pasta and fresh-baked bread.

Oh, her heart cried. In their original plans, the rest of the team was to have driven on to the race site, but Brody had wanted to leave in the morning with her in the Alfa, in time for his afternoon gate training.

Not anymore. She'd changed all that with this interrogation of his ski tech, though she shouldn't be thinking about that with the guy still sitting beside her.

It's now or never, she thought, gambling everything and surreptitiously clicking on her voice recorder. *Please, Steve. Speak.* "How do you feel about Brody's decision to finally tell the truth?"

Steve's face crumpled. "He's making a huge mistake." He wiped his hand across his eyes.

"Yes, but what do you think—"

Steve resolutely exited the car, then strode to her door and opened it, gently but firmly escorting her out.

She had miscalculated badly.

Her heart pounded as she registered into the hotel with her *Paradigm* corporate card taunting her. She'd emailed Chelsea, asking for and receiving extra nights until the day after the final race. From there, the plan was for her to turn in the assignment and return to New York, where she and Brody would balance a long-distance relationship, at least until his season was over. But that wasn't an option now. Above all, Amanda needed to shut out her emotions and discover what he was keeping secret from her.

Inside her room, she locked the door and called up her internet connection. She wouldn't give up until she'd found answers. With her chin set, she did what she should have done before she'd compromised on the angle of her article. She scoured the web, reading every single thing she could find about Brody. Every news update, every statistic, every opinion piece.

The worst she found was a minor equipment check he'd missed because of a scheduling mistake, and then the resulting commentary where a New York–based sportswriter accused him of cheating. Evidently, Brody had been insane with anger. He'd given a diatribe that had been roundly criticized by the sports media. Then, he'd clammed up. No more interviews. No more quotes.

Until now. Until this comeback.

Amanda leaned forward in her chair and racked her brain. His diatribe made sense to her because he took his integrity so seriously. Always, he avoided anything that smacked of cheating. With his father being the man he was, that was no surprise.

But what was the big scandal Steve's reaction confirmed was lurking?

Think.

His injury, she thought. That's what Steve had said. But how did Brody's injury come into play?

She checked the timeline of her dates again. No injuries had been confirmed by his coaching staff, but from the videos she watched, it was evident when one injury happened…two races *after* the diatribe. Brody had slammed his right ankle into a controversially placed gate, and he'd gone down. DNF=Did Not Finish. Then he'd been out for a few races, ostensibly with the flu. Right.

And then…he magically won again.

Here. At Alto Baglio.

Her breath hitched. She found her phone and dialed Brody's number.

It rang, but he didn't pick up.

That's when she knew she was definitely on to something.

BRODY RUBBED HIS ACHING HEAD and trudged up the hotel stairs. Even after everything, he had a crazy wish Amanda would back off her story. But who was he kidding—her character was to fight. To dig. To stand equal.

He hadn't bothered to call her back. The front desk clerk was a skiing fan, and Brody convinced her to slip him a key to Amanda's room. He nudged her door open with his hip while he swung inside with his World Cup trophy. The overall winner two seasons ago, that was him. Supposedly. The trophy had cracked immediately after he'd received it—some irony that was—and the tour officials had taken it to repair it for him. Harrison had chosen today—irony again—to present it to Brody. A signal, he was sure. A message not to forget all they'd fought so hard for.

Brody settled the crystal globe the size of a soccer ball onto the nearest table and blinked to accustom his eyes to the low light.

Amanda was sleeping beneath the white down covers on the hotel bed. She was huddled on her side, and her hair was tousled around her in the way he'd gotten to know so well. Somehow, he wanted to work this out with her. They had compromised before, why couldn't they now?

He set down the room key on the bedside table and clicked off the lamp, then moved the pile of notebooks and papers surrounding her. Knowing Amanda, she'd crashed because they'd caught so little sleep these past snowbound days. Instead, they'd been up nights loving, laughing, exploring each other's bodies. Exploring each other's desires.

Kicking off his boots, he slid under the covers beside her, pulling her close. He felt something hard, saw she was curled around her laptop, so he moved it to the table beside his trophy. Then he returned and rubbed his hand up her belly and over her breasts. She sighed, still asleep.

This was all he wanted, to keep Amanda beside him. Sometime during this past week he'd let her under his skin and near the reaches of his heart. It was the most dangerous thing he'd ever done, yet somehow the thing that felt most right.

He kissed her hair, inhaling the scent that had come to signify comfort. He'd wanted his time with her to last. He'd planned for it to last, even after the season was over.

"Say goodbye to her, Brody." Harrison's voice echoed in his head, and without thinking, Brody ground his teeth.

"No freaking way," he'd told Harrison. "She stays with me through the race, and that's the bottom line." His team had stared at him. Steve had come back from his drive visibly upset, and they'd known that the inevitable was happening: Amanda was getting close to the truth and she'd stop at nothing to expose it. The team had spent the afternoon in the private room of a nearby restaurant discussing what to do.

"Picture this headline: Brody Jones's Record Attained With the Help of Steroids." Harrison had gestured to the block letters he'd written in marker on a yellow legal pad. "Can you deal with seeing that on every sports page in the country? Best Skier in Generations Has Record Tainted."

His fists clenched, Brody had forced himself to listen while Harrison outlined their options. "Every sponsor will drop us like tainted goods. Vivere has one out in their contract—moral scandal. Brody can get sick, be injured, have a bad year, and still they have to pay us. But a steroid allegation? No way—they'll bail on us without question. The same with Xerxes and any others we manage to sign. And Brody's charities? Forget it. No one is going to give money to an Olympic athlete who cheated. Hell, they could strip your medals. They've done it before. And those kids you wanted to help, Brody, they'll lose out, too."

The bald facts had sat in his gut like poison. He wasn't the only one who had everything to lose. Brody had looked from face to face of the guys who stood by him. His team. A few had been with him for twelve years, through the lows to the highs and back again. They'd sacrificed winters with their families, relationships with their kids and job opportunities that had come their way, all to support him and be part of this team.

A winning team. A team with integrity.

A team that didn't cheat.

Brody breathed slowly in and out, struggling to maintain his composure. He knew what he needed to do. He needed to get up from the bed. Put on his boots. Start up his motor home and drive to Alto Baglio without Amanda, in the process keeping everyone around him safe from her interrogations and her questions. Safe from her headlines.

As if sensing his dilemma, Amanda stirred awake, rolling to face him. Her hand fluttered to his chest, and as always, his best intentions disintegrated. Her touch was like balm to him.

"Brody?" she whispered. "I'm glad you came back."

He pulled her into his arms and kissed her, tasting her essence, drinking in all that she was.

I love her. The thought crashed in his consciousness. He felt a tenderness he'd never thought possible. He let his head slip below the covers and he kissed her and touched her all over. He wanted to bring her comfort and pleasure and happiness; he wanted her to feel as good with him as he felt with her.

She moaned and slid off her panties, and, as he'd done so many times this week, he joined himself with her. But this time was different. This time he was truly making love to her, to the person she was. This time he knew he loved her and hoped that somewhere within her heart, maybe she could love him, too.

Afterward, she lay in his arms, tracing her fingers across his chest. "What made you decide to give us a chance?"

He had to be sure she loved him back. "Just finish your story tonight," he said hoarsely. "File whatever you have, and then pack your bags."

Her hand crept around his neck. "You want me to leave you tonight?"

"No, I want you to stay with me tonight." He turned to her, pulling her to him, speaking against the hair at her crown. "Stay through the race at Alto Baglio. And then…stay some more."

He found himself holding his breath. He wanted her to understand, without having to risk telling her what had happened. He wanted her to forgive him. The things he'd told her earlier about his father had been his father's fault, but this—*the steroid use*—he had done that. And somehow, he needed her to show him it was okay.

"That all depends on you, Brody," she said quietly.

He waited, his arms wrapped around her, his lips against her hair. He'd known this moment was coming. He'd known, and yet he'd hoped it wouldn't anyway.

"You're not being honest with me." She lay very still beneath him, her body tense. In her own way, she was probing; she didn't know exactly what he'd done.

"I've been honest with you on everything that counts, Manda." His voice shook.

"If that's what you think," she said, "then you're not being honest with yourself either."

"I've never been more honest," he said bluntly.

She paused. Maybe she was working up her courage. "I need you to tell me the secret you've been hiding from me," she said, bracing her hands against his chest and forcing him to look in her eyes. "And I need you to tell me now, because I do want to build something with you." She shifted her head to look at his trophy, sitting fixed and whole again on the bedside table. She turned back to him. "Whatever that problem represents to you, whatever Harrison is holding over you, we can fix it together."

"You can't fix me, Manda."

"I know that. But we'll never go further than here if you can't share this important part of yourself, whatever it is, that you're keeping hidden from me. It hurts me that you're shutting me out, Brody. It hurts me deeply."

Her eyes radiated with pain, and that was his fault.

"I'll tell you everything when my race is over and you're not investigating me anymore," he said brokenly.

She nodded, swallowing. She seemed to be fighting a battle within herself. Finally she rolled out from under him and gathered her clothes. A bustle of movement that all but killed him.

"Where are you going?" he asked.

"I'm sorry, Brody, but that's not a solution."

"It is to me."

She paused to study him, her clothes pressed to her chest. He'd never seen her look so sad. He waited, but she disappeared into the bathroom, and he heard the faucet running.

She came out fully dressed. She was serious with her decision, and he didn't even try to stop her. Because he knew it was inevitable. Had known all along, if he'd been honest with himself.

"You can't trust me after all we've shared?" she asked.

He said nothing.

With her lips pressed together and quivering, she went back into the bathroom and emerged with her bag of toiletries. She opened her suitcase, still filled with her clothes, and dumped it inside. Then she zipped her suitcase together and reached for her laptop. "Will you stop me? Because you still can."

"This is your hotel room," he said. "I'll leave."

Tears gathered in her beautiful hazel-green eyes. He felt sick at the sight of them, but what could he do?

"You know what your problem is?" she whispered. "You can't forgive yourself. You carry the weight of the world on your shoulders. I saw it, the night of our accident. I didn't understand until now. But you know what, Brody? If you don't stop doing that, you'll never fix anything in your life. Whatever it is, just let it go and then maybe you'll find what you're looking for." And then the door shut, and she was gone.

He waited, but she didn't come back.

He sat, all alone in her empty hotel room. Just him and his repaired World Cup trophy, perched on the bedside table where her laptop had been.

He'd rather have her laptop back. But he didn't see how he could.

CHAPTER SEVENTEEN

INSIDE THE BUSINESS CENTER at the main resort near Alto Baglio, Amanda squeezed her forearms over her stomach. Two days had passed since she'd left Brody and everything hurt.

She'd cried herself to sleep that first night without him, her phone by her pillow, but Brody hadn't called. A hundred times she'd second-guessed her decision to leave him. Most people would think it unreasonable to expect him to tell her everything, especially after such a short relationship. But she and Brody had been through a war together. He knew the most horrible things about her. And she, the things he was most ashamed of.

Or so she'd thought. Whatever this secret was that Harrison held over him, Brody didn't trust her enough to confide it. He'd tricked her with misdirection in order to keep her from seeing what he wanted to keep hidden. He'd used stories about his father to deflect her. That he'd leveraged her guilt and shame about her own father's treatment toward her only made his betrayal worse.

She hated the conclusion she was drawing, but she'd been right to walk away from him. Because another day had passed, and still he hadn't phoned. He wasn't interested in repairing their rift. He wasn't interested in making her an equal partner with him.

And so, on the second morning away from him,

she'd woken to a new understanding, abundantly clear: to choose Brody was to follow her mom's path, a relationship with a man who shut her out.

If this was what Amanda allowed from a relationship, then she would be as powerless as her mom, following a husband around Europe who kept secrets from her, too, to keep her in a weaker position.

Unlike her mom, Amanda refused to be weak.

She turned to her work, knowing she was wiser. She'd fixed her mistake of leaving the hotel room *Paradigm* had paid for by moving to the cheaper hotel where her sister was staying while Massimo helped coach the Italian team. Amanda booked a small, adjoining room that shared a bathroom with theirs, and then buckled down with her quote-gathering. Work would continue to be her salvation.

As always, she covered the pain with busyness and phone calls. Her yellow notepad lay on the desk, the names of Brody's old coaches, teammates and competitors listed and then crossed out in heavy black lines. She'd talked with nearly half of them.

"He's great for the sport." "Everyone loves training with him." "No one works harder and is a better role model to the younger athletes than Brody Jones."

It figures, she thought. No one had a clue about his secret. If she hadn't been so heartsick, she might have laughed at the paradox. Even in breaking up with him, she'd gained nothing.

I can't give up now.

The quest that would give her everything she lacked was almost complete. Once she had her masthead position, no one could make her feel weak again. Not even Brody.

She snapped off a piece of the bittersweet chocolate

that had come with her cup of cappuccino and tried to let it melt in her mouth.

Then she made another call to see what pieces she could excavate next.

"RELAX. YOU'RE GOING TO WIN the race tomorrow."

The words from his coach barely registered with Brody. He'd skied his practice run competently, but his heart wasn't in it.

He kicked out of his rebuilt slalom skis and then passed them off with the rest of his equipment. He noted his time, his placement (first), but then stood at the finish line like an amateur, scanning the stands for Amanda.

Which was stupid. She'd left him. In two days she hadn't called or tried to see him. They'd reached an impasse. Nothing more to say. The only thing left for him to do was win. She wanted him to forgive himself? A win was how he could do that. Because in his world, a person fixed things himself. Made them right. And if she couldn't see that, they could never be together. End of story.

He took off his goggles and rubbed his eyes. The practice runs had ground to a halt because the guy behind him had wiped out badly enough that they were flying in a medical chopper, which was grueling stuff.

The kind of stuff that shook a guy up.

"Brody, let's take a break," Jean-Claude suggested.

He must really look spooked. "No, just let me chill for a while, all right?"

"Where're you going?"

Brody shrugged. How the hell did he know? He just needed to get out of there. He didn't want to think about skiers being hurt in accidents and not having the people they really needed with them.

He turned and tromped through the lodge, heading automatically to the main bar the way he'd done a dozen times before, a dozen seasons before. But this time, the smell of spilled lager and grilling sausage didn't appeal. Was Amanda here, or had she flown back to New York?

"You want to have a drink with me, Brody?"

He stared at one of his former sponsor's reps, a grizzled old-timer for a ski-clothing manufacturer who was patting the empty stool beside him. Harrison would nudge Brody to take the offer, because, hey, business was business and this was part of the game. But he didn't have the heart for it.

"No, thanks," he said.

"You're saying no to a beer with a potential sponsor?" The rep laughed at him. "What kind of alpine racer are you?"

A screwed-up one, apparently. Brody shook his head and walked away. He avoided the tour bunnies and the legends, his friends and the skiing-friendly public. Instead, he found himself wandering the hotel's public rooms, anyplace with internet access and an electrical hookup where a reporter with a laptop and a smartphone might be hanging out.

He found her in the business center, sitting alone while everybody else partied. Brody ground to a halt, his feet rooted to the floor, his heart pounding like a teenage boy's.

Her long, beautiful hair was pulled off her face, and wisps of escaping strands brushed her neck. She wore no makeup and a simple black turtleneck. In no way, shape or form could anyone call her a tour honey, but he was drawn to her as he'd never been drawn to another woman.

He took a step forward. But she wouldn't go back to his trailer even if he asked, because she didn't want him anymore. She wasn't at all interested in fooling around with the great skier, Brody Jones. If he'd ever had a chance with her, he'd blown it completely. From what he'd heard this morning, she'd been calling guys on the tour, asking for quotes, doing her job.

And the truly sad thing was, he understood her better than anyone. He knew why she fought, why she could never give up. He knew exactly what she needed to make herself whole.

All their time together, everything they'd shared, and all she wanted was to know the most important part about him. She'd asked him, more than once, and he had continued to lie to her. He'd lied to himself until Harrison had pointed it out.

It was funny, Brody thought. He'd come back to the tour to prove himself a man of integrity. And yet, the only integrity he'd found had been in her: sitting here at this moment in the business center, aboveboard, honest and pushing through the pain that was etched all over her face.

She had integrity. She was the person he wanted to be. The person he'd fooled himself into believing he already was.

At that moment, as if time had slowed and stopped to show him what he needed to do, from the corner of his eye he noticed MacArthur Jensen walking their way.

As always, Brody stiffened. He willed MacArthur past them.

But, as if by divine intervention, the folder MacArthur carried slid from his hand, the papers scattering across the floor.

Brody's reflexes kicked in. He stepped behind a lamp to shield himself from view until his old coach passed. MacArthur stopped and knelt.

Amanda, hearing the quiet thunk of the pages hitting the floor, looked up. Brody could see her face as she blinked at her father and then stood before him, still clutching her laptop. She had sadness in her eyes as their gazes met and then MacArthur stared straight through her.

MacArthur pivoted and gathered up his papers. In a moment, he would leave. The opportunity passed.

I can fix this for her, Brody thought. With one action he could give Amanda what she really wanted, what she couldn't fix for herself.

I can make this estrangement with her father go away.

But that action would mean the death of his team, and wasn't he responsible for that? Like Harrison said, didn't he have to think of them first?

That's a cop-out. He'd always known it, if he was honest. His team would survive if he left the tour. He would always take care of them, however he could, but he could no longer do it at the expense of his soul.

Brody straightened. The true question was, did he want to spend his life hiding behind lamps, or did he want to face the truth honestly, the way Amanda did?

Brody stepped forward. "MacArthur!"

When his old coach looked up, Brody didn't hesitate. He strode over and took Amanda's laptop from her, then set it down. He clasped her cold, shaking hands and escorted her across the parquet to greet her father.

"Your daughter is one in a million," he said to Mac-Arthur. "You're missing out by overlooking her."

And while Amanda and MacArthur blinked at each other, and then, confused, at him, Brody swallowed and set into motion the machinery that once started he could never stop.

"I don't know if you've heard the news, sir, but Amanda is an excellent writer. She's writing a story about me for *Paradigm* magazine in New York. You should talk with her about it."

And then Brody went back to his motor home, leaving them alone together. And he waited for the ax to fall.

WHAT HAD JUST HAPPENED?

Amanda stood stunned, staring after Brody's retreating form. He'd had a two-day growth of beard and dark circles under his eyes, but he'd never looked better to her. She'd missed him so much.

And yet, something had definitely gone wrong with him, because what was he doing talking to her father? Brody hated him more than anything. Why had he risked approaching him?

He looks through me like I don't exist. Like I'm invisible.

She closed her eyes, remembering her words to Brody. And her afternoon in the gym, telling him her dreams for a relationship she didn't know how to bring about herself. But Brody had tried to help her anyway.

"Amanda?"

She froze. Her father's voice, speaking to her.

She shuddered in her breath and turned to face him.

This time, she didn't see what she'd expected. On the contrary, his heavy dark brows—brows very much like hers—were drawn together and he was quietly studying her for the first time in months.

And, oh, God, for a moment it made her heart glad. Because of all the things she'd hoped for with her dad when she was young, his pretending she didn't exist had never been one.

"What was Brody talking about?" he asked her.

"I...don't know," she stammered. "Please tell me if you figure it out."

Her dad smiled at her. A full smile, spreading across his face and lighting up his eyes. When she was young and she'd done something right, she had lived for those smiles.

"It's good to see you here, Amanda."

She felt as if a heavy burden had lifted from her soul. "Thank you, Daddy, it's good to be here."

"I'm busy just now," he said. "Are you staying with your sister?"

"I am." Jeannie was the glue that kept them all together.

As her father said goodbye and walked away, she felt her mother smiling down on her. And that felt good. She found herself walking in a daze. She looked up, and suddenly she was inside her hotel room. She wasn't sure how she got there, because her head was swimming. But sitting on her hotel bed and staring into space, she felt a huge weight flying from her shoulders.

Amanda was still sitting on her bed a half hour later when Jeannie knocked on the adjoining door, snapping her from her reverie.

"Daddy just called me," Jeannie said, limping inside and then leaning her crutches against the bed before she sat beside Amanda, the mattress sinking with her weight. "He said he talked with you down in the lobby just now, but he forgot to ask for your cell number. Mandy, are you okay?"

"I'm...not sure," Amanda said, shaking her head to clear it. She glanced at Jeannie. "Brody set up the reconciliation between Dad and me. But I don't know why he did it."

"Maybe because he loves you, Amanda," Jeannie said softly.

What she wouldn't give for that to be true. But it couldn't be true, because if Brody did love her, he would have moved heaven and earth to make a future with her. Instead, after the introduction to her father, he'd walked away. She wouldn't see him again.

Her phone rang, causing her to jump. She checked the caller ID, and her heart sank because it wasn't Brody.

"It's my editor. I need to take this." Taking a sip of water from the bottle beside the bed, she connected with the call.

"Amanda! How is my favorite reporter?"

A mess. But her deadline for *Paradigm* was fast approaching, so she forced herself to smile, visualizing confidence and capability flowing through the four thousand miles of airwaves to Manhattan and the heart of the media industry she so desperately wanted to be part of. "I'm fine. You won't be disappointed at what I've got going here."

"I never am, Amanda. In fact, we hear you're doing excellent work." Chelsea's voice echoed as if she was on speakerphone.

Who was with her? And who was telling her about Amanda? "Thanks," she said, buying time. "What's happening in New York?"

"It's snowing. I can't get a cab to save my life."

Chelsea didn't know from snowing. Amanda smiled to herself.

"Listen, Amanda, I have someone special who'd like to speak to you." There was a pause, and then the rattle of a chair rolling across carpet.

"Hello, Ms. Jensen," a deep, masculine voice boomed. "This is Vernon Trowel. I'm hearing tiptop things about your investigative reporting capabilities."

Vernon Trowel? The head of Millan-Rogers Media?

Her mouth dropped open. The billionaire owner never descended into the offices of *Paradigm* magazine. His television and sports media stations on the top floor were more his tot of bourbon.

"Um, hello, sir." What was Vernon doing meeting with Chelsea? She wasn't a direct underling to him, and they certainly weren't close.

He's Daddy's friend. They golf together every Christmas at Hilton Head.

"What's this about, sir?" she asked, her hand shaking on the receiver, the foreboding building within her.

"I'm phoning because I'd like to personally greet our newest staff reporter. Welcome to the masthead, Ms. Jensen."

For a moment her heart didn't beat. Her blood didn't flow. Everything just stopped. A buzzing sounded in her ears, as if she wasn't in her own body.

What had he just said?

"Cat got your tongue, Amanda?" Chelsea laughed in that high, tinkling voice of hers.

I'm on the masthead! I'm on the masthead! I'm on the masthead!

"I'm...thrilled!" Truly, she wanted to throw the phone in the air and scream. This was everything she'd worked so hard for. Everything she'd wanted.

She jumped off the bed and began to pace. What had happened to make them change their minds before she'd even filed her piece?

Vernon boomed into the speaker, "I'll let you get back to your undercover work, Ms. Jensen."

She paused, confused. What undercover work?

"Stay close to those skiers," he ordered. And then a click sounded.

"Amanda?" Chelsea was back on the line. "We've ordered an increase in print run for the month. I'm sending a photographer on tonight's flight, but I'll need you to keep a lid on it until he gets there. Can you meet him at the racecourse?"

"I...already have photos of Brody," Amanda said. Two great ones, in fact, taken at their mountain cabin.

"I'm sure you do, but with the full-bore treatment we hope to give the story, it's time to bring in the professionals." Chelsea's voice cackled. "Leave it to you, Amanda, to dig up a steroid scandal. Vernon is beside himself with happiness."

A steroid scandal?

What? How?

Amanda sank to the bed, her whole body numb. The phone dropped from her hand and she stared at it, lying in the middle of the unmade bed. Even from a distance she could hear the pleasure in Chelsea's voice.

"Haven't I always taught you that absolutely everyone has skeletons in their closets? I knew if you searched hard enough you'd find the dirt."

She shook her head vehemently, as if Chelsea could see her. Because it was Brody they were letting down. He didn't take drugs. He didn't believe in cheating.

Her hands shaking, she picked up the phone. Unbidden, scenes from her memory flashed into her consciousness: Brody, refusing Jeannie's almond drink. Brody, bringing and preparing his own food on tour. Brody, upset with her over her baseball steroids article.

Of course—why hadn't she seen the clues? The steroid allegations were what he'd been hiding, what he'd been determined never to face again.

She passed her hands over her eyes. All of a sudden she understood exactly why no one on his team—including him—thought they could tell her the truth.

The simple fact was: her article *had* broken the story of those athletes who'd tested positive for illicit substances. She'd never followed through with what had happened to the men after her article had been printed, but maybe, if she looked into it, she would find that their careers hadn't been the same since. Whether she'd meant for it to be that way or not.

She hadn't seen it from his point of view then, back in their snowstorm hideaway, and he couldn't risk showing her—because she'd been looking at it as a journalist: present all sides. But what about when presenting certain sides wasn't fair? What if, as he said, even the whisper of a doubt was enough to end his career?

Talk about repercussions. And for proof of those repercussions, look at how excited Vernon was about the simple word *steroids*.

He knew nothing else about the story with Brody, and maybe he needed to know nothing else. Because *steroids* coupled with *Olympic skier Brody Jones* meant career-ending controversy. Career-ending controversy meant more magazine sales. More magazine sales meant more profit for his quarterly income statement, and hence a higher stock price for his company.

Her head pounded, and she wanted nothing more

than to hang up the phone. But she couldn't; she needed to find out all she could about the allegations against Brody.

This is the long con he was worried about.

Oh, God. Her throat felt so tight she could barely get the words out. "Chelsea, who leaked the news to you and Vernon?"

She held her breath, but part of her already knew the answer. Who else with knowledge of Brody's training had the motive and opportunity to place a personal call to Vernon Trowel? Who had both the means and the motivation to punish Brody for his past actions?

"There's no need to be coy, dear. Your father was as proud as punch of you. He says you've found a high-level official who wishes to remain anonymous. Way to use your contacts, Amanda."

Amanda lowered her head. The sinking in the pit of her stomach was the most horrible feeling ever.

She felt the bed dip as Jeannie shifted beside her. Her sister had listened to every word that Chelsea had said. Amanda looked into her quiet face.

And understood that Jeannie had known about Brody's secret, even before this phone call.

CHAPTER EIGHTEEN

"WHY, JEANNIE?" AMANDA ASKED. "Why didn't you tell me about Brody and the steroids rumor?"

Jeannie shook her head sadly. "If you print that word next to his name, Mandy, with your magazine's weight behind it, he'll have his record stripped and his reputation shredded. He won't be able to show his face at a ski lift anywhere in the world. Is that what you want for him?"

No, of course it wasn't. But was this what it came down to? If she were to get what she wanted—the promotion and security at work—did she need to destroy the reputation of the man she cared about?

"He knew that Dad had connections with *Paradigm*," Amanda said, tearing at her hair, "and yet *he's* the one who told him about the article. He set all of this up." She paced across the ski-lodge–themed hotel room, thinking back to the look of intent on Brody's face.

She threw up her hands. "Jeannie, Brody had to know how the revelation would end. He had to know Dad would be tempted to pick up the phone and tell Vernon the dirt about him."

Jeannie slowly nodded. "You're right."

Amanda grabbed for her phone. "I need to talk with Brody."

"Yes, you do."

But instead of Brody answering the call, Harrison picked up. "What?" he said.

"Please," Amanda pleaded, "let me speak with Brody."

"He's preparing for his race. I'll forward your message."

"Harrison, it's urgent. It's life and death for him."

There was a short silence. "Then you had better tell me what it is, and I'll make that determination."

What choice did she have? Amanda swallowed and clutched the phone, her hands ice-cold. "My boss at *Paradigm* received a tip that Brody was involved with steroid use in his last race. She called me about it, and she wants me to investigate that tip. Please, I need to talk with Brody before he does anything reck—"

"No can do, Ms. Jensen, my client is officially on lockdown from you."

"Harrison!"

"You've done more than enough." The phone clicked off.

All her subsequent calls went directly to voicemail.

BRODY CALMLY DRANK THE LAST bottle of Barolo wine he had in his RV, even as Harrison barreled inside his sanctuary, the door slamming behind him.

"It's done," Harrison said, his voice as morose as if someone had died. "The news is out."

Brody sat back at the table and closed his eyes. He palmed his warm glass and drank deeply.

"Don't you understand?" Harrison shouted. "*Paradigm* magazine knows about the positive steroid tests!"

And yet, the world still turns, Brody thought.

His heart was still beating. His blood still flowed. He swirled the wine in his glass and didn't let himself think about the rest of it. His life beyond this moment.

"What are you going to do, Brody?"

He didn't know. He was in uncharted territory here. He looked at Harrison, knowing that Harrison would never have an answer for him.

What would an honest man do?

AMANDA PUT DOWN HER PHONE and cradled her head in her arms. "Why would he do this, Jeannie? Why would he incite Dad to bring him down? That makes it final, with no wiggle room. Even if I refuse to write the story, *Paradigm* will find someone else to do it anyway. I have no power to help him now."

Stupid man. There was no way she could get Brody out of the mess he'd made.

Jeannie blinked her soft gray eyes at Amanda. "You can't build a relationship on lies, Mandy. Obviously, Brody grew to realize that. Love has changed his priorities."

Amanda paced the small sitting room. She wanted to find Brody and shake him. She'd tried to give him the opportunity to come clean with her, but *this* was the way he chose?

"I *hate* that he's destroying himself for me. I wish he'd let me know back at the hotel when I'd asked him, and then I could have toned down my article without anybody having to read the word *steroids* next to his name."

"Would you have done that?" Jeannie asked. "Be honest. Until Brody set the events in motion by bringing your work to Dad's attention, could you have set aside your job as a good investigative reporter and let the steroid story go unchecked?"

The truth burned. Because honestly, as much as Amanda liked to think she would have put Brody first, she probably wouldn't have. And she'd shown Brody this, not only by putting him through the wringer with that emotional interview about his childhood, but then by waylaying his ski tech. Heck, for two days she'd been calling everybody on the tour he'd ever worked with, asking them questions, digging for more information.

"What's it going to take for you to see your worth isn't in your job?" Jeannie asked softly. "That it's in who you are?"

Amanda lowered her head. The terry cloth robe had parted on Jeannie's leg, and she was confronted with the scar from the accident that had ended her sister's skiing career.

As always, Amanda averted her eyes. She wished the bone-shattering crash hadn't happened to her sister, or the resulting surgeries, riddled with complications and infections. Even though Jeannie was accepting of her obstacles and life changes, Amanda never could be. Not completely. Not even close.

"I'm not like you, Jeannie. You lost your identity as an athlete, but you're handling it. I could never handle losing my identity as a writer. I'd be in the worst position of weakness, like Mom. There's no way I could survive that, just like she didn't survive it. *That's* what will happen if I can't write for *Paradigm*. I told Brody this, almost from the beginning. But I don't expect you to understand, because you have your medals to fall back on. And more than that, you have Massimo to take care of you. He loves you. You have a *life* ahead of you with him."

Jeannie pulled back her robe, exposing her injured

leg from upper thigh to ankle. It was the first time Amanda had seen the extent of her injury.

The scar was angry and it was jagged. It ran the full length of Jeannie's left leg, which, she understood, was now an inch shorter than Jeannie's right leg. Amanda sucked in her breath. She didn't want to acknowledge it, so she turned away.

"It's true I can't ski anymore, Mandy," Jeannie said quietly. "I'll most likely never coach and I don't even know if I'll walk normally again, to be honest. Do you think, without Massimo, that means I'm weak?"

"You? No! In a thousand different ways, you're the strongest person I know!"

"I *am* going to be like Mom," Jeannie interrupted. "The way she was her whole life, medal or no medal, husband or no husband." She took Amanda's hand. "At least, I hope I can be. Every day she was strong and compassionate and forward-thinking, no matter what happened. She never felt sorry for herself, and that's how I want to be. Just like you're strong, too, Mandy."

"You think *I'm* strong? *Me?*"

Jeannie rose and then shuffled around the bed, one slow dip of her knee in front of the other. She sat beside her sister and put her arm around her. A wave of emotion swamped Amanda. For a moment they were flashed back in time; Amanda was the ten-year-old big sister and Jeannie just seven. She smiled with that same dimpled grin, but her eyes were older and wiser. Kinder, too, and that was saying something, because Jeannie was born disingenuous.

"Be happy, Mandy. You don't need to fight for power outside yourself, like Dad does, because you have a more potent power inside you. I've always seen it because it's always been there."

"I don't feel strong."

"You *are* strong. Think of this—you stood up to Daddy. Maybe it wasn't effective, but still, you sought him out on Mom's behalf when she was too sick to do it herself, and you fought for her. Mom knew that, and in my mind it counts for everything."

"I *wasn't* effective, was I?" She wished she could have been. She wished she knew how to handle her father the way Jeannie did.

"Don't focus on that now," Jeannie said. "Focus on the fact that you're strong in your heart. No matter what job you do or don't decide to tackle. Or what relationship."

"I don't want to hurt Brody," Amanda whispered. She never had. But maybe her fear of being weak had stood in the way of building something lasting with him. Something that fed her and sustained her as *Paradigm* never could.

"Do you *want* to be with Brody?" Jeannie asked. "Because it's obvious he loves you. He never would have led you to Dad and spoken to him like that if he didn't love you and want you to be happy."

She held her head in her hands. Why hadn't she seen it like this? But it was the only explanation that made sense. Oh, God, Brody must love her.

"I want to be with him more than anything," she whispered. She missed him. She missed everything about him.

The way they laughed together at meals. The infinite patience he had with her, and the way they were drawn together like two pieces of a puzzle that fit, no matter the situation.

"Then do it." Jeannie nodded at her fiercely. "And don't ever mistake following your heart for weakness.

Do you understand? Brody has proven himself a good man for you. That's strength, not a weakness."

She did understand. And he had proven himself the *right* man for her.

So how was she going to fix this dilemma they found themselves in?

And *effectively* this time.

AMANDA SMOOTHED HER HAND over her skirt and prepared to sit down with the man who, prior to this morning's few brief sentences, hadn't spoken to her in almost a year.

Not since the day she'd confronted him in his office in Colorado Springs and, instead of his remorse and help for her mother, she'd received a bony finger pointed at her heart along with the announcement that she was no longer his daughter.

Her heels faltered on the polished wooden floor of the cavernous lobby. So many feelings, all so complicated, swirled within her. In the past, her father had pushed her. He'd made her cry, he'd made her rage and he'd made her feel ashamed. He had that talent of being able to press all her buttons if he wanted to.

But her reactions were up to her, as they always had been. She couldn't let herself dwell on the past and the mistakes she'd made then. Now, she wanted to be effective. She wanted to lay the groundwork for the way her future relationship with him would be conducted. And she knew how to do this. Jeannie was right; above all, if she operated from her inner strength, remembering her compassion for herself and the people she loved, then she would be okay.

Straightening her crisp wool business suit, she strode into the restaurant where her father sat at a table in the darkened room opened just for him, as if he were one of the Medici princes. Yes, dressed all in black, from his Armani jacket and slacks to his expensive handmade loafers, Daddy looked formidable, as he always did.

She paused several feet away on the carpet decorated with swirling gold medallions. When she and Jeannie were kids, he'd instilled in them the belief that nothing was worth doing unless they became champions. Amanda hadn't been the champion of anything back then, and his disappointment in her knew no bounds. She was a terrible skier, a horrendous athlete and then later at college, a poor business student.

And now?

She lifted her chin. Technically she had a new position at *Paradigm*—a position he respected—but Jeannie was right, that wasn't her strength.

I have inner strength, Daddy. Something you might not understand, but to me, it's a quality of the best champions.

Squaring her shoulders, she approached his table. When he neglected to stand or greet her or even get off his phone, she didn't let herself feel cowed. This was who he was, and she knew that about him going in. Instead of getting irritated, she coughed and seated herself across from him. Placing her phone on the table beside her, she caught a server's eye. "San Pellegrino, *per favore.*"

The pretty Italian server smiled and looked questioningly at her father, but he waved her away.

Amanda folded her hands and waited for him, until he decided he was finished making his point with her. She felt acceptance inside, for herself and for Brody, and for her father, too. There was a place inside her heart that had relaxed and unknotted—some of the fury, the wounds, the deep, deep grief at the unfairness of her mom's death. She had done the best she could for her mother, even if he was incapable of seeing what he'd done was wrong.

It wasn't her job to point it out to him. Not today, anyway. Whether he changed or didn't change in his heart toward her mother, wasn't the point of this meeting.

When he finally clicked off his phone and stared at her, his gaze intending to be intimidating, she simply smiled and said, "Thank you for agreeing to meet with me, Daddy."

He stilled, a flash of puzzlement crossing his face. Momentarily, at least, she'd thrown him off balance.

She sipped her sparkling water and carefully set it down. Her purpose was clear: to dig out as much as she could about Brody's steroid use and her father's involvement in it. She needed to extract information from him without threatening him or causing him to shut down. And to do so, she needed to trust that now she better understood how to help the people she cared about. As she hadn't on that day all those months ago when she was scared out of her wits and driven against the wall.

"I spoke with your friend Vernon today," she said. "He told me you called him."

Her father's gaze never left hers. "You got your promotion?"

"I did." She smiled carefully. She felt wiser now, more confident in her power. Because, oh, yes, she did have power. "Vernon mentioned an article he wants me to write involving a high-level official who wishes to remain anonymous. I assume that's you?"

"No, I'm not saying that at all." He waved his hand. From his briefcase, he withdrew a single sheet of paper.

Clicking open his pen, he handed it to her. "You need to sign this first."

A year ago—heck, a day ago—she would have laughed in his face and thrown the pen back at him. But she accepted the sheet of paper and skimmed it.

The document was what she'd expected—a confidentiality agreement. "Everything I say to you is off the record." Standard practice in business. And her father, a graduate of one of the nation's most prestigious business schools, was among the best.

She didn't feel distaste as she signed her name on the indicated line. Her signature, even, looked different. Bigger and bolder. The same as before, but more of itself.

Sitting back, she made eye contact with him. "Anything else we need to get out of the way before we proceed, Daddy?"

"I see you're over your mother," he noted. "Finally."

His voice held a tone of derision. But if she shouted at him, if she flung herself into an argument with him, then he would have succeeded in dragging her down to his level. How effective would that be?

Instead, she calmly handed him his pen and picked up her own. "If you mean am I still angry with you for not helping with her treatment, then you're right, I'm past that. But if you mean am I finished mourning Mom, the answer is no. Someday I hope to be, though I know I'll always miss her."

Her father blinked. His gaze darted to his phone. *A small sign of guilt?* she wondered.

Interesting.

"How very enlightened of you," he said.

"Yes." She smiled. "It's water under the bridge, and I hope you see it that way, too."

He nodded. "You're certainly accepting today."

"I don't want us to be estranged anymore, Daddy. It's not good for me."

He leaned forward. "And I want Brody taken down. Can you arrange that or not?"

So here it was. What he wanted. His "tit for tat."

Very well, she'd been expecting this. At this point in her life, she had no illusions about her father's character or personality. He was a known entity, and that was a plus. Maybe the secret to maintaining a civil relationship with him was to think of him as the willful, emotionally immature child, and herself as the more mature parent who understood how to handle him.

"Daddy, in order to write about the event, I need a source to go on the record. Are you willing to be that credible source?"

He shook his head. "You're not to use my name, ever."

She took her recorder from her purse. "Then I'll need your quotes."

"I won't do that either," he said flatly.

She laid down her pen and laced her fingers together. "Please help me see where there's a story."

"It's simple, Amanda. You do what Vernon asks. You write that there's a high-level member of this team who has knowledge of Brody's steroid abuse, specifically during the last two years of his career. That's it. That's all. Put it out there."

She clicked open her pen. He wasn't going to make this easy for Brody, and she hadn't expected he would.

"To properly investigate the allegation, I need details," she said. "And there's no one else who can give me better details..." She looked into his squinting, recessed eyes. "Than you."

He drew back. He knew that what she said was perfectly logical and said without animosity, but still he hesitated, uncertain of the risk.

Finally, he smirked at her. "Very well." He lowered his voice. "Use this. It started two years ago. Brody twisted his ankle on a slalom run, several gates down. It's on the television footage—look it up."

Amanda made a show of scribbling notes, though she knew the facts well. Had watched the video of Brody's accident, in fact.

Her father fell into a careful, assessing silence, so she nudged him along with another smile and a simple question. "Will you tell me what Brody did next?"

"I'm not intimately aware. As executive director of the federation, I'm removed from the day-to-day operations."

"Of course." She nodded as if she agreed. "Two years ago, you were his main coach. Were you aware of anything then?"

He tapped his fingers on his pad. "I can tell you what my assistants told me."

"That would be helpful."

"They said he became affected by his injury. The tear affected his reflexes, they claimed."

"And did he continue to race?" she asked.

"He was our top-ranked racer," he scoffed. "What do you think?"

They kept him racing because the team needed the money that came with sponsors, advertisers and contracts. Follow the money. Amanda willed out her breath slowly. Now was not the time to feel indignant on Brody's behalf. "And then what happened, Daddy?"

"I'm told, in a nutshell, that Brody took steroids in the belief it would speed recovery of his injury."

"And did it?"

"He won his next slalom race, didn't he?"

This interview was killing her. Indignation for the pain Brody had suffered was threatening to explode through her. But to help Brody, she needed to let it go.

"And then what did he do, Daddy?"

"What he always does—he celebrated in his typical, over-the-top style. Until, of course, the positive result came in on one of the steroid tests and that ended everything."

She bit back her sorrow, forcing herself to jot silly repeated phrases. *Speed recovery, next slalom race, over-the-top.*

Her father suddenly laughed. "Alto Baglio. Don't you love the significance of the timing?"

Her pen shook. Of course. Alto Baglio was the race that was tainted. She hadn't realized before now. *Oh, Brody.* That's why this race was so important to him; he was redeeming himself.

But she focused on her notebook. Let the pen lie loose in her hand. "You were very skilled to keep this scandal out of the press."

"Out of the press?" he asked harshly. "My real skill was in keeping the results from the international federation and the other teams' coaches and skiers. That, my dear, was pure artwork."

She could just imagine. But she simply nodded. "Were any of the testers aware?"

His eyes narrowed. "I saw the results first. I managed it."

He's in it knee-deep.

"Do any of Brody's team members know?"

"Every damn one of them knows. And they'll never say a word about it to you." His face turned mottled.

She had best tread carefully. "How did you think to handle Brody when he was no doubt outraged by your very reasonable assistance toward him?"

Her father leaned back, expanding his chest as if remembering the event. He also seemed to enjoy the ego stroke she'd given him. "My dear, you can't imagine. Brody threw a wild fit. Claimed his food was tainted. Claimed I was the one who had done it to him. Ridiculous."

Then he eyed her. "But you should know his temper well, you've spent the last several days with him, I believe. Stuck in a snowstorm, I'm told." He steepled his hands and studied her.

Amanda kept her face expressionless. She had to use all her control because she needed to find out the truth. For Brody's sake. "Yes, Daddy, I was assigned to write about him. I do whatever it takes to complete my job."

His eyes sparkled. "Like your old man?"

She looked him dead in the eye. Yes, once upon a time, she was like that, too: mistaken in her priorities. "Absolutely."

"It must have been repugnant to you."

She bit her tongue. "Every job has its drawbacks."

"Yet he seems smitten with you. I saw him dancing with you at your sister's wedding."

What could she say? Brody had jumped through hoops in order to be with her, and she loved him for that, but she couldn't show her father. Not while he considered Brody the enemy and was doing everything in his power to destroy him. No way would she alert Mac-Arthur to the fact that he wasn't a good enough father for her to side with him, even over a man she'd only known and loved for such a short time.

"One wants what one cannot have," she quipped.

Her father slapped his knee. "It was a shame you couldn't ski."

And there he was, pushing the old buttons. But she didn't miss a beat. "As it turns out, I have other strengths, Daddy."

Against every expectation, he gave her a nod of approval. Amanda blinked.

"I'm told you have the makings of an excellent investigative reporter," he said.

And then he smiled at her again, that gesture of genuine fatherly pride she'd felt earlier in the morning.

Funny, she thought, with a sense of clarity she'd never had before, but his opinion of her really didn't matter.

Jeannie was right. She didn't need this job or this article to stand equal with him. She was anyone's equal. She was *enough*, with or without outside power. There was power within her. It didn't matter what her job was or what she accomplished in it. Maybe it never had.

She turned the page on her notebook and sat straighter on the leather seat. "Yes, Daddy, it will be my pleasure and my calling to investigate this story. But to do so, I need the specifics on the 'in a nutshell' part of the steroid-taking, and I need to hear it from you." She looked up at him. His brow was creased.

"My name and my interests will not be associated?" he repeated.

"I promised I won't use your name or your title. But you need to be specific on the details with me because I'll never get them from anybody else. I know, I've been trying all week."

She was rewarded. He settled into his seat with the air of a man who had executed his payback and was pleased he had succeeded. Her father's weakness was that he thought integrity was for losers. He thought winning—the result—was all that mattered.

"It was a World Championship year," he began, "and we needed to keep Brody skiing. Within an hour after the injury though, we knew he was in trouble. I used my contacts to call in a coach who'd successfully rehabilitated injuries like his. We needed it done quickly, so it was my idea to push a new treatment we were experimenting with, to heal the sprain faster and more effectively than normal. We experimented with nutritional powders—there was an over-the-counter powder we added to his meals, I'll look up the name and get back to you—because that did the trick. Brody won Alto Baglio, didn't he? I take full credit for that." He smiled smugly.

"But then," he continued, "the positive result came back from one of the tests. I was shocked—no one realized the extent to which some of the products were tainted. How could we? The mistake I made was in showing the results to Brody—thinking it would keep him in line, but instead he lost whatever sanity he had and blamed everyone but himself. Men on his team heard him shouting. There were rumors upon rumors that needed to be explained and covered. It made my week hell."

His upper lip curled. "Brody was always acting the spoiled, backwoods jerk, and I told him I'd had enough, he would regret his outburst. And now that day has come."

"You have your revenge," she said softly.

"No, not revenge." He pointed at her. "Truth. He competed using steroids. I've given you your scoop. Now write it, Amanda. And if you don't, then somebody else will."

She tried to calm her racing pulse, because of everything he'd told her, this last sentence was the most true.

And it broke her heart.

AMANDA STRODE ALONG the busy street with her hand tucked inside her brother-in-law's capable arm. The moon shone overhead and their boots squished in the tromped-down snow as they hurried to the edge of the Italian village.

Thanks to Massimo, she knew where to find Brody. Her sister's husband had worked his network and his phone all evening until he'd found someone who'd seen Brody and his team hunkered down at a tiny, hidden trattoria frequented by locals. She didn't relish facing the guys on his team, particularly Steve, but Massimo had promised to stand by her for whatever she needed. *We're family, and we'll support you until the end,* Jeannie had said.

Yes, at the end of the day, her younger sister had shown Amanda everything she needed to know that was truly important. Grateful, she patted Massimo's jacket. Never would she take him or Jeannie for granted.

"Don't worry, we are almost there, sister Amanda."

"I know, I trust you."

She trusted Brody, too.

The love she felt for him had broken open inside her, especially after she'd heard all the details he hadn't been able to tell her about the motivation behind his comeback. She understood now how guilty and ashamed Brody felt for his mistake, and how responsible he'd made himself for allowing her father to push him into it.

You know what your problem is? You can't forgive yourself.

She'd said those words to Brody at their parting, and while it was a true statement—even truer than she'd realized at the time—she'd delivered it too harshly. She loved this man. She'd wanted to help him, not alienate or blame him.

She had to show Brody that she knew what had happened to him, that she understood, and that she'd commit herself to helping him make it right. For himself, and for the team he felt so responsible for.

She could taste the urgency. The truth was, she cared more about helping Brody salvage his reputation than she did about her promotion. Because she had nothing to prove anymore. She had let it all go. She felt relaxed with herself, finally. She wanted nothing more than to spend the rest of her life living with him and loving him. Being close to her sister and Massimo, and learning to write the way that Sarah wrote.

She'd already left a message with Chelsea:

Cancel the photographer. I talked with the highly placed official, and there is no evidence of steroid use. I've checked and counterchecked, and none of the other skiers believe the allegations to be true. At this point I recommend killing the steroid story entirely.

Yet hours had passed, and Chelsea hadn't called back. Amanda couldn't know if her efforts were enough.

"I just want him to know I've done all that I could," she found herself saying aloud to Massimo.

"I am sure he forgives you." Massimo squeezed her arm.

But Brody hadn't been able to forgive himself; how could he forgive her?

She dug her nails into her palms and tried not to lose hope. It was below freezing in the night air, and if she let herself spiral downward emotionally, she'd be in no shape to help Brody face the coming storm.

Massimo hustled her inside the crowded trattoria bustling with local families. The aromas of sauce and cheese and baking pizza crust hit her hard. Unconsciously she put her hand to her mouth.

"Sister Amanda, wait here."

A beautiful brown-eyed woman with sleek black hair stopped Massimo with a greeting in Italian. The owner, probably asking to seat them. Massimo answered her in a beautiful rush of Italian that rolled off his tongue like poetry.

He turned back to Amanda. "She asks if we will eat, but I tell her we are here to look for a friend. You go, I wait, yes?"

"Come with me, please," she begged. He nodded, his brown eyes somber, and she gripped his arm as they wound through tightly packed tables, dodging waiters carrying baskets of fresh bread and calling out orders.

They turned a corner and came to a room, more like a crowded hall really, with a wooden bar facing the wall and a television playing silently in the corner. Footage flashed from the mountain at the other end of the resort, where the downhill race had run earlier in the day.

All of it served to remind her that Brody had worked for two years, through difficult rehabilitation and exclusion from her father's team, just to make it to tomorrow's slalom race. And maybe, in his mind, if he'd never met her, there never would have been any doubt of his secret staying hidden.

She needed to tell Brody she understood why he hadn't told her. That she would keep her father in the dark about her plans at least through the end of the press conference after the race. Maybe that would be enough to stave MacArthur off. She didn't believe it would be, but she could hope.

"Ah, here is Brody," Massimo said.

Her heart jumping, she followed his gaze. There, in the thick of the noise, the action and the laughter sat Brody, at a table in the corner near the kitchen. Rather than wearing his team jacket like some of the racers she and Massimo had passed in the village, he was dressed in street clothes. He wore the dark parka she knew so well, his V-neck sweater over a faded blue T-shirt and worn jeans.

Her gaze rose to his face and her spirits lifted. It was heaven to see him smile. The only thing that would have felt better was if the smile was for her, but it wasn't. And her worst fear was that it might never be again. His head was cocked as he listened to the people at his table while a grandmotherly woman set a plate of pasta before him and urged him to taste it.

A pang went through her. *He doesn't eat food he doesn't trust is untainted.* Now, after her father's revelations, seeing it nearly broke her heart.

"Go to him." Massimo prodded her. "We have walked all this way, yes?"

But how could she? Though Brody hadn't seen her yet, his team had. The men sat on barstools and two of them faced her, their eyes hooded, their mouths flat, their arms crossed over their barrel chests.

"I'm not sure it's such a good idea at the moment."

"Wait here, dear sister," Massimo said patiently. He approached the largest of the barrel-chested guys and had a low conversation Amanda couldn't hear.

He was back by her side in a moment. "The family he sits with is a local family. They ask for the honor of eating with him." He nudged her. "You will go to him? No one will stop you."

She watched Brody discussing something with the family, whose company he obviously enjoyed. Besides the grandmother they were two middle-aged couples, their phone-scrolling teenagers and a toddler strapped into a high chair.

He's part of a family, she realized. Her eyes grew moist. Of all the scenarios she'd imagined for the night before his race, the last thing she'd expected was to see him sitting with a local skiing family and sharing the joy of the togetherness he'd never had as a kid, and wanted for himself as an adult.

I know him. She dabbed at her eyes with the heel of her hand. If she hadn't been mistaken in her priorities earlier, she could have shared this moment with him, too. Because obviously, Brody had forgiven himself. He was relaxed.

He was happy.

"Amanda?" Massimo asked gently. "Please, he will not bite you."

She composed herself and smiled at Massimo as best she could. "If I leave him as he is, then he'll race better tomorrow."

"Ah." Massimo nodded. "Yes, I see."

She was about to do the hard job of walking away from him, but she noticed his team. On the last stool sat the young ski tech, Steve.

An arrow of guilt hit her hard in the chest. "Give me a minute, please, Massimo."

While he waited, she approached Steve and sat on the empty stool beside him. His head was bowed, his shaggy hair covering his eyes, and his hands were in his lap.

"I want to apologize," she said. "I put you in a bad position that day in the car, and I shouldn't have way-laid you like I did."

"It's done now," Steve mumbled without raising his head. "The secret is out." He wouldn't even look at her.

She was full of regrets, but there was nothing she could do to change the past. "Yes, the secret is out. But I want you to know I'm not writing about it. In fact, I've done everything I can to kill the story. The only thing I can't control is what will happen at the press conference tomorrow after the race."

"Why should I believe anything you say?"

She bowed her head. She'd sat here for a reason, to apologize to Steve and to give him the message for Brody. Not to justify herself. "Please, just make sure Brody races well. Take care of him so he can ski at his best."

Steve fixed his gaze on the label of the beer bottle he'd been peeling. He didn't move, didn't answer, didn't even nod.

"Is there something you're not telling me?"

He raised his shoulder in Brody's direction and shrugged.

With dread in her heart, Amanda turned and looked back at Brody.

And saw that he was eating the meal they'd placed before him. With gusto.

CHAPTER NINETEEN

FORGIVEN.

It's a whole new feeling, Brody thought.

He'd settled into the lift for the second leg of the race and was now swooping over the trees, heading up the mountain. Usually, he had his pre-race thoughts to occupy him, along with his iPod, his visualizations, his process of centering himself in the zone.

But today, all he could think about was how good it felt to ski. For the first time in two years, he felt loose with it.

The sun warmed his face as he pulled on his goggles. He adjusted his gloves and checked his boots in the bindings with new awareness. And then he was in the start house for the second time today. Leaning forward, waiting for the tone to begin.

And then, his reflexes taking over. Muscle memory kicking in.

The crisp winter air bit his cheeks. The click of ski poles vibrated through him. Oh, yeah—rock and roll.

The mountain was a blur as he headed for the first gate. The snow was perfect; just like in the morning run, it crunched beneath his skis and felt as if it was carrying him. Everything felt right; his turns, the placement of his poles, the timing of his breathing, his muscles, his heartbeat. This run was a winner, too; he knew it as he pumped across the finish line with the roar of the crowd in the background, the clang of a hundred cowbells and the loudspeaker announcing his name and his time in three different languages.

He didn't need to tear off his goggles and gaze at the standings to know how he'd fared. The day just smelled right. He was the leader with two competitors left to ski.

The first man wiped out at the course midsection. A DNF—Did Not Finish—nothing to be ashamed of. Wow, did he just think that?

Yeah, he did. Nothing to be ashamed of.

It's over, he thought. *And it's okay. No matter what anybody says or uncovers or accuses me of.*

He'd let it go. Truthfully, it didn't even matter if he finished second. Just by showing up and enjoying every moment of the run, he'd already won.

All that mattered was that he could face himself.

Brody searched the crowd for Amanda. It was true he'd waited until now to seek her out, but he'd wanted to give her time to do what she needed to do. Her deadline wasn't until tonight. And he had so much he needed to tell her.

Instead he saw Sarah Zimmerman. Hans's wife was easy to pick out in a crowd—she dressed in shared Swiss-and-Canadian red, and she always screamed like a banshee after his runs. He made his way to the barrier as she was pushing through the crowd to reach him.

"Brody!" Sarah leaned over the fence and hugged him tight, with Hans two paces behind her, his fist pumping in the air for Brody's success. "I called Amanda's room," Sarah said into his ear, "and left a message like you asked, but I haven't heard back from her yet."

A gust of panic went through him. He hoped she hadn't flown back to New York already. He needed to connect with her more than he needed anything else in his life right now, even his skiing success.

He'd finally realized, lying in bed without her for another lousy night, that he'd shut her out, not because of her father or her job, but because he couldn't forgive himself for what he'd done. He'd shut everyone out, really. He spent time with his team, but never let them get too close, either.

But what he hadn't realized was that by shutting the world out, he'd shut himself in. He'd been in a prison every bit as real as his father's, but he'd made it himself. And he hadn't done his team any favors by locking them in with him.

Amanda had tried to show him that. Until he'd finally skied Alto Baglio this afternoon, he hadn't truly seen it.

Please, Amanda, be here. He had a press conference to attend, and he hoped she would come. He would answer any question she had for him, whatever she needed in order to complete her assignment. Because he loved her and he wanted to build something with her. These days and nights without her had shown him he didn't want to be without her anymore.

He left his skis and poles where he'd planted them and headed for the lodge. But at that moment, the loudspeaker called out his name as winner, and a crush of spectators, competitors and photographers converged on him. Pasting a smile on his face and nodding politely at the congratulations, he was forced to wade along slowly with the crowd. His body thrummed with impatience; all he cared about was finding Amanda.

"Brody, don't go to the press conference!" Steve pushed his way alongside him. He was breathing as heavily as if he'd just battled through Armageddon.

Brody messed up his ski tech's already shaggy hair. "Don't worry. There's nothing they can do to me that I can't do to myself. As for the rest of the guys, tell them I've got their backs."

"*She* thinks something bad's gonna happen there."

She? Did he mean Amanda? He grabbed Steve by the jacket. "When did you talk to her?"

"Last night. She…said she gave up her article for you, but she can't promise that another reporter won't write the story."

Damn it. That wasn't what he'd wanted. She didn't *need* to give up anything for him; he accepted her as she was.

He stalked into the press conference with one thought in mind. A row of folding chairs had been set up in front of a table with a microphone. Reporters and photographers had crowded into the more choice seats. He scanned the faces, and finally found Amanda, sitting quietly in the back row by herself. Her eyes locked onto his, and so many emotions sped through him at once—relief, joy and hope.

He ignored the protocol, and instead strode past the journalists holding bulky cameras and battered voice recorders, until he reached her chair, his helmet in his hand. She wore the same clothes he remembered from their days alone together in the chalet. She'd never looked so beautiful to him.

She stood, too, and her hand fluttered to her heart. "Brody, you won…"

That didn't matter. Not nearly as much as she did.

"I'm sorry I lied to you," he said. "It won't ever happen again."

There was a murmur of interest in the crowd behind him, and she reached for his hand to tug him away from it, but he didn't budge. He didn't care who heard what he had to say. Hell, he wanted the whole world to hear. "Whatever you plan to do with your story, I'm behind you. I'll even help you write it."

But she shook her head. "*Paradigm* is convinced the story is dead. They believed me when I told them it was a mistake, and they've killed the story. Before long, everybody will know."

"You didn't need to do that." He stroked her hair and pulled her close to him. "Your career is important to you—I want you to succeed, Manda."

"Thank you," she whispered. "But I've decided I don't want to work in a job where I'm expected to destroy people for a living."

He felt a lump growing in his throat. He was glad she'd seen that truth. At heart, she wasn't a person who tore people down. She was a nurturer who built them up. She'd built him up, hadn't she?

"You'll never need an insurance policy with me," he said. "I promise you."

"I figured that out, Brody, but not for the reasons you think." She smiled gently. He could kiss this woman all day.

"I love you, Amanda."

Her eyes glistened. "Will you say that again, please?"

He turned to a guy with a microphone in his face. "I love this woman."

But a snort rang out behind him. He turned, and saw Amanda's father standing with a short, squat young man holding a voice recorder.

"Time to go piss in the cup, Brody," MacArthur said.

Amanda's breath hissed in. But Brody already knew the score, had expected it, in fact. The short, squat guy wasn't a drug-test technician, but a known European tabloid reporter.

"Excuse us a minute," Brody said to the reporter. Then he grabbed MacArthur's arm and escorted him away from Amanda. But before Brody could speak, Amanda jumped in.

"Daddy, I'm respectfully asking you not to hurt Brody. And the reason I'm asking is I love him. And I hope that you can accept that. Because you're the only parent I have left, and I love you, too."

A buzzing sounded in Brody's ears. He'd almost stopped listening after the part where she'd said she loved him.

But MacArthur's expression had softened toward Amanda, and that was all the faith Brody needed.

MacArthur turned to Brody. "Do you love my daughter?" he boomed.

"With all my heart, sir," Brody answered.

"If you hurt her," MacArthur said, tapping Brody in the chest with each syllable he made, "I promise you will live to regret it."

As if there was any chance of that happening. "Not a problem, sir."

Amanda beamed at him, probably because MacArthur had actually walked away from the fight. He was heading out of the press conference and past the last row of cameramen, who were waiting patiently for Brody to return to the business at hand.

Let them wait. He had more important things to attend to. Whatever baggage Amanda came with, he was willing to accept. She'd accepted him even though his father was in prison, hadn't she?

He clasped Amanda's hands. "You handled MacArthur better than anyone I've ever seen."

She gave Brody a wistful smile. "It won't be easy having him in my life. Like you said, he's always playing a chess game in his head. But, having him estranged from me, while still on good terms with Jeannie, is worse than having to walk on eggshells around him."

"For you, Amanda, I'll walk on eggshells."

She laughed, a dimple appearing in her cheek. "I'm warning you, they might get sharp sometimes."

"Yeah, and it's a challenge I accept." He brought her hand to his lips and kissed it. "If you'll have me, I'll battle through snowstorms for you."

"And carry me through avalanches?" Her eyes were twinkling.

"There are no avalanches in Manhattan."

Her mouth opened and closed, but for a moment no words came out. "What are you saying?"

Brody cupped her cheek in his hand. "That I'll live wherever you want. In New York, anywhere. Starting today. Just…say that you forgive me."

"You'd die in Manhattan," she said softly.

"Not with you, I won't."

Tears were forming in her eyes. He didn't know if that was a good sign or a bad sign, and he started to worry.

"Brody, I think it's best you stay on the tour for the season like you've committed to your team."

"Amanda, I've already talked with them, and—"

She put her finger to his lips. "I know. And after we return from the tour, both of us together, I want to live in New Hampshire," she whispered. "In your house that you told me about."

"In my…"

"I want to go home. With you." She laughed, and

tears rolled down her cheeks. He promptly wiped them away with his thumbs.

He *would* renovate that house, just like Hans had, now that he would be living there full-time. And it was fitting that he live there with Amanda. He'd never forget their days and nights stuck in a snowstorm in the mountains.

"I'm sorry, Brody. Walking out on you was the hardest thing I've ever done. I only did it because I loved you."

"Loved? As in past tense?"

She bit her lip, making his heart stop beating. "Past, present and future. Even more so since you risked everything to do what's right for yourself."

He wanted to sweep her up in his arms and take her home with him as fast as he could. He settled for a kiss.

While they kissed, applause came from the assembled reporters. But he could only look at Amanda.

Never again would he worry about what he had to prove. About medals or coaches or the past or what might have been.

Because all that mattered was here and now, in his arms.

EPILOGUE

A Year Later

AMANDA OPENED THE FLAPS of the cardboard box from her publisher. There it was, the promotional copies of Brody's story. Her first sports biography, with two more on contract for an Olympic sprinter and a gymnast, both clients of Harrison's.

She danced a little jig and then held the hardcover book against her chest, grinning from ear to ear. This was her first book. And it was all the more special because of Brody's help.

He saw her hopping round the foyer, and his face broke out in a grin, too. He'd already helped her by reading the galleys, so he knew the book as inside-out as she did. "Timely," he said. "You can take a copy to your sister."

"Jeannie will be thrilled."

"Are you ready to go?" He held up their suitcases. Outside, the car service had arrived to take them to Boston's Logan Airport. From there, they would travel on an international flight to Milan, where they would spend two weeks visiting her sister, Massimo and her new baby niece, Ava.

"The question is, are you ready?" She twirled the hanger containing her wedding dress, enclosed in a garment bag.

He leaned over and kissed her. "I was born ready."

"I know that, Coach Jones, but are you ready to marry a writer?"

He nibbled her ear. "No garter thingies, right? You promised me."

"None," she breathed.

"And that thing with selling off the bride to dance with other guys? We're not doing that, either."

"No *buste,*" she agreed.

"Good," he murmured, gathering her close and kissing her more deeply. "Because I'm not interested in sharing you."

She held him for a long time, her hot skier. It was hard to believe that once upon a time, he'd been the last man she'd ever imagined marrying. Now, she couldn't imagine marrying anyone else. "It will be the happiest day of my life." She ran a hand up his hard biceps and licked her lips. His pupils dilated.

"Uh, Manda, the car service sent a limo," he said. "You know, with one of those solid walls that raises between us and the driver. Are you game?"

Yes, she was a very lucky woman.

* * * * *

HEART & HOME

Heartwarming romances where love can
happen right when you least expect it.

Harlequin®
Super Romance

COMING NEXT MONTH
AVAILABLE FEBRUARY 14, 2012

#1758 BETWEEN LOVE AND DUTY
A Brother's Word
Janice Kay Johnson

#1759 MARRY ME, MARINE
In Uniform
Rogenna Brewer

#1760 FROM THE BEGINNING
Tracy Wolff

#1761 JUST DESSERTS
Too Many Cooks?
Jeannie Watt

#1762 ON COMMON GROUND
School Ties
Tracy Kelleher

#1763 A TEXAS CHANCE
The MacAllisters
Jean Brashear

You can find more information on upcoming Harlequin® titles,
free excerpts and more at www.HarlequinInsideRomance.com.

HSRCNM0112

REQUEST YOUR FREE BOOKS!
2 FREE NOVELS PLUS 2 FREE GIFTS!

Harlequin®

Super Romance®

Exciting, emotional, unexpected!

YES! Please send me 2 FREE Harlequin® Superromance® novels and my 2 FREE gifts (gifts are worth about $10). After receiving them, if I don't wish to receive any more books, I can return the shipping statement marked "cancel." If I don't cancel, I will receive 6 brand-new novels every month and be billed just $4.69 per book in the U.S. or $5.24 per book in Canada. That's a saving of at least 15% off the cover price! It's quite a bargain! Shipping and handling is just 50¢ per book in the U.S. and 75¢ per book in Canada.* I understand that accepting the 2 free books and gifts places me under no obligation to buy anything. I can always return a shipment and cancel at any time. Even if I never buy another book, the two free books and gifts are mine to keep forever.

135/336 HDN FC6T

Name	(PLEASE PRINT)

Address	Apt. #

City	State/Prov.	Zip/Postal Code

Signature (if under 18, a parent or guardian must sign)

Mail to the Reader Service:
IN U.S.A.: P.O. Box 1867, Buffalo, NY 14240-1867
IN CANADA: P.O. Box 609, Fort Erie, Ontario L2A 5X3

Not valid for current subscribers to Harlequin Superromance books.

**Are you a current subscriber to Harlequin Superromance books
and want to receive the larger-print edition?
Call 1-800-873-8635 or visit www.ReaderService.com.**

* Terms and prices subject to change without notice. Prices do not include applicable taxes. Sales tax applicable in N.Y. Canadian residents will be charged applicable taxes. Offer not valid in Quebec. This offer is limited to one order per household. All orders subject to credit approval. Credit or debit balances in a customer's account(s) may be offset by any other outstanding balance owed by or to the customer. Please allow 4 to 6 weeks for delivery. Offer available while quantities last.

Your Privacy—The Reader Service is committed to protecting your privacy. Our Privacy Policy is available online at www.ReaderService.com or upon request from the Reader Service.

We make a portion of our mailing list available to reputable third parties that offer products we believe may interest you. If you prefer that we not exchange your name with third parties, or if you wish to clarify or modify your communication preferences, please visit us at www.ReaderService.com/consumerschoice or write to us at Reader Service Preference Service, P.O. Box 9062, Buffalo, NY 14269. Include your complete name and address.

HSR11

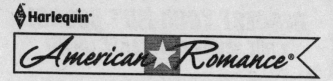

New York Times *and* USA TODAY *bestselling author*
Maya Banks presents book three in her miniseries
PREGNANCY & PASSION.

TEMPTED BY HER INNOCENT KISS

Available March 2012 from Harlequin Desire!

There came a time in a man's life when he knew he was well and truly caught. Devon Carter stared down at the diamond ring nestled in velvet and acknowledged that this was one such time. He snapped the lid closed and shoved the box into the breast pocket of his suit.

He had two choices. He could marry Ashley Copeland and fulfill his goal of merging his company with Copeland Hotels, thus creating the largest, most exclusive line of resorts in the world, or he could refuse and lose it all.

Put in that light, there wasn't much he could do except pop the question.

The doorman to his Manhattan high-rise apartment hurried to open the door as Devon strode toward the street. He took a deep breath before ducking into his car, and the driver pulled into traffic.

Tonight was the night. All of his careful wooing, the countless dinners, kisses that started brief and casual and became more breathless—all a lead-up to tonight. Tonight his seduction of Ashley Copeland would be complete, and then he'd ask her to marry him.

He shook his head as the absurdity of the situation hit him for the hundredth time. Personally, he thought William Copeland was crazy for forcing his daughter down Devon's throat.

Ashley was a sweet enough girl, but Devon had no desire

to marry anyone.

William had other plans. He'd told Devon that Ashley had no head for the family business. She was too softhearted, too naive. So he'd made Ashley part of the deal. The catch? Ashley wasn't to know of it. Which meant Devon was stuck playing stupid games.

Ashley was supposed to think this was a grand love match. She was a starry-eyed woman who preferred her animal-rescue foundation over board meetings, charts and financials for Copeland Hotels.

If she ever found out the truth, she wouldn't take it well.

And hell, he couldn't blame her.

But no matter the reason for his proposal, before the night was over, she'd have no doubts that she belonged to him.

What will happen when Devon marries Ashley?
Find out in Maya Banks's passionate new novel
TEMPTED BY HER INNOCENT KISS
Available March 2012 from Harlequin Desire!